Phantom Lines

Eliza Hunt

Published by Eliza Hunt, 2024.

This is a work of fiction. Similarities to real people, places, or events are entirely coincidental.

PHANTOM LINES

First edition. November 6, 2024.

Copyright © 2024 Eliza Hunt.

ISBN: 979-8227960016

Written by Eliza Hunt.

Chapter 1: Unwelcome Encounters

The crisp autumn air of Willow Creek carries the scent of pine and impending change, wrapping around me like a familiar, albeit uneasy, embrace. My first day as the lead actress in the community theater's ambitious production of "Shattered Dreams" finds me backstage, standing amid a labyrinth of painted flats and forgotten props. The soft murmur of fellow actors mingles with the rustling of costumes, the soft thud of shoes on worn wooden floors echoing my own pounding heart. I take a deep breath, inhaling the mingled aromas of old paint, sawdust, and the faint trace of sweat that lingers in the air, a reminder of countless performances before mine.

"Anna, are you ready?" calls out a voice from the shadows. It's Sarah, my best friend and the show's stage manager, her clipboard clutched to her chest like a shield. Her eyes shine with excitement, but I can see the hint of nerves beneath her bright smile.

"Ready as I'll ever be," I reply, forcing a grin that I hope is convincing enough. In truth, my stomach churns with a cocktail of exhilaration and dread. This is my moment, my chance to shine, yet the spotlight feels heavier than I anticipated. I glance at the script, my lines swimming in a sea of anxiety, and wish I could dive into the safety of the audience instead.

As the rehearsal begins, the air thickens with anticipation. The cast members take their places, and I close my eyes for a moment, picturing the character I'm about to embody—Elena, a woman trapped in the confines of her own shattered dreams, desperately seeking redemption. My heart quickens as I think of the weight of her journey, one I am determined to convey with honesty and depth. Just as I open my eyes, ready to embrace the role, the theater door swings open, and in walks Lucas Sterling.

He's everything they warned me about: tall, with tousled dark hair that looks perpetually windswept, and a presence that commands attention without uttering a word. His reputation as a demanding theater director precedes him, and the aura of authority he carries seems to suppress even the most spirited of actors. The moment our eyes meet, I feel a spark that ignites the air between us, electric and unsettling.

"Ah, the leading lady graces us with her presence," he remarks, his tone a perfect blend of sarcasm and arrogance. "I hope you know those lines better than you look like you do."

"Charming," I retort, crossing my arms defiantly. "I didn't realize I signed up for a critique session before rehearsal even started."

He smirks, the corner of his mouth curling upward as if he's amused by my audacity. "It's called preparation, Anna. Something that you might find helpful in this line of work."

Before I can respond, the rehearsal begins, and I dive into my character, trying to forget the man watching from the sidelines. Each line I deliver feels like a step into a treacherous dance, the kind that requires precision and trust. But every time I glance at Lucas, I feel the tightrope of our interactions wobble beneath my feet. His gaze is penetrating, as if he's peeling away the layers of my performance to expose the raw truth beneath. It unnerves me, yet somehow, it fuels my passion for the role.

Just when I think I might find my rhythm, disaster strikes. A wayward stage prop—a cardboard tree meant to symbolize Elena's entrapment—topples over, crashing to the ground with a resounding thud. I barely manage to dodge it, but Lucas is quick to react, stepping into the chaos with reflexes honed from years of experience.

"Are you okay?" he asks, concern slipping through the cracks of his typically cool demeanor. The tension in his voice disarms me, and for a split second, the rivalry fades, replaced by a fleeting sense of camaraderie.

"I'm fine, just... theatrical flair," I reply, attempting to mask my embarrassment.

He raises an eyebrow, a challenge glinting in his eyes. "Theatrical flair? You should consider a career in acrobatics."

With a deep breath, I summon my bravado. "You should consider a career in being less of a jerk."

He laughs, the sound rich and unexpected, and I can't help but feel a rush of warmth flood my cheeks. The laughter brings with it a shift, a fragile truce in the stormy seas of our burgeoning rivalry. Yet, the moment is short-lived. Lucas quickly regains his composure, his director's mask slipping back into place.

"Let's take it from the top," he orders, his tone sharp and commanding. "And Anna, try to connect with your character a little more this time. She's not just a pretty face."

The words cut deeper than he likely intends, but there's a flicker of something—perhaps admiration—beneath the harsh surface. I nod, unwilling to let him see how deeply his comment has affected me. With renewed determination, I throw myself into the scene, determined to prove that I can meet his expectations.

As the rehearsal unfolds, our interactions grow more charged. The push and pull of our chemistry become almost palpable, a tension that dances in the air around us. The sharpness of his critiques and the unexpected moments of vulnerability form a complex tapestry that keeps me on my toes. Just when I think I've deciphered his intentions, Lucas surprises me again, his gaze softening as he offers a piece of advice that feels almost personal.

"Let go of the fear of failure, Anna. The best performances come from embracing the imperfections."

His words linger in the air long after they're spoken, echoing the very essence of Elena's struggle. It's a reminder that perhaps the greatest tragedy is not the dreams we shatter, but the ones we let slip away out of fear. The rehearsal continues, weaving its way through the chaos and laughter, and despite our rivalry, there's an undeniable connection forming, one that I can't quite grasp but can't ignore.

Each moment spent in Lucas's presence pulls me deeper into a world where passion and ambition collide, crafting a narrative that feels as vibrant and unpredictable as the leaves falling outside, painting the town in hues of gold and crimson.

The days drift by in a colorful blur, the vibrant leaves outside whispering tales of change as rehearsals for "Shattered Dreams" unfold like a well-worn script. Each evening, I find myself falling deeper into the role of Elena, a woman grappling with her failures while seeking a glimmer of hope amidst her despair. Yet, intertwined with my journey on stage is an unpredictable current of banter and tension that flickers between Lucas and me, as intoxicating as it is infuriating.

As we work through scenes, I've noticed how Lucas's critiques shift. Initially, his feedback felt like a relentless barrage, sharp enough to draw blood, but gradually, there's a softness creeping into his eyes. It's as if the more I embody Elena's struggle, the more Lucas reveals his own vulnerabilities, veiled beneath layers of stubbornness and pride. Our dialogues have morphed from icy confrontations to exchanges laden with witticisms that crackle in the air.

"Anna, darling," he begins one evening, his voice rich with mockery, "if your performance were any more wooden, I could use you as a prop."

"Oh please, Lucas," I shoot back, unable to resist the urge to volley. "If I'm a prop, then you must be the scenery—perfectly stationary and entirely overdramatic."

He chuckles, the sound unexpectedly warm, melting the frost that often coats our interactions. "Touché. But at least I'm not flailing around like a windmill caught in a hurricane."

The playful exchange bounces between us like a well-tossed ball, a welcomed distraction from the mounting pressures of performance. Yet, beneath the surface, an undercurrent of tension bubbles, hinting at something deeper that neither of us is quite ready to acknowledge. Every lingering glance seems charged, every moment filled with an electricity that makes my heart race. It's maddening and exhilarating all at once.

As the weeks wear on, the theater transforms into a second home, filled with familiar faces and the comforting chaos of creativity. The smell of freshly brewed coffee mingles with the scent of paint and fabric softener, forming a sensory tapestry that wraps around me as I arrive for rehearsals. The cast has become my makeshift family, their laughter echoing off the walls, mixing with the sounds of rehearsal—a symphony of lines, laughter, and the occasional mishap.

One afternoon, during a particularly intense scene where Elena confronts her past, I decide to dig deeper into the emotional turmoil she faces. I take a breath, plunging into the depths of the character's pain, channeling the frustrations and disappointments I've experienced in my own life. The room fades away, leaving only the pulse of Elena's heartbeat reverberating through me. I deliver my lines with raw honesty, pouring every ounce of myself into the performance.

Just as I reach the climax of the scene, where Elena must confront her greatest fear, I spot Lucas leaning against the wall, arms crossed, his eyes fixed on me. I feel the weight of his gaze, the scrutiny turning my insides into a tempest. It ignites something within me—a reckless determination to prove my worth. I'm so immersed in the moment that I barely register the audience of fellow cast members hanging on my every word.

When I finish, the silence hangs heavy for a heartbeat before the room erupts into applause. I'm breathless, the performance leaving me raw and exposed, but the look on Lucas's face is what truly steals my breath. There's admiration flickering in his eyes, a mix of respect and something else—something deeper. But before I can dwell on it, he straightens up, slipping back into his role as director.

"Not bad, Anna. If only we could get the rest of the cast to match your level of commitment," he quips, the glimmer of pride in his voice almost unnoticeable.

"Thanks for the vote of confidence," I reply, unable to mask the grin spreading across my face. "I'll be sure to pass it along to the others, assuming they survive your rehearsals."

The banter becomes our secret language, a coded exchange of mutual respect and simmering attraction, each retort drawing us closer even as we pretend to be enemies. But that closeness brings its own complications. With every shared laugh and lingering glance, I feel myself teetering on the precipice of something I'm not sure I'm ready to embrace.

One evening, as we gather for a read-through of the final act, I arrive early to prepare. The theater is silent, a stark contrast to the chaos of the previous days. The air hangs thick with anticipation, but also with something else—something electric. I lean against a prop table, flipping through my script when Lucas walks in, his footsteps echoing against the wooden floor.

"Didn't expect to see you here so early," he remarks, arching an eyebrow, a hint of amusement dancing in his eyes.

"I thought I'd get a head start on my lines," I reply, playing it casual, though my heart races at the sight of him.

"Ah, the overachiever. Tell me, do you ever take a break from being the best?" he teases, stepping closer.

"Only when the best is busy trying to keep the worst in line," I shoot back, grinning, my confidence swelling. The tension swells like a taut string, vibrating with unspoken words and unshed emotions.

Just then, a commotion erupts outside as a group of teenagers bursts into the theater, laughing and shrieking. They've arrived to check out the production, eager for a glimpse behind the scenes. In an instant, the atmosphere shifts from intimate to chaotic, and I feel the moment with Lucas slip through my fingers like sand.

The teenagers scatter through the aisles, eyes wide with excitement, oblivious to the tension that has been brewing in the air.

"Perfect timing," Lucas mutters, shaking his head as he moves to greet the new arrivals, the opportunity for a deeper connection vanishing like smoke in the wind. I can only watch as the spell we shared is broken, the moment disappearing into the fray of enthusiasm and youthful exuberance.

As the rehearsal continues with the interruptions, I steal glances at Lucas, each one igniting a spark of frustration and longing. I wonder if he feels it too—this strange connection that we're both trying to deny. The distractions pull us apart, and I'm left grappling with the swirling emotions that threaten to overwhelm me. The laughter of the teenagers mingles with the tension of our rivalry, creating a tapestry of confusion that leaves me questioning everything.

When the day finally draws to a close, I leave the theater with a heavy heart and a mind filled with questions. The vibrant colors of the leaves outside seem to mock my inner turmoil, each one falling to the ground as if echoing my own spiraling thoughts. I can't shake the feeling that my connection with Lucas is both a blessing and a curse, one that may lead to revelations I'm not prepared to face. The sweet scent of pine fills the air, promising change, but I'm left standing at the edge of uncertainty, caught between the woman I am and the one I might become.

The days unfurl like a vibrant autumn tapestry, each rehearsal weaving its way into my routine with increasing intensity. I've settled into the rhythm of the production, a whirlwind of lines and blocking, laughter and late-night coffee runs, yet a palpable tension lingers in the air—specifically between Lucas and me. We have become a curious duo, caught in a perpetual dance of wit and rivalry that ignites every interaction, both on and off the stage.

One evening, as we dive into a particularly emotional scene, I can feel the weight of my character's heartbreak settle heavily upon my shoulders. I channel the pain of Elena, and with each line, I'm confronted not only with her struggles but with my own fears of inadequacy. Just as I reach a fever pitch in my delivery, Lucas interrupts.

"Hold," he calls, his tone sharp but not unkind. "You're all fire and brimstone, but I need to feel the vulnerability underneath. Can you dig deeper?"

The words spark a flame of indignation within me. "Are you suggesting I'm too much?" I challenge, unable to mask my irritation.

"I'm suggesting you have layers, Anna," he replies, a smirk dancing on his lips. "You know, like an onion. Or maybe a parfait."

"Why don't you just stick to directing?" I shoot back, crossing my arms in defiance. "I'll handle the emotions."

"Fine, but remember that I only want what's best for you... and the show." He winks, the playfulness of his words smoothing over the rough edges of our earlier clash.

And yet, his teasing only deepens my resolve. I'm determined to prove to him—and to myself—that I can embody Elena's struggles authentically. As rehearsals progress, Lucas's critiques morph from biting to constructive, nudging me closer to uncovering the complexities of my character. It's infuriating and invigorating in equal measure, a push-and-pull that keeps me on my toes.

As autumn begins to shed its leaves, the community theater buzzes with energy. The production is just weeks away, and excitement courses through the cast and crew like a living thing. Yet, beneath the surface, I sense the storm of emotions brewing between Lucas and me, a tempest of unspoken words and untamed feelings. Each time our eyes meet, there's a flicker of something that sets my heart racing, but it's always swiftly smothered by our banter and rivalry.

One chilly evening, after a particularly intense rehearsal, the cast disperses into the night, leaving just Lucas and me in the dimly lit theater. I linger by the edge of the stage, contemplating my performance as I collect my thoughts, when Lucas approaches, his silhouette framed by the soft glow of the stage lights.

"Anna," he says, his voice unexpectedly soft, "you were incredible tonight. The way you captured Elena's despair... it was haunting."

"Thanks," I reply, surprised by his sincerity. "I was just trying to keep up with your demanding standards."

He chuckles, the sound low and warm. "I can be a hard ass, but you're worth it. You just need to believe that."

"I believe I'm tired of your constant need to critique," I counter, unable to resist the urge to throw a playful jab. "But that doesn't mean I don't appreciate the feedback."

We share a moment of silence, the air thick with unspoken possibilities. It's as if the world around us fades away, leaving only the two of us suspended in this delicate balance of rivalry and something more. Just when I feel the tension shift, ready to bridge the gap between us, a loud crash echoes from the wings.

"Is that a prop or a person?" I ask, breaking the moment, my voice laced with humor as I glance towards the shadows.

Lucas sighs, shaking his head. "Let's hope it's just the set design throwing a tantrum. I'll check it out."

As he strides toward the source of the noise, my heart races with a mix of adrenaline and uncertainty. There's a strange weight in the air, as if something is about to unfold—something I can't quite put my finger on. The theater feels charged, alive with the thrill of anticipation.

I follow him cautiously, heart thudding in my chest, and as we round the corner, we find Sarah, the stage manager, grappling with a fallen piece of set—a half-collapsed backdrop that has decided to stage its own coup.

"What happened?" Lucas demands, his director's voice returning to full force.

"I tripped on the cable," Sarah explains, brushing herself off with a sheepish smile. "But hey, I saved the backdrop from hitting the ground. You're welcome."

"Next time, maybe try not to perform your own stunts," he quips, rolling his eyes, but I can see the relief in his demeanor.

As we help her reassemble the scene, the lightheartedness returns, and I find myself stealing glances at Lucas, the earlier tension still crackling in the corners of my mind. I can't help but wonder if we'll ever bridge the gap between our rivalry and the undeniable chemistry that simmers beneath the surface.

The rehearsal winds down, and we gather to discuss the next steps. The laughter and camaraderie are infectious, filling the space with a sense of community. I feel a flicker of hope that perhaps this journey might lead to something beautiful—both on and off the stage.

Later that night, as I leave the theater, the cool air bites at my cheeks, and the stars twinkle above like a thousand watchful eyes. I'm lost in thought, reflecting on the whirlwind of emotions that have tangled around me in the past weeks. Just as I reach my car, a voice calls out from the shadows.

"Anna!"

I turn to find Lucas striding toward me, a determined look etched on his face. "Can we talk?"

"Sure," I say, curiosity piqued, a thrill running down my spine.

He steps closer, the streetlights illuminating the intensity in his eyes. "I've been thinking about what we talked about earlier. About the layers..."

My breath catches as I realize that this might be the moment I've been waiting for—the moment when we finally address the tension that has woven itself into the very fabric of our rehearsals.

But before he can continue, the ground beneath us rumbles violently. The shock reverberates through my body, the lights flickering ominously, and a low growl echoes from the distance, shaking the very foundations of the theater.

"What was that?" I gasp, eyes wide, heart racing in fear and confusion.

Lucas's gaze snaps toward the sound, a mix of concern and urgency flooding his features. "We need to get inside. Now!"

As we race toward the theater, the world around us spirals into chaos. I feel the weight of uncertainty crash over me, like a storm rolling in to shatter the fragile peace we've created. Just as we reach the door, a blinding flash lights up the night sky, illuminating the chaos unfolding before us.

And in that moment, as the theater doors swing open, I realize that whatever happens next will change everything.

Chapter 2: Secrets Beneath the Surface

The wooden floorboards creaked beneath my feet as I stepped onto the stage, the scent of dust and old paint hanging in the air like a shroud. Sunlight streamed through the high, grimy windows, illuminating motes of dust that danced lazily in the shafts of light. The theater had seen better days; peeling wallpaper clung desperately to the walls, and faded velvet curtains framed the stage with a melancholic elegance that belied its grandeur. This place was my sanctuary, a realm where the whispers of the past mingled with the present, but lately, an unsettling tension wove through the air, knotting my stomach.

Rehearsals had been exhilarating, a whirlwind of laughter and creativity. I found solace in the camaraderie of my fellow actors, each of us tangled in our dreams, striving to carve our names into the annals of this production. Yet, as the days stretched on, the atmosphere shifted, thickening with an unnameable dread. Lucas, the enigmatic leading man, had become an unintentional catalyst for my unease. He was everything I admired—talented, charismatic, and maddeningly secretive. His dark hair fell effortlessly across his forehead, framing deep-set eyes that seemed to hold shadows of a life untold.

Every time I dared to peel back the layers of his aloofness, he simply smiled that infuriating smirk, as if he enjoyed the game of withholding the truth. "Curiosity killed the cat, you know," he teased one afternoon, leaning against the brick wall of the rehearsal space, arms crossed. I rolled my eyes, desperately trying to mask my fascination with irritation.

"Curiosity also led to some pretty great discoveries, like penicillin and chocolate," I shot back, planting my hands on my hips. His laughter echoed in the empty theater, rich and warm, but it only served to fuel my determination. There was something in his past—a scandal, they said—that had forced him to leave his previous theater company in disgrace. The whispers had been soft at first, mere shadows flitting through our rehearsals, but as time passed, they grew louder, more insistent.

Every night, after the last of the cast had departed, I lingered in the theater, pretending to organize the props, but really I was eavesdropping on the echoes of conversations hidden behind closed doors. "He's got a reputation," I overheard one of the actresses say to another as they huddled near the backstage curtain. "People say he was involved in something awful—something that drove the company to the ground."

I feigned disinterest, but the words burrowed into my mind like a burr, scratching at my insides, urging me to dig deeper. I caught glimpses of Lucas in the wings, his shoulders tense, his gaze often distant, as if he were battling unseen demons. He would throw himself into rehearsals, his performances electric, but I sensed a storm brewing just beneath the surface.

Then came the peculiar incidents. It began subtly—a misplaced prop here, an odd thump from the darkened corners of the stage there. But soon, it escalated into something far more unnerving. During one rehearsal, as the cast prepared for a particularly rousing scene, the lights flickered ominously, casting eerie shadows that danced across the stage like specters. A collective shiver passed through us, yet Lucas merely shrugged it off, his grin a mask of casual indifference.

"Just the old wiring, nothing to worry about," he said, but I could see the flicker of concern in his eyes, the briefest glimpse of uncertainty that hinted at a deeper turmoil.

Another night, just as we were about to start, the sound of a glass shattering echoed from the prop room. Everyone jumped, their faces a mixture of confusion and fear. When I rushed to investigate, I found the floor littered with shards of what had been a beautifully crafted vase—a beloved relic of the theater's past. My heart raced. Who would destroy something so precious? I glanced at Lucas, who had followed me, his expression unreadable.

"Maybe it was an accident," he offered, but the tightness in his voice told a different story.

"Or maybe it was something more." I could feel the tension between us, electric and palpable, as if we were teetering on the brink of something monumental, yet still lost in the throes of misunderstanding.

Our rehearsals grew increasingly chaotic, with strange occurrences multiplying like a bad dream. One actor swore he heard whispers in the dark when he was alone on stage. Another insisted the temperature had dropped so dramatically that he could see his breath. Fear and suspicion began to circulate among us like a disease, twisting friendships into fragile alliances.

Late one evening, after a particularly fraught rehearsal, I found myself wandering the theater alone, unable to shake the feeling that we were not alone. The echo of my footsteps sounded hollow in the empty space, and the shadows seemed to stretch and shift, watching me with a conspiratorial gaze.

"Isn't it a bit late for a solitary stroll?" Lucas's voice sliced through the silence, startling me from my reverie. He stepped from the shadows, his features illuminated in the dim light, casting a mysterious aura that sent a thrill racing down my spine.

"Maybe I'm looking for ghosts," I replied, a teasing lilt in my tone, but my heart raced with the thrill of his proximity. "Or perhaps just a little excitement."

"Excitement? Here?" He chuckled, but it held an edge that hinted at something more—something that lay just beyond the veil of our banter. "You should know by now that theater is fraught with its fair share of drama."

"Then perhaps it's time to uncover what's truly going on," I challenged, meeting his gaze with steely determination. "The whispers, the accidents... There's something beneath the surface, Lucas, something we need to address."

For a moment, the air thickened with tension, an unspoken challenge hanging between us. His expression shifted, and I saw a flicker of vulnerability before he masked it with a practiced smirk. "And what if what we uncover isn't what you want to hear?"

"Then I'll take my chances," I declared, my resolve solidifying as I faced him head-on.

The night stretched on, a fragile thread of tension binding us, the uncharted territory ahead laden with secrets that begged to be unearthed. Each heartbeat echoed the mounting anticipation, a promise that whatever lay hidden beneath the surface would soon be revealed.

The air crackled with a tension I could hardly ignore, as if the very walls of the theater were holding their breath. Rehearsals transformed from playful collaborations into a battleground of unspoken fears and veiled glances. The whispers that had circulated among the cast about Lucas's past hung in the air like a heavy fog, and I found myself straddling the line between fascination and dread. His presence loomed larger with each passing day, igniting my curiosity and simultaneously raising my defenses.

"Do you think we'll ever get through this rehearsal without the universe trying to sabotage us?" I asked, casting a sideways glance at Lucas as we took a break during one particularly tense run-through. He leaned back against the stage, arms folded, an impenetrable wall of confidence.

"Probably not. It seems to be our new normal," he replied, his smirk a mask for something deeper lurking behind those stormy eyes. "Maybe the theater is trying to tell us we're not cut out for this."

"Or maybe it's just trying to keep things interesting," I shot back, trying to keep the mood light. But my heart wasn't in it; the strange occurrences had taken on a life of their own. Every creak of the floorboards seemed to echo louder than before, every misplaced prop felt like an omen. I could feel the cast's nerves fraying, a collective anxiety that manifested in hushed conversations and sidelong glances.

As we gathered for another rehearsal, I noticed that the air was thick with something more than the usual apprehension. The absence of our stage manager, who was usually a calming presence, left a void that heightened everyone's unease. "Has anyone seen Sam?" I asked, glancing around the group.

A chorus of shrugs greeted my inquiry. "Maybe he got lost in the labyrinth that is our prop room," Lucas quipped, but even he couldn't disguise the concern that flickered across his face.

"Or maybe he's trapped under a pile of cursed costumes," I added, trying to inject a bit of humor into the situation. Yet, I couldn't shake the feeling that something was amiss.

With every rehearsal, the strange incidents escalated. Props vanished without explanation, seemingly absorbed into the ether of the theater. The unsettling sounds—a low thud, a faint whisper, or the rustle of fabric—grew more pronounced. Each unexplained event felt like a subtle warning, urging us to tread carefully. I could almost sense the theater breathing around us, its very essence weaving the fabric of our fate, but what was it trying to tell us?

During one rehearsal, as we gathered for a particularly intense scene, the lights flickered dramatically, plunging us into darkness for a heartbeat before illuminating the stage again. "A bit dramatic, don't you think?" I remarked, my heart racing as I tried to maintain a façade of nonchalance.

Lucas's brow furrowed slightly. "The place has its quirks, that's all," he said, his voice smooth, but the slight tremor in it belied his bravado. I caught the tension in his posture, the way he instinctively moved closer to me as if my presence offered some small comfort against the encroaching darkness.

The rehearsal dragged on, but the unease hung around us like an unwanted guest. Finally, when we called a break, I seized the opportunity to corner Lucas. "What do you really know about this theater? About what's happening?"

He glanced around, ensuring no one else was listening, then leaned in closer. "What I know is that every theater has its ghosts, some more literal than others. You can't let the past overshadow what we're trying to create here."

"But isn't it the past that shapes us?" I countered, my heart racing as I probed further. "You're acting like it's a forbidden topic, and I can't shake the feeling that it has something to do with what's happening."

He studied me, an unreadable expression flickering across his features. "Sometimes, it's better not to dig too deep. You might not like what you find."

My stomach twisted at the thought of unseen horrors lurking in the shadows. "You're saying we should just ignore the strange happenings? Pretend it's all in our heads?"

He shrugged, the smirk returning, but I sensed the tension underneath. "What do you suggest? A séance?"

"Honestly, that might not be a terrible idea," I shot back, half-joking but entirely serious. The idea of summoning the spirits of the theater was absurd, yet there was something appealing about confronting whatever forces seemed determined to disrupt our work.

"Let's just hope they're friendly," he said with a laugh, but his eyes darted toward the exit as if he were already considering an escape route.

In the following days, my resolve only strengthened. I began to notice patterns in the disturbances—missing props that were essential for specific scenes, sounds that only occurred during moments of high tension. It was as if the theater were responding to our collective emotions, twisting them into a reflection of our fears and doubts.

One evening, after a particularly grueling rehearsal, I found myself unable to sleep, my mind racing with the events of the day. The darkness of my room felt heavy, oppressive, almost as if the shadows were trying to suffocate me. I tossed and turned, but every time I closed my eyes, I was pulled back into the theater, the echo of the past surrounding me.

Driven by an impulse I couldn't ignore, I threw on a sweater and slipped out into the night, the moonlight guiding my way to the theater. As I stepped through the heavy wooden doors, the familiar scent of dust and history washed over me, welcoming and haunting all at once.

Inside, the theater felt alive, the silence crackling with energy. I wandered to the stage, the wooden boards cool beneath my feet. I stood in the center, breathing in the memories that lingered in the air. "If you're out there," I called softly, "I'm listening."

For a moment, all was still. Then came a soft rustling, a whisper that curled around me like smoke. I froze, heart pounding in my chest, straining to decipher the sound. It wasn't my imagination; something stirred in the shadows. I took a step back, caught between fear and intrigue.

Suddenly, the lights flickered to life, illuminating the theater in stark brilliance. I blinked against the brightness, searching for the source of the sound. Was it my imagination, or had the air shifted?

Then I saw it—a shadow flitting at the edge of the stage. "Who's there?" I demanded, my voice echoing in the vast emptiness.

A moment of silence followed, thick and suffocating, before the shadow coalesced into a figure—familiar yet unrecognizable. My heart raced. It was Lucas, standing at the back of the theater, a haunted look in his eyes.

"What are you doing here?" I breathed, both relieved and startled.

"Looking for answers," he said, stepping into the light, his features etched with a mix of determination and fear. "And maybe a bit of mischief."

The tension between us crackled like static, igniting a flame of curiosity that I couldn't extinguish. Whatever secrets lay beneath the surface, we were about to uncover them together, whether we were ready or not.

The air in the theater was thick with anticipation, a charged silence that hung like fog just before a storm. I stood on the edge of the stage, watching Lucas as he paced the worn wooden floor, lost in thought. His presence was magnetic, drawing my gaze despite the storm brewing in my mind. "So, what's the plan? Ghost hunting?" I ventured, attempting to break the tension that had settled over us like a heavy blanket.

Lucas stopped mid-step, a flicker of amusement lighting up his features. "I thought that's what you wanted when you showed up in the middle of the night." He leaned against the side of the stage, arms crossed, the playful glint in his eye at odds with the shadows under them. "You seemed so eager for answers."

"Maybe I was hoping for more than just spooky sounds and missing props," I replied, matching his playful tone while keeping my voice low. "But now that we're both here, it feels like the universe is trying to tell us something."

"Or just messing with our heads," he said, straightening up and glancing around, as if expecting an apparition to jump out at us from the darkness. "Still, I'm all for digging deeper. But let's tread carefully; we don't want to end up like the last cast—what was it? Driven mad by their own production?"

A shiver ran down my spine at the thought, yet I couldn't ignore the thrill of discovery that coursed through me. "Let's start with the backstage area," I suggested, feeling bold. "That's where most of the strange occurrences have happened."

Together, we made our way down the narrow corridor that led to the prop room. My heart thudded in my chest with each step, the atmosphere thick with mystery and unspoken fears. The walls were adorned with faded posters of past productions, their vibrant colors dulled by time, but each one seemed to whisper secrets of its own.

As we reached the door to the prop room, I paused, glancing at Lucas. "Are you ready for whatever we might find in there?"

He smirked again, a mixture of confidence and apprehension dancing in his eyes. "Ready as I'll ever be. Just promise me if we find anything too spooky, we'll turn tail and run."

I laughed softly, but the tension simmered just beneath the surface. "Deal."

I pushed the door open, and it creaked ominously, the scent of aged wood and dust enveloping us. Inside, props were haphazardly strewn about—everything from old costumes to set pieces that had seen better days. My eyes were drawn to a large trunk in the corner, its brass fittings glinting faintly in the dim light.

"What do you think is in there?" I asked, pointing it out.

"Probably someone's rejected ideas," Lucas replied, stepping closer to inspect it. "Or maybe the remnants of a failed production. Either way, it's probably best left closed."

But the trunk beckoned to me, a mystery begging to be uncovered. "Or it could hold the key to understanding what's happening here," I insisted, moving toward it.

"Or it could hold a cursed script," he quipped, but I could see the spark of curiosity in his eyes as well.

With a deep breath, I knelt before the trunk and pulled at the latch. It clicked open with a reluctant groan, and I hesitated, glancing back at Lucas. "Here goes nothing."

The lid creaked open, revealing a jumble of old scripts, yellowed and frayed at the edges. But as I sifted through them, something else caught my eye—a small, leather-bound journal, its cover cracked with age. "What's this?" I murmured, pulling it out and brushing off the dust.

"Looks like a diary," Lucas observed, leaning closer. "You're not actually going to read it, are you? It could be someone's personal thoughts."

"Or it could provide insight into the theater's history," I countered, unable to resist the allure of the unknown. Flipping it open, I scanned the first few pages, my heart racing with each handwritten line.

"Dear Diary," the first entry read, "today marked another round of rehearsals, but tension lingers in the air. Rumors swirl like smoke, and I fear for the future of our company..."

I glanced up at Lucas, excitement and unease swirling within me. "This is it! This could explain everything!"

"Or it could be a collection of grievances from a melodramatic actor," he said, but the intrigue in his voice was undeniable. "What else does it say?"

I continued to read, the entries revealing a tale of ambition, jealousy, and a growing sense of paranoia among the cast. "It seems they had their share of strange occurrences too," I said, my voice lowering as I turned the pages. "People disappearing, arguments breaking out over nothing... It sounds like history is repeating itself."

"Maybe it's just the theater," Lucas offered, his tone light, but I could sense a flicker of worry behind it. "They say it's haunted by the spirits of those who didn't make it."

"Maybe we should pay them a visit," I replied with a smirk, but inside, a knot of unease tightened.

As I reached the final pages, the entries grew darker. "I can feel the shadows closing in. Something terrible happened during our last performance—something that shattered the company. I must uncover the truth before it's too late."

I looked up sharply, my heart racing. "Lucas, do you think—"

Suddenly, a loud crash echoed from the wings, jolting us both. We exchanged a panicked glance, adrenaline flooding my veins. "What was that?"

"Let's find out," he suggested, and I could see the flicker of challenge in his eyes, igniting my own sense of adventure.

We moved cautiously toward the sound, stepping into the shadowy corridor that led backstage. The air felt charged, as if the theater itself were holding its breath, waiting for us to make a move.

As we crept around a corner, the dim light revealed the source of the noise—a prop that had toppled over, lying in a chaotic heap on the floor. But just as we were about to approach it, the lights flickered again, plunging us into darkness.

"Lucas?" I called out, my voice trembling slightly.

"I'm here," he replied, but I could hear the tension in his voice as he moved closer to me, his presence a reassuring anchor in the unknown.

Just then, a low, echoing laugh reverberated through the air, sending chills down my spine. It was a sound filled with malice, a mocking tone that seemed to emerge from the very walls of the theater.

"Did you hear that?" I whispered, my heart racing.

"Yeah, I did," he said, his eyes wide as he scanned the darkness around us. "We should probably—"

Before he could finish, the lights burst back to life, and we were greeted by a sight that froze us in place. Standing in the shadows at the back of the stage was a figure cloaked in darkness, their features obscured but an unmistakable glint of something dangerous gleamed in their eyes.

"Looking for something?" the figure asked, their voice dripping with amusement, sending a jolt of fear through my chest.

My breath hitched, and for a moment, I couldn't move, entranced by the figure's presence. Lucas stepped slightly in front of me, the tension in his shoulders radiating as he prepared to confront whatever we had uncovered.

"Who are you?" he demanded, his voice steady despite the fear coursing through me.

But the figure merely chuckled, a sound that echoed ominously in the vast theater. "You really shouldn't be here. The past has a way of catching up with those who pry too deeply."

I could feel the weight of their words hanging in the air, a sinister promise laced with a threat that sent a shiver racing down my spine.

And just like that, the theater transformed from a stage of creativity into a battleground of shadows and secrets, with the truth lurking just out of reach. I could only wonder what lay ahead—if we would uncover the hidden history or become another ghost in the theater's tapestry of tales.

Chapter 3: Revelations in the Shadows

The theater's atmosphere thickened with the weight of the past as I paced the empty stage, rehearsing my lines under the flickering glow of the overhead lights. The air smelled of aged wood and dust, a comforting mix that whispered of countless performances and hidden stories. I wrapped my arms around myself, trying to absorb the energy swirling around me, hoping to draw inspiration from the echoes of actors long gone. The grand chandelier overhead sparkled like trapped stars, casting fragmented light across the worn velvet seats, each one a silent witness to dramas that had unfolded long before I'd even dreamed of stepping onto this stage.

As I meandered backstage, the creaking floorboards beneath my feet seemed to hum a tune, one I had yet to learn. The theater felt alive, each shadow breathing with secrets. Curiosity pulled at me, stronger than the gravity of my rehearsals. I ventured further, my heart thrumming in time with the distant rumble of thunder outside. The storm had finally decided to unleash its fury, pounding against the windows like a desperate lover seeking entry. I found myself drawn to a narrow corridor, one I had always ignored in my countless trips through the theater. Dimly lit and draped in cobwebs, it seemed to beckon me closer.

I pushed open a door at the end, its hinges groaning in protest. What lay beyond was a world frozen in time. The hidden room was a treasure trove of history—walls adorned with old posters advertising productions from decades past, yellowing scripts piled haphazardly on rickety shelves, and photographs that captured moments of joy, despair, and everything in between. A shiver ran down my spine as I stepped inside, the musty air wrapping around me like an old friend. It was intoxicating, the way the past lingered here, as though waiting for someone to breathe life into it again.

My fingers danced over the spines of the scripts, feeling the weight of the words that had once burst forth from them. I imagined the actors who had stood where I stood, the laughter and tears that had filled this space. Yet, it was a particular photograph that caught my breath—a faded image of Lucas, the theater's enigmatic director, his infectious smile captured alongside a woman whose striking resemblance to the ghostly figure haunting our backstage chilled me to the bone. I studied it closely, my heart racing as the puzzle pieces began to shift and align in my mind. Who was she? What story had entwined her with Lucas, and why did the air grow colder as I pieced together the fragments of this mystery?

Just as the realization began to settle, the door swung open with a jarring bang. Lucas stood there, his silhouette framed by the stormy night, an unexpected flash of vulnerability in his usually confident demeanor. Our eyes locked, and the air crackled with unspoken words.

"What are you doing here?" he demanded, a hint of annoyance lacing his tone.

I could feel the tension thickening like the storm clouds outside, but there was an undeniable thrill in the discovery that compelled me to answer defiantly. "Looking for ghosts, apparently," I shot back, gesturing toward the photograph in my hand. "Or maybe just trying to uncover some hidden secrets of the theater."

Lucas's brow furrowed, his lips pressing into a thin line. "You shouldn't be here. This place—there are things you don't understand."

"Maybe I want to understand," I challenged, stepping forward, emboldened by the shadows that clung to me like a second skin. "Who is she?" I asked, holding up the photograph, the weight of it heavy between us.

His expression darkened, and the storm outside raged on, its fury echoing our rising conflict. "That's not for you to know," he replied, his voice strained yet low, a thread of something deeper weaving through his words.

"Why not?" I pressed, my heart pounding with a mixture of fear and excitement. "This theater is filled with ghosts, and not just the ones we see. It feels like you're hiding something, Lucas. Something important."

"Sometimes," he said, taking a step closer, his frustration morphing into something more intense, "the past is better left buried. You might think you want to know, but trust me—some secrets are meant to stay hidden."

His eyes glinted in the low light, a tempest of emotions swirling just beneath the surface. I could feel the magnetic pull between us, igniting a fire that was both unsettling and exhilarating. "Why do you care?" I challenged, my voice wavering slightly as I tried to maintain my bravado.

"Because this theater is my life," he snapped, and in that moment, the distance between us narrowed, filled with unspoken histories and tangled emotions. "And I don't want you getting hurt."

"Maybe I want to get hurt," I retorted, my breath hitching in my throat. The vulnerability in his gaze made my resolve falter. "Maybe I'm tired of running from things I don't understand."

The air around us crackled with tension, the storm raging outside mirroring the tempest brewing between us. In an instant, the room seemed to shrink, and the world outside faded away. I could almost hear the pulse of the theater, the heartbeat of its stories calling to us.

"Don't say that," he whispered, his voice thick with urgency. "You don't know what you're asking for."

But before I could respond, before the storm could unleash its final fury, the distance between us shattered as our lips collided in a fierce, unexpected kiss. It was a collision of confusion and passion, of secrets and desires, leaving us both breathless, reeling from the moment. As the storm howled outside, we stood in the eye of our own tempest, two souls drawn together by the ghosts of the past, each moment echoing the promise of revelations yet to come.

The kiss hung between us, a fragile thread woven with uncertainty and wild energy. My heart raced, its rhythm echoing the storm outside, where the rain lashed against the windows with a ferocity that seemed almost jealous of our moment. Lucas pulled away, his breath uneven, and for a heartbeat, the world outside faded into insignificance. All that existed was the warmth lingering on my lips, the heat of his body still close enough to feel, and the tension thickening the air like the humidity before a summer storm.

"What just happened?" he asked, his voice a low rumble, a mixture of surprise and something darker.

"Something unexpected," I replied, my own voice a breathy whisper, aware of the weight of the photograph still clutched in my hand. The image of the woman and Lucas had burned into my mind, intertwining with the moment we'd just shared. "Maybe we both needed it."

"Or maybe it was a mistake," he countered sharply, stepping back, putting a wall between us that felt as tangible as the dusty shelves lined with old scripts. I could see the conflict raging in his eyes, a storm of emotions battling for dominance.

"Is that how you really feel?" I asked, my heart sinking at his words. "Because it didn't feel like a mistake to me." The passion we had just ignited was still flickering, a flame caught in the draught of our complicated circumstances.

His gaze shifted to the floor, the faint light catching the glimmer of unshed frustration. "I can't afford to let my emotions cloud my judgment, especially when there's so much at stake."

I bit my lip, torn between the exhilaration of our kiss and the weight of the secrets that seemed to loom over us like the gathering storm clouds outside. "What do you mean by that?" I pressed, unwilling to let him retreat into his fortress of solitude. "What's at stake, Lucas? Is it the theater? The productions? Or is it...us?"

The air grew heavy with unspoken words, and I felt a rush of boldness, as if the very essence of the theater urged me to push forward. "You can't keep burying your past, Lucas. It's in everything we do, in every performance. If we're going to work together, we have to confront it."

He ran a hand through his tousled hair, revealing the tension etched on his features. "You think it's that easy? You think just because you found a picture in some dusty corner, you understand everything? This isn't just about you and me. It's about a legacy, about lives that were changed here. You have no idea what you're stepping into."

"Then tell me!" I exclaimed, the frustration bubbling to the surface, igniting my determination. "Stop treating me like I'm a child who needs to be sheltered from the truth. I want to know."

He looked at me then, really looked at me, and I saw the flicker of something—a glimmer of hope, perhaps, or fear. "You really want to know?" he challenged, his voice low, almost conspiratorial. "Fine. But once you know, there's no turning back."

"I'm not afraid," I declared, the weight of the photograph heavy in my pocket, a talisman of the ghosts that danced between us.

"Good," he said, his tone shifting, a playful spark igniting in his eyes. "Because it's going to take more than courage to face what's lurking in the shadows of this theater. Are you ready to dive deep? Because once we start pulling back the layers, there's no telling what we'll uncover."

His words sent a shiver down my spine, and suddenly the thrill of the chase felt almost intoxicating. "I've been waiting for something real to happen in this place," I replied, determination lacing my words. "If this theater is haunted, then let's find out why."

Lucas studied me for a long moment, a smile breaking through the seriousness like sunlight piercing storm clouds. "Alright then, Miss Braveheart. Let's uncover the ghosts of our past."

As we stepped deeper into the hidden room, the air thick with anticipation, I felt a shift in our dynamic. The lines between director and actress began to blur, and in that moment, we became partners in a shared quest, the remnants of our argument slipping away like the sound of thunder fading into the distance.

He led me to a dusty old trunk tucked away in the corner, its leather cracked and worn. "This belonged to the woman in that photograph," he said, pointing to the faded image still clasped in my hand. "Her name was Amelia, and she was the brightest star this theater had ever seen. But her story... it's tragic."

I leaned in, my heart pounding as Lucas opened the trunk. Inside, layers of silk costumes and handwritten scripts spilled out like secrets begging to be shared. The delicate fabric shimmered even in the dim light, the colors vibrant with memories of performances long past.

"Amelia was an incredible actress," he began, his voice steady yet tinged with emotion. "She was my mentor, and when she vanished... it sent this theater into a tailspin. Rumors of her ghost began to spread, and ever since, every time a new production opens, people claim to see her. They say she's searching for something—or someone."

I looked up at Lucas, my breath catching as I processed his words. "What happened to her?" I asked, the weight of the moment settling on my shoulders.

"They say she fell in love with the wrong person," he replied, a shadow passing over his features. "Someone she was never meant to be with. And in the chaos that followed, she disappeared without a trace."

"Just like that?" I breathed, intrigued by the intertwining tales of love and loss. "What if she's not just haunting this theater? What if she's trying to tell us something? What if she wants us to find her?"

Lucas met my gaze, the flicker of doubt in his eyes slowly shifting to something more profound, a kindred spirit rising to the challenge. "Then we're in for a wild ride," he said with a hint of a smirk, the connection between us sparking anew. "Are you ready to play detective?"

With a deep breath, I nodded, my heart racing at the adventure ahead. "Absolutely. But remember, I'm not just your sidekick. I'm in this as much as you are."

As we began to sort through the remnants of Amelia's life, the theater hummed with possibilities, each script and costume a fragment of a tale waiting to be unraveled. Little did we know, our search for the truth would lead us to revelations we never anticipated, shifting the very foundations of our understanding—of the theater, of ourselves, and of the ties that bound us together, unearthing ghosts far more tangible than we had ever imagined.

The air felt charged as Lucas and I began to sift through Amelia's belongings, a palpable energy swirling around us. Each costume we unwrapped and each script we opened felt like a step deeper into a story that was both beautiful and tragic, a tangled web of dreams and heartaches woven into the very fabric of the theater. My fingers brushed against the delicate lace of a gown, its elegance timeless despite the dust that clung to it. "Can you imagine the magic this must have created on stage?" I mused, a smile creeping onto my lips as I imagined Amelia twirling beneath the bright lights, her laughter mingling with the applause of enchanted audiences.

Lucas's eyes sparkled with the same nostalgia, but then they darkened, his thoughts pulling him into a place I couldn't quite reach. "She had a way of captivating people," he replied, his voice barely above a whisper. "But the theater can be a dangerous place for those who lose themselves in its stories. I learned that the hard way."

"What do you mean?" I pressed, wanting to pry the layers off his guarded heart like the costumes we were uncovering. "What happened to you?"

He hesitated, a flicker of something raw crossing his features. "Amelia wasn't just a friend; she was everything to me. When she disappeared, it broke me. I thought I could save her, that I could pull her back from whatever darkness had taken hold. But in trying to save her, I lost myself."

I looked at him, really looked, and for the first time, I saw the scars hidden beneath his confident exterior. "You never really let go, have you?" I asked softly, wanting to bridge the distance that still clung between us.

"No," he admitted, his voice thick with emotion. "I thought if I buried myself in this theater, in her memory, maybe I could keep her alive somehow. But it only became a prison."

I felt a pang of empathy, the kind that twisted my heart in a way I hadn't expected. "Lucas, you don't have to bear this alone. We can figure this out together. Maybe finding the truth about Amelia will help you let go."

He paused, his gaze piercing into mine as if searching for some hidden strength within me. "What if the truth is more painful than you realize? What if it reveals something about this place that we can't change?"

"Then we'll face it," I replied firmly, my conviction echoing in the stillness of the room. "We owe it to Amelia to know her story."

Lucas's lips curved slightly, the tension between us shifting once more as he took a deep breath, resolve filling his eyes. "Alright. Let's find out what happened to her."

Together, we began to piece together the fragments of her life. Scripts led us to scribbled notes and letters tucked within the folds of elegant costumes, stories penned in moments of vulnerability. Each discovery felt like a thread unraveling from the tapestry of Amelia's existence. We laughed at her youthful exuberance and cried for the heartbreak etched into her words, recognizing our own reflections in the hopes and fears she expressed.

As the hours slipped away, the storm outside intensified, rain battering the theater with a ferocity that matched the intensity of our search. With every passing moment, I felt us moving closer—not just to Amelia's truth but to each other. Lucas's hand brushed against mine as we sorted through an old trunk, the contact igniting sparks that danced between us like fireflies in the night. The chemistry was undeniable, a current of electricity that coursed through my veins.

Just then, a sudden crash echoed through the theater, shattering our intimate bubble. Startled, I whipped my head toward the door, where the wind howled as if the spirits of the theater were warning us. Lucas stood frozen, his expression shifting from concern to something darker. "Did you hear that?" he whispered, a tension radiating from him.

"Yeah," I breathed, the hairs on the back of my neck standing on end. "It sounded like it came from the stage."

"Stay close," he said, his tone suddenly serious as he moved toward the door, and I followed, my heart pounding like a drum. The dimly lit corridor felt alive with an unsettling energy, shadows flickering as if the very walls were watching us.

As we stepped onto the stage, the world felt different. The air was thick, saturated with a weight that made it hard to breathe. The lights above flickered, casting eerie shadows that danced along the floorboards. I glanced around, my pulse quickening. "What could have caused that noise?"

Lucas motioned for silence, straining to listen. The sound of something dragging across the floor reached us, an unsettling rhythm that seemed to echo the very heartbeat of the theater. "It's coming from the prop room," he said, his voice low and steady.

"Should we check it out?" I asked, trying to sound braver than I felt. Every instinct screamed at me to turn back, but a sense of adventure held me firm.

With a determined nod, Lucas took the lead, his shoulders squared against the unknown. We moved cautiously through the dimly lit hallway, our footsteps muted by the thick carpet, each creak amplifying the tension that had settled between us.

When we reached the prop room, the door stood ajar, an ominous invitation. I felt a chill ripple through me as Lucas pushed it open slowly, the hinges groaning in protest. The room was a mess—props scattered about, shadows lurking in the corners, but nothing seemed out of place, nothing explained the noise.

Then, from the corner of my eye, I caught a flicker of movement—a flash of white fabric darting behind a tall stack of old scenery. I gasped, my heart racing. "Did you see that?"

Lucas nodded, his expression shifting from curiosity to concern. "Stay behind me."

He stepped forward, and as he did, the air felt charged again, like the stillness before a storm. We rounded the stack, and there it was—a costume, a shimmering gown that looked eerily familiar. My breath caught as I realized it resembled the one from the photograph of Amelia.

But just as I reached out to touch it, a cold wind swept through the room, extinguishing the lights in a blink. Darkness enveloped us, and a figure emerged, ethereal and flickering like a candle in the wind.

I squeezed Lucas's arm, the breath escaping my lungs as the ghostly silhouette of Amelia hovered before us, her eyes wide with a sorrow that seemed to reach across time.

And then, in a voice that echoed with both longing and despair, she whispered, "Help me."

Just as the words settled in my mind, the prop room door slammed shut behind us, trapping us in a shadowy embrace. The walls seemed to pulse, a heartbeat resonating with every fiber of my being, and I knew, without a doubt, that our lives were about to change forever.

Chapter 4: A Fractured Alliance

The air in the cramped rehearsal room buzzed with a nervous energy that mirrored the tangled web of emotions in my chest. Sunlight streamed through the tall windows, illuminating the dust motes dancing in the golden light, and for a moment, it felt like the world outside was untouched by the chaos that was brewing inside. The scent of fresh paint from the newly installed set pieces mingled with the faintest hint of stale coffee, creating a blend that was oddly comforting, yet charged with tension. I could almost convince myself that this was just another day of rehearsal for our high school production, but I knew better. Everything had changed after that kiss.

Lucas had a way of infuriating me like no one else. His confidence was infectious, his arrogance unbearable, and yet somehow, I couldn't shake the feeling that beneath his bravado was a vulnerability that intrigued me. We had danced around each other for weeks—two rival leads vying for the spotlight—until that moment. The kiss had been unexpected, a sudden collision of our contrasting personalities that left me breathless, and not just from the surprise. It was a jolt of electricity, a reminder that beneath the banter and bickering lay an undeniable chemistry that neither of us wanted to acknowledge.

Now, as we settled into our usual spots on the creaky wooden stage, the air felt thick with unspoken words and unresolved feelings. I stole a glance at Lucas, his dark hair tousled, eyes focused on the script. He caught my gaze and smirked, the corners of his mouth curving in that infuriatingly charming way that made my stomach flip. "Ready to embarrass yourself again, Hayes?" he teased, his voice low and dripping with sarcasm.

I rolled my eyes, forcing a smile. "I wouldn't dream of letting you steal the spotlight without a fight, Drake. Just try not to trip over your ego on your way to the stage."

The rehearsals had taken on a different tone since that kiss. Gone were the easy jibes that had defined our rivalry; now, each exchange was laced with a tension that was both thrilling and frustrating. It was a game of cat and mouse, and I was uncertain whether I was more cat or mouse. The atmosphere crackled with a mixture of attraction and annoyance, a precarious balance that made it hard to breathe.

Just as our director, Ms. Holloway, clapped her hands to gather our attention, a vibration in my pocket startled me. I glanced down at my phone, heart racing as I read the message that flashed across the screen: "Back off the play, or you'll regret it." A chill crept through me, and I instinctively glanced around, half-expecting to see a shadow lurking in the corner.

"Is everything okay, Hayes?" Lucas asked, concern etched in his features as he leaned closer. His playful demeanor shifted, and for a moment, I saw the real him—the one who cared, despite the front he put up.

I hesitated, the words stuck in my throat. "It's just a prank," I finally managed, forcing a laugh that felt hollow. "You know how it is—kids being kids."

"Right," he said, skepticism lacing his tone. But I could see the worry in his eyes, and it only added fuel to the fire of my growing anxiety. What if it wasn't just a prank? What if someone really wanted me out of the play?

As the rehearsal began, I tried to focus on my lines, forcing myself to ignore the tightening knot in my stomach. The scene unfolded around me, filled with laughter and camaraderie, yet I felt like a ghost among them, my mind drifting back to the message.

The words replayed in my head like a haunting melody, each note a reminder of the stakes I had unwittingly become a part of.

In the midst of a particularly intense moment, Lucas's voice broke through my thoughts. "Hayes, are you even paying attention?" He was smirking again, but there was a hint of genuine concern behind his playful jab. "Or are you too busy daydreaming about my stunning performance?"

"Right, because that's the only thing on my mind," I shot back, irritation mixing with an inexplicable urge to reach out to him, to pull him into my chaos. "But seriously, can you try not to be so distracting?"

His laughter echoed through the room, light and infectious. "If I'm distracting you, I must be doing something right."

But as the rehearsals continued, my mind was anything but focused on our flirtatious bickering. The messages kept coming, each one more menacing than the last, and Lucas's skepticism gradually turned into curiosity. "You're really going to let this get to you?" he asked one day after practice, his brow furrowed with concern. "It's just some idiot trying to scare you off."

"It's not just some idiot," I snapped, the frustration spilling over. "It feels...personal."

"I get it," he said, his tone shifting from teasing to earnest. "But I'm not going to let you face this alone." His words hung in the air, a surprising offer of solidarity that shattered the barriers we'd carefully constructed.

The rehearsals took on a new rhythm, marked by our ongoing bickering as well as moments of unexpected camaraderie. Lucas began to shadow me, a persistent presence at my side, and while our arguments continued to spark like flint on steel, I sensed a growing bond beneath the surface. The more we battled, the more I realized how much I craved his company. There was something intoxicating about the way he challenged me, pushing me to dig deeper, to confront the chaos swirling around us.

As the final curtain call loomed closer, the weight of the threats began to suffocate me, twisting in my gut. But with Lucas by my side, I found a sliver of strength I hadn't known I possessed. Even amid the uncertainty, I began to believe in our fractured alliance—a precarious truce that might just lead us to something unexpected. Something real.

With every rehearsal, the unease continued to weave itself into the fabric of our interactions, turning our rivalry into a dance of wits that was both invigorating and exhausting. I found myself caught in a relentless cycle of bickering and camaraderie with Lucas, each quip a prelude to an unexpected spark of connection that left me questioning everything I thought I knew about him—and myself.

"Hey, Hayes! Care to share what thrilling revelation has you lost in thought again?" Lucas called out one afternoon, his voice teasing yet edged with genuine curiosity. He had a knack for zeroing in on my moments of distraction, as if he could sense the undercurrents of my anxiety. His brows arched playfully, challenging me to keep up with his banter.

I shot him a look that was meant to convey annoyance, but I could feel the corners of my mouth twitching upwards. "Oh, I don't know. Just trying to decipher the nuances of your ego. It's like a complex play without a script," I replied, crossing my arms as I leaned back against the cool brick wall of the rehearsal space.

"Touché," he said, folding his arms in mock defeat. "But you have to admit, my ego does add a certain flair to this otherwise dreary production."

"Flair? More like a clown at a funeral," I retorted, laughter bubbling up despite the heaviness that had settled over me since the threats began. I appreciated the way our banter offered a momentary escape, a reprieve from the lurking shadows that threatened to engulf me.

As the days crept forward, the messages became more frequent, each one tauntingly cryptic, like a puzzle I was never meant to solve. "You don't belong here. Back off, or else." They were accompanied by a sense of dread that clung to my shoulders like an unwanted cloak. Lucas, however, seemed to embrace my turmoil with an odd intensity, refusing to let me wallow alone.

"Why are you still acting like this is just a game?" he pressed one day, frustration tinging his tone as we stood alone in the dim rehearsal space. The flickering fluorescent lights overhead hummed in protest as I struggled to keep my thoughts from spiraling. "You know it's not. Whoever's sending these messages means business."

I shrugged, feigning nonchalance. "It's probably just some bitter understudy with too much time on their hands. I can handle it."

His gaze pierced me, sharp and unwavering. "That's not how it works, Hayes. You can't just brush off a threat. This is serious."

"I'll deal with it," I insisted, my voice wavering despite my bravado. I could see the concern in his eyes, the way it softened the edges of his typically cocky demeanor. It made me uneasy, as if he were peering into the depths of my guarded heart, unearthing fears I was not yet ready to confront.

"Together, then," he said suddenly, and the weight of his words hung between us like a fragile thread. "We'll face it together. You might think you can tackle this solo, but I'm not letting you go down without a fight."

I opened my mouth to argue, to protest the idea of having him as my ally, but the warmth of his commitment quelled my rising frustration. There was a strange comfort in knowing that someone cared, even if that someone was Lucas—my rival turned reluctant partner in crime.

The following week, we decided to approach the issue head-on. We crafted a plan to investigate the source of the threats, transforming our rehearsals into a mix of drama and detective work. The air crackled with energy, tension vibrating between us as we whispered theories while preparing for our scenes.

"Maybe it's Ms. Holloway. You know, her creative juices have to come from somewhere," Lucas joked one day, gesturing dramatically to our director, who was engrossed in her notes, oblivious to our plotting. "After all, what better way to spice up a dull rehearsal than with a good old-fashioned villain?"

"Right, because making us jump through hoops and worry about our lives is the hallmark of great direction," I quipped back, laughing despite the unease in my chest. "You're ridiculous."

"Ridiculously brilliant," he shot back, a glint of mischief in his eyes. "But seriously, we should at least consider everyone. Trust no one."

As rehearsals dragged on, the blending of our two worlds—one filled with threat and the other with an insatiable desire to perform—created a strange sense of solidarity. During one particularly intense scene, where our characters were meant to confront their inner demons, Lucas and I exchanged glances that spoke volumes. It was as if our private battle had become an integral part of the performance itself, adding an authenticity to our acting that neither of us had anticipated.

Then came the moment when everything shifted. I had just finished a scene, heart racing, when my phone buzzed violently against the wooden floor. Picking it up, I found another message, the words cutting through my newfound courage like a knife. "One more chance, Hayes. Leave the play, or face the consequences."

The world around me faded, the laughter of my fellow castmates dulling to a distant echo. Panic tightened its grip on my throat, and

I looked up to find Lucas watching me, his expression shifting from playful to concerned in an instant.

"What is it?" he asked, stepping closer, his eyes narrowing in scrutiny. The energy in the room changed, and for a moment, the only sound was the soft thrum of my heartbeat.

"It's getting worse," I whispered, the gravity of the situation finally crashing down on me. "They're not playing around anymore."

Before I could catch my breath, Lucas took my phone from my hand, his gaze skimming over the message, brows furrowing deeper with each word. "This isn't just some prank, is it?" he said, his voice dropping to a serious tone that sent chills racing down my spine.

"No, it feels...personal," I admitted, the truth finally spilling from my lips. "I think they really want me out."

Lucas's jaw clenched, a look of determination igniting in his eyes. "Then we have to take this seriously. We're going to figure this out together, whether you like it or not."

The raw intensity in his voice grounded me, the flickering embers of fear igniting a fire within. I had been fighting this battle alone, but perhaps with Lucas by my side, I wouldn't have to anymore. In the middle of our fractured alliance, a thread of hope began to weave itself through the chaos, promising that together, we could face whatever darkness awaited us.

The energy in the rehearsal space had morphed into something almost tangible, a current that hummed beneath the surface of our interactions. With each passing day, the stakes felt higher, the threat looming like a dark cloud overhead. Yet, somehow, Lucas and I had stumbled into an unspoken agreement—one where we supported each other while still taking our jabs, and it felt both comforting and chaotic.

"Do you think whoever is behind these messages has a flair for the dramatic?" Lucas mused one afternoon, flipping through the script as we prepared for our next scene. The light from the tall windows cast long shadows across the floor, creating an ethereal atmosphere that felt more fitting for a thriller than our high school production.

I arched an eyebrow, unable to suppress a smirk. "Oh, absolutely. Maybe they're hoping for a starring role in our tragic tale of teenage angst and threats. We should consider casting them."

He laughed, the sound lightening the weight on my shoulders for just a moment. "Right? I can picture them now, lurking in the shadows, wearing a beret and clutching a notepad, composing their next piece of poetic intimidation."

"Only if they come equipped with an overly dramatic monologue," I added, a teasing glint in my eyes. "You know, something like 'I will have my revenge unless you abandon this pathetic play!'"

But as laughter bubbled between us, I felt a sudden chill run down my spine, a reminder of the danger that lingered just outside our bubble of humor. I pushed the thought aside, forcing myself to focus on our upcoming rehearsal. The play was set to open in a week, and I was determined to not let these threats ruin the only thing that mattered to me right now.

That evening, as we wrapped up for the day, Lucas leaned against the doorframe, arms crossed, watching me with that familiar intensity that sent butterflies fluttering in my stomach. "You're not actually going to let this go, are you?" he asked, genuine concern weaving through his teasing tone.

I shook my head, feeling a surge of determination. "No way. If anything, it's made me more determined to give the best performance of my life. I won't let anyone scare me off."

"Good," he said, pushing himself off the wall and stepping closer, the warmth of his presence somehow bolstering my resolve. "But we still need to dig into this. I don't like the idea of you facing this alone."

I met his gaze, the spark of camaraderie igniting something deeper between us, a connection that made my heart race for reasons I wasn't quite ready to explore. "What do you suggest? We turn into amateur detectives in our spare time?"

"Exactly," he replied, the mischief returning to his eyes. "I can't believe I'm saying this, but we need to gather intel. Time to channel our inner Sherlock Holmes."

The next day, we devised a plan to confront our fellow cast members, casually gathering information while feigning nonchalance. Our strategy felt like a bizarre combination of spy movie and school drama, and every whispered conversation and scrutinizing glance held the potential for revelation.

We approached Olivia, the ever-enthusiastic stage manager, who was flitting about, organizing props and checking cues. "Hey, Liv," I called, catching her attention. "Have you heard anything weird going around? You know, aside from Lucas's constant need for attention?"

"Funny, Hayes," Lucas quipped, shooting me a playful glare.

Olivia frowned, glancing between us. "Weird? You mean besides the fact that you two are practically inseparable now? I mean, what happened? One minute you're rivaling for lead, and now you're practically a team."

"We're just... exploring new dynamics," I said, forcing a casual smile. "But seriously, have you noticed anything strange? Anyone acting... suspicious?"

Her brow furrowed in thought. "Now that you mention it, I overheard some whispers. People have been talking about you, Hayes. A couple of the techies mentioned something about wanting you out of the play."

"Of course they have," Lucas muttered, rolling his eyes. "It's not jealousy; it's just good old-fashioned melodrama."

"Right, because everyone loves a tragic heroine," I shot back, my heart racing. "But what exactly did they say?"

"Just something about you being a distraction," Olivia said, shrugging. "People are nervous about the performance. It happens, you know?"

I nodded, but the knot in my stomach tightened. It felt like every passing hour was drawing us closer to the truth, and I wasn't sure if I was ready to face it.

Later that week, as the final rehearsal approached, the atmosphere shifted. The whispers had intensified, but there was also an unspoken solidarity forming among us. Lucas seemed to pick up on it too, his competitive spirit tempered by a protective instinct that was unexpected yet comforting.

On a particularly tense afternoon, we found ourselves alone in the theater, the hushed silence enveloping us. I could hear the faint echoes of past performances, memories lingering in the corners of the empty seats. "Do you ever think about how quickly things can change?" I asked, my voice barely above a whisper.

"Every day," he replied, his tone suddenly serious as he leaned against the back of the stage. "One moment you're riding high on adrenaline, and the next, you're dodging anonymous threats and wondering who you can trust."

"Exactly," I said, meeting his gaze. "It's like we're in some twisted drama, and I'm not sure I want to know how it ends."

"Maybe we just need to rewrite the script," he suggested, a hint of that trademark mischief returning to his eyes. "Make it a thriller instead of a tragedy."

I chuckled, appreciating his ability to lighten the mood even when everything felt heavy. "You think we can pull that off?"

"Together, we can pull off anything," he said, the sincerity in his voice making my heart race.

But before I could respond, a sudden noise shattered the silence—an unmistakable crash from backstage. Our eyes widened as we exchanged a look of alarm. "Did you hear that?" I breathed, my heart racing.

"Yeah, let's check it out," Lucas said, his voice low, a protective edge creeping in as he stepped ahead of me, leading the way into the shadows.

As we approached the source of the noise, the tension in the air grew palpable. "It's probably just a prop falling," I whispered, trying to convince myself.

"Or something much worse," Lucas replied, glancing over his shoulder, his expression grave.

We stepped cautiously into the dimly lit space, the smell of dust and old wood surrounding us. Shadows flickered in the corners, and the hairs on the back of my neck stood on end. "What if it's just a misplaced scene change?" I suggested, though I didn't truly believe it.

But as we rounded the corner, the sight that greeted us was anything but benign. A figure stood amid the scattered props, their back turned to us, frozen in the act of—what? Vandalism? Sabotage? Before I could process the scene, the figure spun around, and my breath hitched in my throat.

The familiar face emerged from the shadows, their expression unreadable. "Well, well, look who decided to play detective."

Chapter 5: Shadows of the Past

The theater stood as a relic of forgotten glamour, its once-vibrant facade now cloaked in shadows that twisted like whispered secrets in the night. I felt the weight of the place pressing down on me, the air thick with the scent of aged wood and lingering perfume, remnants of a bygone era where laughter and applause had danced in the aisles. Now, a sense of foreboding hung heavy in the velvet-draped air, as though the very walls had absorbed the sorrow and triumph of those who once tread its stage.

As I walked through the dimly lit corridors, the flickering lights above cast playful shadows that flickered and darted like mischievous spirits. Each step echoed with the history of countless performers who had poured their hearts into this space, yet my mind was clouded by the threat that had surfaced, an unsettling harbinger of what was to come. I clutched my notebook—a steadfast companion in this labyrinth of intrigue—while my heart raced with an insatiable curiosity. My investigation had taken a dark turn, revealing an undercurrent of terror that threatened to unravel everything I had worked for.

Then there was Lucas. He had become an enigma I couldn't quite decipher. His sharp wit and unnerving charm had initially thrown me off balance, positioning him firmly as my adversary in the battle to reclaim this theater. But beneath the layers of his bravado, I sensed a vulnerability, a flicker of pain that sparked my interest. It was during one of our late-night discussions in the empty dressing room, illuminated by the ghostly glow of a single overhead bulb, that the truth began to unfold like an intricate tapestry woven from despair and hope.

"Did you know," Lucas began, his voice low and gravelly, "that the theater holds onto its past? The echoes of every performance, every life that graced this stage, they linger like smoke from a long-extinguished fire." His gaze drifted, distant, as if he were peering into a realm I could not access.

I leaned forward, intrigued. "What do you mean? Are you talking about the haunting rumors? The actress who disappeared?"

His eyes flickered with an intensity that sent a shiver down my spine. "Her name was Eliza Hartley. A brilliant star—one of the best this theater has ever seen. She vanished without a trace one fateful night, and they say the theater has been cursed ever since."

I could feel the atmosphere shift, thickening around us, suffocating in its solemnity. The tragic story poured from Lucas like the slow drip of a tap, revealing layers I hadn't anticipated. "They found her costume, torn and bloodied, behind the curtains. But no sign of her body. Some say she was taken by the spirits that roam these halls, others whisper about a lover scorned. No one knows for sure, but her presence lingers."

I could see the pain etched on his features, the way he wrestled with the weight of the narrative. This was no longer just a ghost story; it was a wound that had never healed. I felt an unexpected pang of empathy for him, and for the woman who had lived a life consumed by ambition and tragedy.

"Why are you telling me this?" I asked, my voice a mere whisper, as if the shadows were listening.

His gaze met mine, and for a moment, the playful banter that had defined our interactions evaporated, leaving something raw and unguarded in its wake. "Because I think you deserve to know what we're up against. This isn't just about a production anymore. It's about uncovering the truth, about bringing justice to a soul that was wronged."

My heart raced at the shift in our dynamic. The lines that had been so clear—friend and foe—began to blur, softened by our shared quest for understanding. I had seen Lucas as an opponent, yet now, in the dim light of that dressing room, he appeared more like a kindred spirit, burdened by the echoes of the past.

"What if we could find out what really happened to her?" I proposed, the idea igniting a flicker of hope within me. "What if we brought her story back to life? It could be the heart of our production."

Lucas regarded me with a mixture of surprise and admiration. "You're willing to risk everything for a ghost story?"

"I'm willing to risk everything for the truth," I countered, my conviction strengthening with each word.

He chuckled, the tension easing slightly. "Well, I guess we make quite the pair, don't we? Two fools chasing shadows in a haunted theater."

And just like that, the tension shifted again, the air crackling with a new energy. Together, we embarked on this unexpected journey—two determined souls drawn together by fate, entwined in the tangled threads of history and mystery. As we pieced together the fragmented echoes of Eliza's life, I began to see Lucas not just as an adversary but as a man shaped by sorrow, desperately seeking redemption in the shadows of his past.

Outside, the world continued its indifferent march, but within the theater's walls, we were cocooned in our own universe—a realm where the past breathed life into the present, where every corner held the potential for discovery. As we moved deeper into the enigma of Eliza Hartley, I couldn't shake the feeling that perhaps our fates were intertwined, echoing the tragic tale we were about to unravel together.

The theater's energy shifted, an electric charge thrumming between us as I considered the weight of Lucas's revelations. It felt as if the very walls conspired to keep Eliza's secrets buried, and yet, there was a thrill in the pursuit—a sense of purpose that ignited a fire within me. I'd entered this world as an outsider, determined to protect my vision and uphold our production, but now I found myself entangled in a web of history and heartache, each thread pulling tighter around us.

With the burden of our discovery heavy in the air, I leaned closer to Lucas, the tension between us palpable. "So, what's our next move? We can't just sit here and let Eliza's story fade into oblivion."

He scratched his chin, an adorable habit I hadn't noticed before, and I caught a glimpse of a hesitant smile tugging at the corners of his mouth. "We could start by digging into the archives. There's an old newspaper in the library that might have details about her disappearance. And, who knows, maybe a few eyewitness accounts."

"Great idea. I'll grab my flashlight," I quipped, half-joking, but there was a part of me that knew I would dive headfirst into this mystery. The shadows of the past beckoned us, and I felt a strange kinship with the ghost of a woman I'd never met, her story resonating with the faint echoes of my own struggles.

As we made our way to the library, the sound of our footsteps echoed in the cavernous space, each thud against the polished floor reverberating like a heartbeat. The musty scent of old books welcomed us, and I couldn't help but feel that we were intruders in a sanctum of forgotten tales. I swept my gaze across the room, my fingers grazing the spines of countless volumes, each one a testament to lives lived, dreams pursued, and hearts broken.

"Why are you so eager to unearth this?" Lucas asked, his curiosity tinged with skepticism as he flipped through a dusty tome. "It's just a ghost story, after all."

I turned to him, my heart pounding with an urgency I couldn't quite articulate. "It's more than that. Eliza's disappearance is a mystery that deserves to be solved. She was a person with dreams and aspirations, and she deserves to be remembered—not just as a specter haunting the stage, but as a real woman who lived and loved."

Lucas regarded me with an intensity that made my stomach flutter. "You're right. She deserves that. But what if we find something that complicates things? Something that doesn't fit our narrative?"

"Then we adapt," I replied, my voice steady, trying to channel my resolve into something palpable. "We tell the whole story, the messy parts included. That's what art is about, right? The truth, however painful."

He nodded slowly, the tension in his shoulders easing slightly. "Okay, let's dig. But if we uncover a scandal, I'm going to make you promise not to shy away from the juicy bits. This isn't just a history lesson; it's theater."

We shared a conspiratorial grin, and I couldn't help but feel the spark between us ignite, a warmth that softened the edges of our earlier friction. Together, we navigated the labyrinthine shelves, a quest for knowledge binding us closer.

After hours of rummaging through old newspapers, yellowed with age, we stumbled upon an article that sent chills racing down my spine. It detailed a gala held at the theater the night Eliza vanished, complete with names of attendees, whispered rumors, and a photograph that captured her radiant smile. I traced the outline of her face, a ghost of a woman who had once dazzled audiences with her presence, and a pang of sorrow washed over me.

"Look at this," I whispered, turning the page to reveal a sketch of the stage, vibrant with performers dressed in elaborate costumes. "She was part of something beautiful, and now she's just... gone."

Lucas leaned in closer, his breath warm against my ear. "It's haunting, isn't it? This was her life. But then, there's something unsettling about this photo. If Eliza was so beloved, why did no one seem to care when she disappeared?"

The question hung between us like a specter, and I felt a knot tighten in my stomach. "Maybe they were afraid. Or maybe there was something more sinister at play. You don't just vanish without leaving a trace."

His brow furrowed as he processed my words, and in that moment, I saw the flicker of understanding cross his features. "Let's not forget the theater's reputation. It thrives on secrets. Maybe someone wanted to keep hers buried."

A tension built, twisting like a coiling vine, each revelation deepening the shadows that danced around us. The air crackled with uncertainty as we pieced together the fragments of Eliza's life. Every clue seemed to lead us further into a maze of darkness, and I could feel the weight of our discoveries pressing down like a storm on the horizon.

"I want to meet someone who was there that night," I declared suddenly, resolve surging within me. "There has to be someone left who remembers her. We need firsthand accounts."

Lucas's eyes sparked with mischief. "I like your style. How do you feel about crashing a few parties, then? Digging up dirt can be exhilarating, you know."

I laughed, a lightness blooming within the heaviness of our quest. "You mean, we're going to charm the pants off the local socialites? I'm in. But I get to choose the outfits."

"Of course," he replied, the warmth of his voice wrapping around me like a comfortable embrace. "But just remember, if we're going to dig up ghosts, we might as well do it in style."

And just like that, amid the darkness and uncertainty, we transformed our shared burden into a thrilling adventure, the thrill of discovery glimmering in the dim light of the library. We were no longer just adversaries locked in a battle of wills; we had become unlikely partners, bound together by our determination to uncover the truth that had eluded so many. The ghosts of the past beckoned, and together we would step into the shadows, ready to illuminate the darkness.

Our plan to infiltrate the local social scene took shape over the following days, an exhilarating mix of strategy and spontaneity that left me buzzing with anticipation. The theater, with its peeling paint and whispered secrets, had become a cocoon of possibility, and I felt a shift within me—an awakening, perhaps—drawing me closer to Lucas. Each time we strategized, a current of tension flickered between us, teasing at the edges of something deeper, something that tangled together our shared quest for truth and the unspoken feelings simmering just beneath the surface.

As we prepared for our first social event—a gala held at the estate of one of the theater's most prominent benefactors—I scoured my closet, searching for an outfit that would say, "I mean business" while still allowing me to blend in among the polished elite. The night arrived with a cascade of stars twinkling above, mirroring my own excitement. I slipped into a deep emerald gown that flowed like liquid silk, the color accentuating my eyes in a way that made me feel both fierce and vulnerable. The mirror reflected a woman ready to face the ghosts of the past, both literal and metaphorical.

When Lucas arrived, I almost forgot to breathe. He stood at my door, clad in a tailored navy suit that seemed to mold perfectly to his frame. The sharp lines of his attire highlighted the casual confidence that he wore like a second skin, and for a fleeting moment, all thoughts of Eliza Hartley and our mission fell away.

"Wow," he said, taking a moment to appraise me, his gaze lingering a little too long before a smirk played on his lips. "If I knew a ghost hunt could look this good, I would have signed up ages ago."

"Just wait until you see my dance moves," I shot back, feigning a playful confidence that masked the nerves prickling beneath my skin.

As we stepped into the gala, the opulence of the estate unfolded before us, a sprawling tapestry of laughter, clinking glasses, and the soft strains of a string quartet weaving through the air. Chandeliers glimmered like stars trapped in glass, casting a warm glow over the elegantly dressed guests. The atmosphere crackled with the electric energy of high society, a world that felt both intoxicating and utterly foreign to me.

Lucas was in his element, gliding through the crowd with a charm that turned heads. I found myself caught up in the tide of people, his presence a comforting anchor amidst the sea of unfamiliar faces. With every introduction, he deftly navigated conversations, dropping names and anecdotes like breadcrumbs, drawing me into the fold.

But it was a chance encounter with a woman named Beatrice that set the stage for our next move. Beatrice, a silver-haired matron with an eye for gossip sharper than any dagger, had been a close friend of Eliza's during her final days. She held court by the grand fireplace, regaling a small audience with tales that sparkled with scandal and intrigue. As Lucas and I approached, her eyes flickered with interest.

"Ah, young lovebirds!" she declared, her voice laced with a playful teasing that made me want to squirm. "What brings you two to this sea of drab conformity?"

"Just fishing for stories," I said, matching her wit with my own, though my heart raced at the implications.

"Stories are my specialty," she winked, the glimmer in her eye promising secrets buried beneath layers of decorum. "But what you seek is dangerous. Eliza's tale is a double-edged sword, and some truths are best left undiscovered."

My stomach tightened at her words, but Lucas leaned in, unfazed. "We're not afraid of the truth, Beatrice. We want to honor her memory."

Her gaze shifted between us, a silent calculation playing out in her expression. "Honor, you say? How noble. But be warned—those who seek to unveil the past often find themselves ensnared by it."

I could feel Lucas's tension beside me, a quiet understanding passing between us as we took in Beatrice's warning. But I wouldn't back down. Not now. "We're not looking for trouble, just clarity. Can you help us?"

Beatrice considered for a moment, her smile tinged with mischief. "Very well, my dears. Meet me tomorrow at the café by the old mill. Bring a notebook, and be prepared for a story that twists like a vine. Eliza's life was not merely a tale of beauty and loss; it was a tapestry woven with envy, ambition, and heartbreak."

With that tantalizing promise hanging in the air, Beatrice melted back into the crowd, leaving us both reeling from her words. Lucas turned to me, his eyes alight with determination. "This is it. If anyone can guide us, it's her. We need to be ready for whatever she reveals."

We spent the rest of the evening mingling and dancing, laughter echoing in the grand hall, but beneath the surface, I could feel the tension brewing, a palpable anticipation for what was to come. As the night wore on, I found myself increasingly aware of Lucas's presence, the way our hands brushed as we navigated through the throngs, the electricity that danced between us igniting a spark of something deeper.

The gala ended, and as we stepped back into the cool night air, the world felt impossibly vast. The stars twinkled above us, mirroring the tension in my chest as I contemplated the path ahead. "What do you think Beatrice will say?" I asked, my voice barely rising above the night's whispers.

"Whatever it is, we'll face it together," Lucas replied, his tone steady, yet I sensed an undercurrent of apprehension.

The next morning, a storm rolled in, dark clouds swirling ominously as if nature itself were bracing for our confrontation with the past. When we arrived at the café, I found Beatrice seated at a table in the corner, a stack of papers piled before her, her expression grave.

As we approached, she looked up, her eyes narrowing in scrutiny. "You're here for the truth, but remember—truth is a fickle companion."

Before I could respond, the door burst open, and a figure stood silhouetted against the stormy sky. My heart raced as I recognized him—James, a prominent director with ties to the theater and a man whose name was whispered in hushed tones among the staff. He looked directly at us, a dark smirk playing on his lips.

"What do you think you're doing?" he asked, his voice dripping with contempt, the atmosphere shifting abruptly with his presence. "You don't want to dig too deep into Eliza's past. It's a place best left undisturbed."

The air crackled with tension as Beatrice's expression turned from curiosity to icy resolve, and in that moment, the storm outside felt like the perfect backdrop to the chaos unfurling within the café. My pulse quickened as I exchanged glances with Lucas, the stakes rising higher than ever. What secrets had Eliza's life held, and how far would those in power go to keep them buried?

Chapter 6: Twisted Alliances

The air was thick with the scent of freshly painted sets, the lingering aroma mingling with the salty tang of popcorn from the lobby. The dim lights of the theater flickered like nervous fireflies, casting shadows that danced along the walls. It was the night before opening, and the cast buzzed with a frenetic energy that both exhilarated and exhausted me. I could hear snippets of conversation—half-hearted jokes and frantic last-minute preparations—colliding with the deep rumble of the orchestra tuning their instruments. In this cacophony, I found a strange comfort, yet a tremor of anxiety lay just beneath the surface.

Rehearsals had become a battleground, each of us fiercely guarding our roles like prized possessions. I could feel the weight of competition hanging over us, thick as the velvet curtains that framed the stage. Lucas stood across the room, his dark hair falling in messy waves over his forehead, an intense focus gleaming in his hazel eyes. The way he moved through the space was almost magnetic, a force that drew attention even in the chaotic swirl of our pre-show madness. We had shared heated debates about our characters, pushing each other to dig deeper, to perform better. Yet, each exchange ignited a different fire, one that crackled with unspoken words and shared glances that lingered a moment too long.

As the rehearsal dragged into the evening, a tension began to unravel. Whispers echoed about a series of mishaps that had plagued the production—lights flickering ominously, misplaced props, and a shadowy figure seen lurking backstage. No one could pinpoint what was happening, but the whispers grew louder, fueled by fear and paranoia. I could see it in the eyes of my fellow cast members; the shared glances, the hushed conversations. Everyone was on edge, as if the very walls of the theater were closing in around us.

"Can you believe this?" I muttered to Jenna, my best friend and fellow cast member, as we waited for our cue. "It's like we're in a horror movie."

"Don't say that! You'll jinx us," she replied, rolling her eyes but not hiding her own unease. "Just focus on your lines. We can't afford to mess up tomorrow."

The lights dimmed, and we resumed our positions. My heart pounded in my chest as I prepared for my entrance. I was about to step into a world where the ordinary faded into the background, replaced by the melodrama of the stage. Yet, as the rehearsal progressed, a feeling of dread settled over me. I brushed it off, telling myself it was simply nerves, but the unsettling sensation continued to swirl in my gut.

After a particularly heated scene, I found myself wandering backstage, the echoes of the performance fading behind me. The narrow hallway felt claustrophobic, shadows clinging to the corners as I made my way toward the storage room, where the costumes hung like ghostly figures. I paused, hearing a rustle behind me, and my breath quickened. It was nothing—a stray prop or a wayward breeze—but I couldn't shake the feeling of being watched. I pressed onward, the overhead lights flickering sporadically, adding to my disquiet.

Just as I reached for a coat to check its fit, a sudden crash echoed from the main stage area, followed by frantic voices. Adrenaline surged through me, and without thinking, I turned to run back toward the sound. That's when I saw him—a dark figure darting away from the scene, blending into the shadows like a wraith. Panic coursed through my veins, and I instinctively called out, "Hey! Stop!"

My voice trembled as I pushed through the backstage chaos, desperate to make sense of what was happening. Suddenly, a pair of arms wrapped around me from behind, pulling me to safety just as

I was about to collide with the wall. I gasped, my heart racing, and turned to see Lucas, his expression a mixture of concern and fury.

"What were you thinking?" he demanded, his voice low and urgent, eyes scanning the space around us. "You can't just go chasing after someone like that."

"I saw someone!" I exclaimed, breathless. "They were right there!"

"I don't care! This isn't the time to be a hero," he snapped, the intensity of his gaze sending a shiver down my spine. For a moment, we stood there, the tension between us palpable, the heat of our argument swirling like the chaos around us.

"I'm not trying to be a hero," I retorted, my voice sharp, yet I could feel the crackling connection between us, a raw current that both scared and thrilled me. "I just wanted to make sure everyone was safe."

He softened slightly, his features easing as he studied my face. "You're too brave for your own good, you know that?" The hint of a smile broke through, the fierce look in his eyes melting into something more tender, something unexpected.

"Someone has to be," I replied, our arguments often blurring into this uncharted territory where rivalry danced with something deeper, something fragile and delicate that neither of us wanted to acknowledge.

Before I could say more, the commotion escalated, and our moment shattered like glass. The clamor of voices erupted, and as we hurried to rejoin the others, my heart thudded in rhythm with my racing thoughts. We were stepping onto a precipice where alliances would twist, and loyalties would be tested. My gut twisted in anticipation; I could feel the weight of unspoken words between us, a bond forming under the pressure of the unknown.

As we rejoined the group, the atmosphere crackled with tension, and I couldn't shake the feeling that we were all pieces on a chessboard, precariously balanced as the stakes rose higher. The night loomed before us, the curtain ready to rise on something far more than just a play, a treacherous game where trust was as fleeting as the stage lights that flickered overhead. And as I glanced at Lucas, I wondered if our growing closeness could survive the chaos that was about to unfold.

The stage was set for chaos, the kind that unfolded in unexpected bursts like confetti in a windstorm. I could feel the anticipation humming in the air, the pulse of the theater resonating through the very floorboards beneath my feet. Each tick of the clock echoed in my mind, a countdown to the opening night that felt both thrilling and utterly terrifying. We had spent countless hours rehearsing, each of us weaving our characters into something real, something tangible, but now the weight of our performances loomed larger than ever.

As I navigated the labyrinth of backstage, the shadows stretched like dark fingers reaching for me, the dim light flickering ominously. I spotted Jenna, pacing nervously by the prop table, her fingers anxiously twisting the fabric of her costume. "I'm going to throw up," she muttered, her eyes wide and panicked. "What if I forget my lines? What if the lights go out again?"

"Then we'll improvise. Besides, you could pull off a dramatic monologue about the existential dread of an ill-fated prop," I quipped, trying to infuse some humor into the situation. Jenna shot me a look that was half amusement, half disbelief. "You know, something like, 'Alas, poor Yorick, you were once a glorious hand mirror, but now you're nothing but a broken shard of glass!'"

Her laughter echoed softly in the tension-heavy air, and for a fleeting moment, the anxiety lifted like a curtain, allowing us a brief respite. Yet, as we exchanged playful banter, I felt the heaviness creeping back in, a subtle reminder of the unseen threat lurking in the shadows. The whispers had spread, each cast member muttering about accidents and strange occurrences. I couldn't shake the feeling that something more sinister was at play, an undercurrent of dread that surged through our rehearsal.

As the clock ticked closer to midnight, the rehearsal began to resemble a surreal blend of reality and the fantastical. The director called for a run-through of the final act, and as we took our places, the atmosphere crackled with palpable tension. I stood in the wings, peering out at the dimly lit stage, where our world would soon come to life. It was in this moment of anticipation, just before the curtain rose, that I spotted Lucas moving with a quiet intensity, a determined set to his jaw that sent a shiver down my spine.

He caught my eye, and for a heartbeat, the noise of the rehearsal faded away, leaving just the two of us suspended in a moment of shared understanding. He gave me a nod, a silent promise that we were in this together. The connection between us had deepened unexpectedly, forged through shared fears and the raw vulnerability that bubbled beneath the surface. The rivalry that had once defined our interactions now felt like an intricate dance, each step leading us closer to something we had yet to name.

The rehearsal proceeded with a chaotic elegance, our performances intertwining in a way that felt both exhilarating and dangerous. The energy in the room surged, each laugh and gasp drawing us deeper into the world we had created. Yet, in the back of my mind, I remained hyper-aware of the lingering threat. Shadows seemed to stretch longer, and the sudden clang of metal made my heart leap into my throat.

Then it happened.

In the midst of a particularly dramatic scene, I heard a crash, sharp and jarring, cutting through the air like a knife. I turned, my heart racing, to see one of the set pieces topple ominously toward me. Instinct kicked in; I lunged to the side just as Lucas bolted from the other side of the stage, his body a blur of motion. He reached me just in time, his arms wrapping around me and pulling me out of the way with a force that knocked the breath from my lungs.

The heavy prop crashed to the ground where I had just stood, sending up a cloud of dust and a collective gasp from the cast. "Are you okay?" Lucas asked, his voice low and urgent as he stepped back to assess my state. The intensity of his gaze burned into mine, and I could see the fear etched in the lines of his face, the worry that sent a thrill of warmth coursing through me.

"I'm fine," I managed, still trying to regain my composure. "Just a little startled."

"Startled? You could have been seriously hurt!" He ran a hand through his hair, frustration boiling just beneath the surface. "What if I hadn't been here?"

"Thank you for the heroic save," I replied, attempting a teasing tone to mask the tremor of adrenaline that still coursed through me. "Next time, I'll make sure to wear a cape."

"Seriously, though," he continued, his voice dropping to a near whisper, "this isn't just bad luck. Something feels off. We need to be careful."

A chill skittered down my spine at his words, and the laughter of our fellow cast members faded into the background as the weight of reality settled heavily upon us. I could feel the tension in the air shift, the camaraderie of the rehearsal replaced by a cautious wariness.

"I know," I replied, my voice barely above a whisper. "It's like we're being watched. It's all... too much."

"I won't let anything happen to you," he declared, the fierce protectiveness in his voice a balm against the rising unease. "You mean too much to this show, and, well, to me."

The confession hung between us, heavy and electrifying. I could feel my cheeks warm, and the vulnerability in his eyes mirrored my own. Our roles as rivals began to blur, the lines of competition dissolving in the face of something far more profound. Just as I opened my mouth to respond, a loud voice cut through the moment, pulling us back into the reality of our surroundings.

"Can we get back to rehearsing?" our director snapped, breaking the spell that had formed around us. "We're not paying you to stand around looking pretty! Let's take it from the top!"

With that, we reluctantly returned to our positions, the previous tension simmering just below the surface, threatening to erupt again at any moment. But I could still feel Lucas's presence, the warmth of his body lingering in my mind, a reminder that even amidst chaos, we had each other's backs. In a world fraught with uncertainty, it was a small comfort, but a comfort nonetheless, one that would lead us deeper into the tangled web of our lives. As we resumed our roles, I steeled myself for the unpredictability of the night ahead, knowing that whatever lay in wait, I wouldn't have to face it alone.

The night dragged on, a cacophony of footsteps and frantic whispers reverberating in the theater as we moved through the final rehearsals. The atmosphere was charged, a simmering blend of anxiety and excitement that thickened the air like smoke. I could sense the tension in every corner, every creak of the floorboards, every shadow flickering across the walls. It felt as if we were on the brink of something monumental—or something disastrous.

Jenna flitted around the stage, adjusting her costume and muttering lines under her breath. "I think I'm one line away from becoming the dramatic ghost of this production," she quipped, her eyes darting nervously. "You know, the one who haunts the backstage, warning everyone to leave while they still can."

"Only if your ghost costume has a fabulous cape," I teased, trying to lighten the mood. But my heart wasn't in it. The backstage whispers had taken on a more frantic tone, filled with hushed concerns and furtive glances. Someone had mentioned a series of pranks escalating into outright sabotage, and each mention felt like a frayed thread pulling us closer to unraveling.

Lucas lingered at the edge of the stage, his eyes scanning the room with a guarded intensity. I could see the wheels turning in his mind, the weight of responsibility settling heavily on his shoulders. "We need to stay focused," he said quietly, stepping closer to me, the proximity sending an electric jolt through my body. "Whatever's happening, we can't let it derail the show."

"Agreed. But what if it's more than just pranks?" I asked, my voice barely above a whisper. The fear that had settled in my gut felt like an anchor dragging me down. "What if someone is really trying to hurt us?"

He stepped even closer, his expression resolute. "Then we'll figure it out together. No one is going to take this from us."

I held his gaze, the intensity of the moment magnifying the growing tension between us. In that charged silence, I felt the walls of rivalry and fear begin to crack, exposing the raw emotions simmering beneath the surface. I could see the reflection of my own fears mirrored in his eyes—an acknowledgment of the stakes we were playing for.

But before I could respond, the director's voice cut through the air, demanding our attention with a commanding shout. "Let's get back to it! From the top, people! We don't have all night!"

With a reluctant nod, we returned to our places. The rehearsal resumed, but the air felt different, fraught with the unspoken understanding that we were navigating more than just our characters' arcs. Each line I delivered felt weighted, infused with the tension that thrummed through the theater like a live wire.

As the final act approached, I could feel the energy shift once more. Jenna, usually a ball of laughter, had fallen quiet, her eyes darting around the stage, scanning for the slightest hint of danger. "I don't like this, not one bit," she murmured as we prepared for our climactic scene. "It feels like we're being hunted."

"Just stick to the script," I replied, though my heart raced at her words. The idea of being hunted echoed in my mind, sending a fresh wave of unease coursing through me.

We moved through the scene with practiced precision, but as I stepped into the spotlight, I felt the familiar thrill of performance mingling with dread. The audience would soon be here, and with them, all the eyes that had turned our intimate world into a spectacle. I could hear the murmur of voices from the front rows, an audience slowly gathering, their excitement palpable.

But in that moment, a sound pierced through the rehearsal—a loud crash echoed from the props area, followed by a strangled cry. My heart dropped, and I turned to see the shadows shift near the entrance. Lucas was already moving, his body a blur as he rushed toward the sound. I followed instinctively, fear propelling me forward, every nerve in my body tingling with the instinct to protect those around me.

As we burst through the doorway, we found a scene that sent my heart racing. A heavy prop had fallen, narrowly missing Jenna, who stood frozen in shock, her face pale. But it wasn't just the prop that drew my attention; a figure cloaked in shadow stood nearby, their outline barely visible in the dim light.

"Who are you?" I shouted, my voice trembling but fierce, the protective instinct rising within me.

The figure turned, and for a fleeting moment, our eyes locked. A chill coursed through me as recognition sparked—someone from our cast, a once-trusted ally now obscured by an air of menace. "This is your fault," they hissed, voice dripping with anger. "You've ruined everything!"

Before I could process their words, they took a step back, retreating into the darkness. "Wait!" I called, but they melted into the shadows, disappearing from sight. Lucas was right beside me, his expression tense. "We have to get Jenna out of here. This isn't safe."

"But they know us," I replied, my mind racing. "What if they come back?"

"We can't dwell on that now. We need to secure the area and make sure everyone is accounted for." He turned to Jenna, who still looked shaken. "Let's go."

As we retraced our steps, the atmosphere thickened with uncertainty. The theater felt different now, like a living entity filled with secrets and hidden dangers. I could sense the rest of the cast gathering, anxious murmurs echoing through the halls as they sensed something had changed.

Then, from the far end of the stage, I heard a voice rise above the others, loud and clear. "Everyone, we need to talk about what's been happening!" It was our director, her face etched with concern. "There are things we need to address, and we can't ignore them any longer."

A knot tightened in my stomach as I caught Lucas's eye, the unspoken understanding of the precarious situation we were in hanging heavy between us. The director's call felt like a summons to face whatever dark forces had infiltrated our world.

And just as I took a step forward, the lights flickered overhead, plunging us into a moment of darkness. The collective gasp from the cast reverberated through the air, and when the lights flickered back on, the figure from the shadows was standing there again, now at the center of the stage, their face illuminated and unmistakable.

The tension snapped tight, and I could feel the impending dread settle in the pit of my stomach as I realized we were all staring at the very person I had once called a friend, their eyes glinting with something that felt dangerously close to malice.

"What do you want?" I breathed, the question hanging in the air like a storm cloud ready to burst. The gravity of the moment felt suffocating, and as they smiled, a chilling revelation settled in: this was only the beginning.

Chapter 7: Unmasking the Villain

The velvet curtains of the theater hung like heavy drapes of blood-red fabric, a somber backdrop to the electric tension that pulsed through the air. I stood in the dimly lit backstage, the scent of fresh paint and aged wood filling my lungs, mingling with the faint aroma of popcorn wafting from the lobby. It was a deliciously chaotic setting, where dreams collided with reality and the stage whispered secrets of those who dared to step into the spotlight. I had always adored the theater, but tonight, the thrill of performance had been eclipsed by something far more sinister.

"Do you really think it's going to happen tonight?" Lucas's voice cut through the low hum of anticipation, laced with an urgency that matched the erratic flutter of my heart. He leaned closer, his warm breath tickling my cheek, and I caught the glimmer of fear in his otherwise steadfast gaze.

"I don't know, but we need to be ready," I replied, glancing towards the entrance where shadows danced like specters, taunting our resolve. The looming threat had taken on a life of its own, morphing from mere whispers of concern to a tangible danger that threatened to unravel everything we had worked for.

In the past few weeks, our efforts to unearth the identity of the person behind the threatening notes had spiraled into a shared obsession. What had begun as an innocuous search for answers had morphed into a web of intrigue, drawing us deeper into each other's lives. Lucas had become my partner in crime, and with every late-night brainstorming session and hushed conversation, the chemistry between us ignited like an unexpected spark in the dark.

We had spent countless hours combing through old theater records, cross-referencing names with a timeline that seemed to twist and turn with every revelation. My fingers danced across the pages of the dusty archives, tracing the stories of actors long gone, their dreams buried beneath the weight of the past. Each name carried a haunting resonance, a reminder that the theater was more than a stage; it was a living tapestry woven with ambition, jealousy, and desire.

"Look at this," Lucas murmured, pulling a frayed newspaper clipping from the pile. His fingers brushed against mine, sending a shiver of electricity up my arm. The article detailed a scandal involving a former starlet whose career had been mysteriously cut short. "This could be a connection."

I leaned closer, my breath hitching as I read the headline: Tragedy Strikes: Rising Star Disappears from the Limelight. The photo depicted a stunning woman, her smile bright yet shadowed by the weight of her eyes. "She was involved in some messy drama with the theater's director at the time," I noted, feeling the threads of the past weave into our present.

Lucas's expression shifted, the shadow of realization dawning upon him. "What if someone is using her story as a way to manipulate the present? To exact some twisted revenge?"

The thought sent a chill racing down my spine. As we delved deeper, we uncovered more names, each revealing a layer of a scandalous history that lingered like an unwelcome ghost. It was a tapestry of betrayal that seemed to echo through the theater's hallowed halls, and I couldn't shake the feeling that we were merely scratching the surface of something much darker.

"Do you believe in ghosts?" I asked, attempting to lighten the mood, though my voice trembled with the weight of the words.

Lucas chuckled softly, the sound rich and warm against the backdrop of our anxiety. "Only the ones that haunt my past." His gaze softened, a mixture of pain and understanding flickering across his features. "But I'd rather face them head-on than hide in the shadows."

The sincerity in his voice struck a chord deep within me, resonating with the unspoken fears that had lingered beneath the surface of our investigation. I had come to admire his strength, the way he confronted his demons with unwavering resolve. In those moments, our connection deepened, threading us together in a way that felt both exhilarating and terrifying.

With the clock ticking down to opening night, we couldn't afford to let our guard down. As the house lights began to dim, signaling the start of the performance, we made our way toward the front of the theater, scanning the audience for any sign of trouble. The energy crackled around us, a chaotic symphony of laughter and murmurs that concealed the growing unease in my chest.

"Stay close to me," Lucas urged, his voice low but firm. I nodded, feeling the warmth of his presence envelop me like a protective shield. Together, we navigated through the sea of spectators, weaving between clusters of patrons engrossed in pre-show chatter.

But as the first act unfolded, I couldn't shake the feeling that we were being watched. The flickering lights cast eerie shadows across the stage, and I could swear I saw a figure lurking just beyond the fringes of the spotlight. A chill skated down my spine as I caught a glimpse of movement out of the corner of my eye—an indistinct shape cloaked in darkness, its intentions hidden.

"Did you see that?" I whispered urgently to Lucas, my heart pounding in my chest.

He nodded, his jaw set in determination. "Let's check it out after the first act."

As the applause erupted and the actors took their bows, my mind raced with possibilities. We had come too far to let fear dictate our actions. As the curtain fell, we slipped into the shadows, ready to confront whatever awaited us. The air crackled with tension, each heartbeat echoing in the silence as we approached the darkened corners of the theater, unaware of the revelations that awaited us, lurking just beyond the edge of our understanding.

The backstage hallway stretched before us, dimly lit and adorned with dusty old photographs of past productions, their frames tarnished by years of neglect. Each image whispered tales of triumph and tragedy, reminding me that every performance held its secrets—like a theater filled with ghosts of forgotten dreams. I followed Lucas, our footsteps echoing softly against the wooden floorboards, each step laced with an electric mixture of dread and determination.

"Is it just me, or is it getting darker in here?" I quipped, trying to lighten the mood despite the knot tightening in my stomach. My voice was a little too loud in the silence, but I couldn't help it. Humor was my armor, a shield against the encroaching shadows.

Lucas shot me a sidelong glance, amusement flickering in his eyes. "That's because you're just imagining it. A few more moments, and I might start to believe in those ghosts you were joking about."

"Please, if there were real ghosts here, they would have sent us packing by now," I said, rolling my eyes. "I'm sure they've seen far worse than two nervous wrecks in search of a threatening note."

He chuckled, the sound warming the chill in the air. "You'd think they'd be used to it by now. A theater full of drama is practically a ghost's buffet."

We reached the end of the hallway, where the light from the stage spilled into the darkness, illuminating a corner that felt infinitely more welcoming. I took a deep breath, letting the scent of fresh paint and old wood settle into my bones. It was the essence of creation, of life being breathed into the performance. But as I turned to Lucas, the weight of our task pressed down on us both.

"Let's just take a quick peek," he urged, stepping toward the edge of the stage. I nodded, my pulse quickening as he pulled aside the curtain, revealing a world that felt both magical and menacing.

The stage was deserted, the props left in disarray from the last rehearsal. A pile of discarded costumes lay crumpled in the corner, their vibrant colors muted by the dim lighting. I could feel the remnants of the actors' energy lingering in the air, but that familiarity felt overshadowed by an unseen presence. Something was off.

"Do you hear that?" Lucas whispered, and I strained my ears, catching the faintest hint of rustling fabric behind the backdrop. A wave of apprehension washed over me, and I instinctively stepped closer to him, the comfort of his presence grounding me.

"Maybe it's just a loose prop," I suggested, though I didn't quite believe it myself. "Or a stray cat. You know how they love the theater."

His lips quirked into a wry smile. "Or it could be the specter of a long-lost understudy seeking revenge for a role not played."

Before I could retort, the rustling grew louder, a sharp sound that broke the tension like glass shattering on a tiled floor. Lucas and I exchanged a glance, and without a word, we crept toward the source of the noise. My heart raced as we rounded the edge of the stage, peering into the shadows behind the curtain.

What we found was not a ghost or a stray animal but a figure cloaked in darkness, half-hidden behind an old set piece. The breath caught in my throat as the realization hit me—a familiar shape and a flash of anger so palpable it sent shivers down my spine.

"Emily?" Lucas's voice was low, but the question hung heavily in the air, charged with surprise and unease.

The figure stepped into the dim light, and I was met with the cold glare of Emily, a fellow actress whose talent shone brightly until jealousy twisted her ambition. "What are you two doing here?" she snapped, her tone laced with defiance, but her eyes darted nervously, betraying her bravado.

"Looking for answers," I shot back, unable to hide the fire igniting within me. "And I think you might have some."

"Oh, please. You think I'm responsible for all this? You've got it all wrong." Her laugh was brittle, echoing in the silence. "I have enough on my plate without chasing shadows."

"Then why are you hiding back here?" Lucas pressed, stepping closer, his eyes narrowing as he assessed her. "What do you know about the threats?"

She hesitated, and for a brief moment, I thought I caught a glimpse of vulnerability beneath her fierce exterior. "I'm not hiding. I'm... just trying to keep out of the way."

"Out of the way? Or out of sight?" I challenged, feeling a mix of anger and pity for her. "You've been here too long, Emily. It's not just about you anymore."

"Look, you don't know what you're dealing with," she shot back, her voice barely contained. "This isn't just about a few threats—it's bigger than all of us."

Bigger than us? My heart thudded loudly in my chest as her words sank in. What did she mean? I glanced at Lucas, who wore an expression that mirrored my own confusion.

"What do you mean by that?" Lucas's voice was steady, urging her to elaborate.

Emily took a deep breath, her façade cracking just enough for us to see the fear lurking behind her bravado. "There are things happening here, things I thought were in the past. I didn't ask for any of this, but it keeps coming back."

"Things like what?" I pressed, my pulse quickening with each passing moment. "Are you saying someone is targeting us because of something you did?"

A flicker of uncertainty crossed her face, and she glanced around as if the shadows themselves were listening. "Not just me. This place has history—secrets buried so deep, they've come back to haunt us."

The urgency in her tone sent a jolt of adrenaline coursing through me. "If you know something, you have to tell us. We can help you."

Emily's eyes flickered with indecision, and I sensed the weight of her dilemma. "Help? You think you can help? This isn't a play, and there aren't any heroes in this story."

"Maybe not," I replied, stepping closer, my resolve hardening. "But we're not going to let fear control us. You can fight this."

The moment hung in the air, thick with the unspoken truths swirling around us. I could see her wrestling with the choices before her, the past clawing at her, but the flicker of hope in her eyes ignited a fire within me. "What do you need from us?"

As if considering her next move, she finally spoke, her voice barely above a whisper. "I'll tell you everything. But first, you need to understand how dangerous this is. You're in way over your heads."

We shared a look, a silent agreement forging between us. Lucas stepped closer, the intensity of his gaze focused on Emily. "We can take it. Just tell us the truth."

The tension thickened as she contemplated our request, the shadows creeping closer, eager to swallow us whole.

The air felt electric, a charged moment hanging between us as Emily shifted, caught in the throes of her inner turmoil. Shadows flickered around her, the dim light casting an almost ethereal glow that did little to mask the tension. "You don't know what you're asking," she murmured, her voice barely above a whisper, yet it resonated deeply within me.

"We're asking you to trust us," Lucas interjected, his gaze steady, revealing a glimmer of the determination that had pulled us through this mess thus far. "We're already in this together, whether we like it or not. If there's a threat, we need to face it head-on."

Emily's eyes flickered, the fight within her wavering as she processed our words. "You have no idea what's at stake here. It's not just about me. This place... it holds so many secrets, and those secrets don't want to stay buried."

I took a step forward, grounding my voice with resolve. "Then help us unearth them. We can't fight shadows if we don't know what they are. If there's something lurking in the dark, we need to know what it is."

She hesitated, glancing back toward the stage, where the curtain rustled softly as if echoing her indecision. "All right," she finally said, her voice barely above a whisper. "But you need to understand—the deeper we go, the more dangerous it gets."

"Dangerous is our middle name," I quipped, trying to lighten the atmosphere while my insides twisted in apprehension. "Besides, we've survived this far without being completely terrified. What's a little more danger?"

Lucas shot me a warning glance, but I pressed on, desperate to keep the momentum. Emily's guarded demeanor cracked just slightly, a flicker of amusement passing across her features. "Oh, is that so? I'll have to remember that when the ghosts come knocking."

"Trust me, I have a plan for them too," I shot back, unable to resist a smirk. The tension shifted, lightening just enough to coax Emily into our world.

She took a deep breath, steeling herself as if preparing to dive into frigid waters. "It started years ago. A production that went terribly wrong. A leading lady with too many secrets. She wasn't just an actress; she was the daughter of someone powerful, someone who would do anything to keep the truth hidden." Her voice trembled slightly, revealing the weight of what she was about to share.

I felt the gravity of her words, the stories of ambition and betrayal swirling around us like ghosts. "And you were involved?" I asked, my curiosity piqued.

"I was her understudy," Emily confessed, her gaze drifting to the floor. "I was supposed to take over if anything happened to her.

But then...she disappeared." The air grew thick with her unspoken fears. "No one knows what happened. Some say she ran away, others say she met a darker fate. But her father... he made sure the theater fell into chaos. Anyone who dared to ask questions was dealt with harshly."

Lucas and I exchanged glances, the weight of her confession settling heavily in the space between us. "So the threats are connected to this mystery? Someone is trying to silence us?" Lucas pressed.

Emily nodded, her expression darkening. "I thought it was all behind me until those notes started appearing. Someone is watching, waiting for the right moment to strike. I can't let it happen again. I can't let them destroy another life."

My heart raced, an unsettling sense of foreboding wrapping around me like a shroud. "What do we need to do?"

"We need to find out who's behind this," she replied, her eyes steely with determination. "If we can uncover the truth, maybe we can put an end to it once and for all."

"Great, where do we start?" I asked, adrenaline pumping through my veins.

Emily's gaze drifted toward the props piled against the wall, and she pointed. "There's an old trunk in there. It belonged to the leading lady. It's been locked away, but there might be something in it—something that can give us a clue."

"Let's do it," Lucas said, moving toward the pile with a sense of urgency. I followed close behind, the air heavy with anticipation.

As we pried open the trunk, the hinges creaked like a warning. Inside lay a collection of faded costumes, old scripts, and a few personal effects. I lifted a delicate scarf, the fabric soft yet tinged with the weight of forgotten dreams. But it was Lucas who unearthed the real treasure—a leather-bound diary, its pages yellowed and fragile.

"Do you think it's safe to read it?" I asked, glancing at Emily, who was peering over Lucas's shoulder, her breath hitching slightly.

"We have to," she insisted, her voice barely a whisper. "It could hold the key to everything."

With bated breath, Lucas opened the diary, the first page revealing elegant handwriting that danced across the paper like a fleeting memory. Each entry was filled with the youthful exuberance of a girl in love with the theater, but as we flipped through the pages, the tone shifted. Darker emotions began to seep through—the anxiety of a hidden past, fear of powerful connections, and whispers of betrayal that chilled me to the bone.

"Here," Lucas said, stopping abruptly on a page. "This entry mentions someone named Victor. He was supposed to be involved with the production. The last entry talks about a meeting that was never to happen."

"Victor?" Emily echoed, her eyes narrowing. "That's the name of the director who…"

Her voice trailed off, and I could see the pieces falling into place behind her eyes. "Who what?" I prompted.

"Who disappeared right after the show went south. He knew something. Something about her."

The implications hung in the air, thick and suffocating. "So we need to find Victor," I suggested, my mind racing with possibilities.

Before Emily could respond, the lights flickered, casting erratic shadows around us. My heart dropped as a creaking sound echoed from the stage, a slow, deliberate sound that set my nerves on fire.

"What was that?" Lucas whispered, instinctively stepping in front of Emily as if to shield her from whatever lurked beyond the veil of light.

"Let's find out," I said, adrenaline coursing through me as I edged toward the stage, my heart thundering in my chest.

As we moved closer, the air thickened with tension, the world narrowing to that singular point of focus—the stage, where the shadows danced like phantoms, waiting. The door at the back of the theater creaked open slowly, a figure slipping through the darkness, silhouetted against the dim light.

I gasped as recognition washed over me. "It can't be..." My breath caught in my throat as the figure stepped into the light, revealing a face I thought I'd never see again.

"Hello, old friends." The voice dripped with malice, laced with secrets long buried. "I believe it's time we had a little chat."

The atmosphere crackled with tension, a palpable danger radiating from the figure before us, and I knew, without a doubt, that our journey into the shadows had only just begun.

Chapter 8: A Dangerous Performance

The theater pulsed with a heartbeat of excitement, a rhythm thrumming through the worn floorboards and settling deep into the very bones of its walls. Gold-trimmed curtains, once vibrant, now faded to a buttery hue, hung heavy, whispering secrets to those who dared to listen. The scent of freshly painted backdrops mingled with the faint tang of popcorn, creating an intoxicating blend that danced through the air like an eager specter. I stood in the dimly lit wings, feeling the weight of the night settle upon my shoulders, every inch of me tingling with anticipation.

As the clock ticked closer to the hour, the atmosphere thickened. There was an electric hum of whispered fears—were the rumors of sabotage mere figments of our collective imagination, or was there a ghost among us, ready to strike? I glanced toward the stage where the spotlight would soon gleam like a watchful eye, illuminating not just the performance but the growing unease nestled in the hearts of my fellow cast members. Tension simmered beneath our jovial banter, turning playful quips into barbed exchanges. Each laugh held an undercurrent of doubt, every friendly gesture edged with suspicion.

"Did you hear about the missing prop?" Aiden, our brooding lead, leaned in close, his breath a whisper of worry. His dark hair fell across his forehead, and in the flickering backstage light, his eyes sparkled with a mix of intrigue and fear. I had always found comfort in his presence, a steady anchor amid the storm, but tonight, his intensity sent a shiver down my spine.

"What do you mean missing? I just saw it—right before the last rehearsal!" I shot back, my voice a tad sharper than I intended. The words hung between us, heavy like the velvet curtains draping the stage.

"It was there," he confirmed, crossing his arms tightly. "And now it's not. I don't know if it's just nerves or something more... sinister."

The stage manager, a no-nonsense woman with a penchant for efficiency, bustled by, her clipboard clutched like a lifeline. "Focus, everyone! This is our moment! We can't let the rumors get to us." Her voice, authoritative yet reassuring, momentarily steadied my racing heart.

Yet, as the audience began to filter in, their laughter and chatter melding into a singular murmur of expectation, I felt the familiar thrill of the stage morphing into a tightening knot of apprehension in my gut. My palms were clammy, and I wiped them discreetly against the fabric of my costume—a flowing gown that swirled around my ankles, shimmering with the promise of magic and dreams. Tonight, I was not just a character in a story; I was the embodiment of hope and creativity, and yet, the shadows lurking beyond the spotlight felt ready to pounce.

"Break a leg!" whispered Lisa, my closest friend and a vibrant spirit in our otherwise serious ensemble. Her smile was bright, though I could see the fear flickering behind her hazel eyes. She reached for my hand, squeezing it as if we could channel our worries into something tangible.

"Let's just give them a show to remember," I replied, attempting to inject some levity into our fraying nerves. "What's a little sabotage compared to our dazzling performance?"

But as the curtain rose, revealing the set that glimmered under the stage lights, the laughter of the audience began to dissolve my bravado. I stepped forward, my heart pounding a frantic tattoo in my chest, the audience's eager gazes pinned on me like butterflies on display. The first notes of music enveloped me, and I surrendered to the rhythm, letting it carry me away.

Each line I delivered felt charged with a weight I hadn't anticipated, a tension woven intricately into the fabric of our narrative. The plot twisted and turned, much like the real-life chaos swirling just outside our beautifully crafted world. Aiden and I danced around one another on stage, our characters embroiled in a tangled web of love and betrayal, and for a moment, I lost myself in the performance, allowing my fears to melt away.

But then, the lights flickered. A collective gasp rippled through the audience. The disruption was subtle yet jarring, like a crack in the façade of our fantasy. I exchanged a glance with Aiden, and in that brief moment, I saw the same confusion reflected in his eyes. It was no longer just a performance; something was amiss.

As the scene reached its climax, I felt a strange tension building, a frisson in the air that made the hair on my arms stand on end. The shadowy corners of the stage seemed to pulse with life, and I could swear I heard faint whispers that sent chills skittering down my spine. Just as our characters leaned into their passionate confrontation, a loud crash echoed from behind the scenes—a prop, a light, or something worse?

"Keep going!" Aiden urged, his voice low but urgent, propelling me forward even as uncertainty threatened to paralyze me. I played my part, forcing my emotions to rise to the surface, but the danger looming in the dark cast a long shadow over my performance.

Then, in a moment of sheer instinct, I turned to face the darkness that lurked just beyond the stage. The flickering lights revealed a figure—a silhouette against the backdrop, poised to disrupt everything we'd worked for. The air thickened with suspense, the audience's collective breath hitching as I prepared to confront whatever chaos was about to unfold.

"Who's there?" I called out, my voice cutting through the charged atmosphere. My heart raced, each beat echoing in my ears, and as I braced myself for the unexpected, the lines of our story blurred with the reality we found ourselves in, challenging everything I thought I knew about trust, courage, and the love that had started to bloom amidst the chaos.

The figure stepped into the weak light, and my breath hitched. Dressed in dark clothing that seemed to absorb the light around it, the person's face was obscured by shadows, an eerie silhouette that sent a shiver racing down my spine. "Who are you?" I managed, though my voice trembled despite my efforts to sound brave. The audience gasped, the tension in the theater now palpable, thick enough to slice through.

"What a delightful question," the figure replied, voice smooth like velvet yet laced with an unsettling edge. They took a step forward, revealing the glint of something metallic tucked into their belt. A prop knife, perhaps? Or something more sinister? My heart drummed a frantic rhythm against my ribs, a wild animal desperate to escape.

Aiden, ever the protector, positioned himself slightly in front of me. "This is not part of the show," he stated, his voice steady, though I could see the tension coiling in his muscles. "You need to leave. Now."

The audience was entranced, perhaps thinking this was an audacious part of our performance. They leaned forward, wide-eyed and breathless, mistaking our panic for dramatic flair. I could see some whispering, exchanging glances, as if trying to decipher whether they were witnessing a new level of immersive theater. I wanted to scream that this wasn't a game, that real danger lurked here, but my words felt lodged somewhere deep, caught in the clutches of fear.

"Danger? How quaint," the figure said, amusement dancing in their voice. They tilted their head, and for a moment, a shaft of light caught the edge of their jaw, revealing a smirk that chilled me. "Don't you see? This is the most authentic performance of your lives."

"Get off my stage!" I shouted, stepping out from behind Aiden, emboldened by an unnameable fury. The moment hung suspended, the air electric. A challenge glimmered in the darkness, a standoff brewing in the space between us. "This is our moment, and you don't get to ruin it."

The figure's laughter was sharp, slicing through the tension like glass shattering. "Such spirit! But spirit won't protect you." With a sudden, fluid motion, they withdrew the metallic object from their belt. It gleamed menacingly under the stage lights, and I caught the audience collectively holding its breath. A knife? No, it was a fake, a prop, but the sheer audacity of its presence struck fear into my heart.

"Enough!" Aiden stepped forward, his eyes fierce. "You want authenticity? Here's some for you!" In an unexpected move, he lunged toward the figure, embodying the very role of a hero he had played on stage. But just as quickly, the figure sidestepped him with an agility that caught us all off guard.

"Now, now, let's not make this any more dramatic than it needs to be," the figure taunted, spinning to face Aiden. Their movements were fluid, almost graceful, as if they were playing a dance rather than a dangerous game. "After all, you all seem so keen on playing your parts. Let's see how well you improvise."

In that moment, everything turned chaotic. I could hear Lisa screaming from backstage, and the soft murmur of the audience transformed into a cacophony of confusion. Some clutched their phones, ready to record what they likely thought was an elaborate stunt. Others looked around, trying to understand if this was indeed part of the show.

"Everybody stay calm!" I shouted, but my voice felt small, lost amid the growing chaos. I glanced at Aiden, whose expression had shifted from anger to concern as he realized the audience had become a part of this unpredictable drama. The reality of the situation struck me—the danger was real, and we had unwittingly invited our audience into a world that had become dangerously blurred.

The figure turned to me, their eyes gleaming with mischief. "Why don't you tell them the truth? About your little secrets? The fears you've tucked away like forgotten props?"

I recoiled, heat flooding my cheeks. "What are you talking about?" My voice wavered, though I held my ground.

"Oh, don't play coy," the figure retorted, leaning closer, their presence overpowering. "I know about the whispers, the doubts. I've seen the cracks in your facade." They waved a hand toward the audience, who watched, spellbound, like children captivated by a bedtime story. "Let's give them a show, shall we?"

Before I could respond, the figure darted forward, and the blade—an innocent-looking plastic knife, though still intimidating—glinted under the stage lights. They lunged toward Aiden, but he sidestepped again, catching my eye for a fleeting moment. I could see the gears turning in his mind, the determination hardening in his jaw.

"Run!" he shouted to me, and instinctively, I turned. The adrenaline surged through me as I dashed toward the back of the stage, heart racing, mind racing faster. I could hear the figure's laughter trailing behind me, a haunting echo.

But I wasn't about to let fear dictate my actions. The thought of the audience, their curious faces turned toward the chaos, fueled my resolve. If this was a performance they wanted, I would show them a finale worth remembering.

As I reached the backstage, I could hear the scuffle between Aiden and the figure escalating. I grabbed a nearby stage prop—an oversized rubber mallet—and took a deep breath. "You want authenticity?" I muttered under my breath, stepping back into the fray. With each step, my courage bolstered by sheer will, I felt the weight of the moment settle on my shoulders.

Emerging back onto the stage, I confronted the figure. "You've got a strange definition of authenticity, friend!" I declared, brandishing the mallet with a dramatic flair. The audience gasped, their reactions a mix of shock and delight, but my heart pounded for an entirely different reason.

The figure's expression shifted, surprise flickering across their face, and in that split second, I charged. "Game on!" I cried, swinging the mallet with all my strength, the air crackling with tension as I aimed not just for the figure but for the control we had lost amid this twisted performance. The stage was ours, and I would reclaim it, regardless of the chaos surrounding us.

The mallet soared through the air, a comical contrast to the tension that filled the theater. I aimed for the figure, but they ducked with an agility that took my breath away. The rubber struck the stage with a loud thud, causing a ripple of laughter mixed with nervous gasps from the audience. "Nice try!" they jeered, spinning to evade me like a dancer expertly sidestepping an awkward partner.

"You think this is funny?" I shot back, my heart racing as I adjusted my grip on the mallet, a makeshift weapon in a surreal game of cat and mouse. Aiden, meanwhile, was still locked in a desperate struggle, grappling with the figure, his determination palpable as he fought to regain control of the situation.

"Just wait until the final act!" the figure taunted, eyes glinting with an unsettling glee. They were reveling in this, the chaos spiraling into something neither planned nor expected. "You'll be the punchline!"

"Funny how you're the one about to get whacked!" I retorted, my voice louder than I intended, a rush of adrenaline granting me the confidence I desperately needed. With a swift motion, I lunged again, this time closer, the audience hanging onto every moment, their eyes wide with a mixture of fear and excitement. They didn't know that this was not a performance; it was a battle for survival, and I was determined not to lose.

Just as I lunged again, Aiden managed to gain the upper hand, catching the figure's wrist. But it was a fleeting victory; with a twist, the figure broke free and stepped back, giving me a split-second opening. My instincts kicked in, and I swung the mallet once more, a wild arc of rubber and desperation. The audience collectively gasped, as if sensing the turning tide.

"Stop this!" Aiden shouted, but the figure merely laughed, their voice slicing through the air like a knife. "You're all too late! This isn't about you anymore. This is my stage now!"

In that moment, something flickered behind them—an unusual reflection that caught my eye. I hesitated, curiosity mingling with my instincts to fight. I was so close to confronting this threat, but the glimmering reflection pulled me in, a hint of something lurking in the shadows. It wasn't just a prop. It looked like a real weapon, concealed behind the curtain but now revealed in the chaotic light of the stage.

"Watch out!" I yelled, my warning coming too late. The figure launched themselves at Aiden, pushing him aside as they reached for whatever it was that glimmered in the dark. My heart dropped as realization dawned—it wasn't just a knife; it was a blade, menacing and sharp, and it was now in their hands.

"Aiden!" I cried, racing forward, desperation clawing at my chest. The audience erupted into a flurry of chaos, panic sweeping through them like wildfire. Chairs scraped against the floor, and a few brave souls stood, peering over the seats as if they could somehow intervene. "Get away from him!"

But the figure's confidence grew, fueled by the frenzy around us. They brandished the blade, eyes shining with a wild mix of triumph and madness. "This is the moment where the curtain falls for all of you. You thought you could put on a show without consequences?"

Aiden, ever the stalwart hero, stepped between me and the figure, determination etched on his face. "You won't get away with this. We're not afraid of you!" His voice was firm, but I could see the tremor in his hands, the way he braced himself for the inevitable clash.

"Oh, sweet naïve actors. You misunderstand," the figure sneered, their stance shifting. "This is all a part of the performance—the real drama is about to unfold." They glanced at the audience, and I could see the flicker of uncertainty cross their face. "You'll be part of history tonight!"

Before I could respond, they lunged forward, aiming directly for Aiden. My heart raced, instinct kicking in again as I shifted my weight. "No!" I shouted, raising the mallet instinctively, my vision narrowing to a pinpoint focus on the unfolding danger. I swung with all my might, feeling the rush of adrenaline surging through me, but my aim faltered. Aiden ducked just in time, but I lost my balance, stumbling forward as the figure sidestepped me, the blade glinting dangerously close.

"Is this your idea of a dramatic climax?" the figure taunted, their laughter echoing in the now chaotic space. "How quaint."

The audience gasped again, the tension thickening to a point where it felt as though the air itself was holding its breath. In that split second of confusion, everything seemed to happen in slow motion. The figure turned, and I caught a glimpse of their expression, a mix of glee and malice, the kind that ignited a primal fear deep within me.

Then, with an unexpected flick of their wrist, they threw the blade toward Aiden, not with the precision of a practiced fighter but rather with reckless abandon. Time stood still as I gasped, my hands instinctively reaching out in a futile attempt to stop the inevitable.

"Aiden, watch out!" I screamed, and the world shrank to the singular focus of that moment—the blade glimmering as it soared through the air, aimed right at him. My heart sank, the weight of dread settling like a stone in my gut.

But then, something shifted. As if propelled by fate, Aiden dodged just as the blade whizzed past him, embedding itself into the wall behind him with a sickening thud. The audience erupted in a mixture of gasps and murmurs, their reactions a cacophony of disbelief.

"Is this part of the act?" someone shouted from the back, their voice cracking with confusion.

"No!" I shouted back, stepping forward. "This is not a show!" My voice rang out, cutting through the chaos as I looked back at Aiden, whose face was a mixture of shock and resolve.

The figure's smile faltered, the mask of confidence slipping just enough for me to see the crack in their facade. They were starting to realize that we were no longer playing their game; we were fighting back.

But just as I thought I could regain control, the lights flickered again, plunging the stage into darkness. The audience gasped, the atmosphere thickening with tension and uncertainty. Then, a single spotlight flickered to life, illuminating the figure, but not before I felt a hand grip my arm from behind, yanking me into the shadows.

"Aiden!" I cried out, fear clawing at my throat.

"Stay close!" he shouted back, but the words faded as the figure began to move again, circling us like a predator assessing its prey. My heart raced as I tried to shake off the hand gripping my arm, but it held firm, pulling me deeper into the darkness that cloaked the edges of the stage.

"Where do you think you're going?" the figure called, their voice dripping with amusement and menace. "The show isn't over yet."

I felt the grip tighten, panic coursing through my veins. Whatever had grabbed me was pulling me away from the chaos of the stage, away from Aiden, and into the depths of shadow where the truth was more dangerous than I had ever imagined.

The theater was no longer just a place of performance; it had become a battleground. And as I was dragged further into the dark, I realized the true performance was just beginning, the stakes higher than any of us had anticipated. I struggled against the grip, but the world around me faded, leaving only the chilling certainty that the ending was far from written, and I was about to learn just how dangerous this performance would become.

Chapter 9: Whispers in the Dark

The moon hung low in the sky, casting a silver veil over the old theater, its cracked facade whispering tales of the past. I found myself drawn back to the stage, where the air still buzzed with the energy of our opening night. The applause had faded, leaving behind a heavy silence that clung to the shadows like cobwebs. Lucas and I had exchanged words of comfort, our shared smiles acting as a fragile truce in the aftermath of a night that had shaken us both. Yet, despite our efforts to mask it, the weight of what had transpired lingered in the corners, as palpable as the dust motes dancing in the dim light.

As I moved through the empty rows of seats, my footsteps echoed like whispers, and I felt the weight of countless eyes upon me. It was a feeling I had grown accustomed to during my time on stage, but now, it felt different—intimate yet unsettling. The theater, with its peeling paint and velvet drapes, seemed to breathe around me, the history imbued in its very structure throbbing like a heartbeat. Each performance had left a mark, but tonight, I could feel an undercurrent, a pulse of something more alive and restless than the applause we had received.

I retreated backstage, seeking the comfort of familiarity. The dressing rooms, still littered with the remnants of our hurried preparations, held an air of intimacy. Makeup brushes lay abandoned beside half-opened lipstick tubes, and costume pieces draped haphazardly over chairs, remnants of the personas we had donned. Lucas's costume, a tailored suit that fit him like a second skin, hung in stark contrast to the chaos. I reached out to touch the fabric, the memory of his grin warming me against the chill that settled deep within my bones.

My thoughts turned to the fleeting glances we had exchanged, the way his eyes sparkled with mischief even in the throes of chaos. Yet, lurking beneath the surface was an unspoken tension, a shared understanding of the shadows that loomed over us. It felt like we were standing at the edge of an abyss, tethered together by the fraying threads of our pasts. I took a deep breath, steeling myself for what lay ahead, when a soft sound pierced the silence—a voice, faint and sorrowful, like a haunting melody that beckoned me closer.

Following the sound, I made my way through the narrow hallways, each step guided by an unseen force. The voice seemed to whisper secrets, intertwining with my own thoughts, pulling me deeper into the heart of the theater. I felt like a moth drawn to the flickering flame of a candle, each heartbeat a testament to my curiosity. My fingers grazed the cool, worn banister as I climbed the creaky staircase that spiraled upward into the attic, the air thick with dust and mystery.

The attic opened before me, a cavern of forgotten relics, where time itself seemed to stand still. The dim light spilled through the small window, illuminating the dust that swirled like tiny galaxies. It was a treasure trove of discarded dreams: faded costumes draped over old trunks, framed photographs of actors long gone, their smiles frozen in time. But it was the diary that caught my eye, resting on a rickety table, its leather cover cracked and weathered. I felt a shiver run down my spine as I reached for it, as if I were unlocking a door to a world that had been sealed for too long.

Flipping through the yellowed pages, I was enveloped by the delicate scrawl of the actress who had vanished—her hopes and fears etched in ink that seemed to pulse with life. Each entry was a window into her soul, revealing a woman vibrant and full of passion, longing for the applause and adoration that came with the spotlight. But there was darkness there too, an undercurrent of despair that echoed through her words like a mournful refrain. The final pages trembled with emotion, a raw honesty that made my heart ache.

As I read, a chill swept through the attic, the temperature dropping as if the room itself mourned the loss of its inhabitant.

I couldn't shake the feeling that I wasn't alone; the very air felt charged, crackling with the echoes of her dreams. A distant sound broke my reverie—a door creaking open, the soft shuffle of footsteps. Panic flickered in my chest as I turned, heart racing, fully expecting to find Lucas there, curiosity written across his handsome features. Instead, I was met with darkness, the shadows swirling like phantoms, taunting me.

"Hello?" I called out, my voice barely more than a whisper. The sound felt swallowed by the vastness of the attic, lost among the remnants of a forgotten past. I stepped further into the room, compelled by a mix of dread and intrigue. The voice I had followed felt closer now, wrapping around me like a shroud, urging me to uncover its secrets. I could almost hear it speaking, urging me to listen more closely, to delve deeper into the life that had been lost.

With each passing moment, the urgency of the moment intensified, and I felt the weight of the diary pressing against my chest, a talisman linking me to the actress who had come before me. I knew, without a doubt, that the answers I sought lay within these pages, and as I turned back to the diary, I felt the chill of the room turn into a warmth, igniting a spark of determination within me. I was on the brink of uncovering something profound, a truth that had been buried for too long, and I was ready to face whatever shadows awaited me.

The pages of the diary, a delicate testament to dreams that had slipped through time, felt both fragile and insistent beneath my fingers. I leaned against the rickety table, the wood cool against my skin, absorbing the weight of the words that spilled forth like whispers from the past. Each entry drew me deeper into a world painted in both vibrant colors and muted grays, a spectrum reflecting the highs of the stage and the crushing lows of a life overshadowed by longing.

The actress had poured her heart into those pages, recounting the thrill of applause and the ache of solitude that followed once the curtain fell. "The stage is my home," she had written in one particularly poignant passage, "yet it is also my prison. I am both queen and captive, adored by many but known by none." I could almost hear her voice in my mind, the lilting tones and the heavy sighs that would have accompanied her words. What had driven her to vanish, leaving behind not just her dreams, but the echo of her presence in this very theater?

A shiver ran down my spine as I reached a passage that sent a chill through my heart. "The shadows in this theater are my friends," she had scrawled, "but they hold secrets I am not yet ready to uncover." I could almost feel her spectral hand guiding my own as I turned the pages, breath hitching at the intimacy of her thoughts. The attic, filled with dusty relics and the scent of old wood, felt alive with her spirit, each breath I took heavy with the weight of her unfulfilled desires.

Suddenly, a loud crash echoed from below, jolting me from my reverie. The sound rattled the rafters, sending a shower of dust cascading from the beams above. Heart racing, I set the diary down and crept toward the attic door, the floorboards creaking underfoot as if they, too, were in a state of alarm. What could possibly be happening? Was Lucas behind the noise, playing a prank to lure me out of my thoughts?

With a cautious push, I swung open the door and peered down the narrow staircase, the darkness below cloaking everything in mystery. I hesitated, torn between the desire to uncover what lay ahead and the urge to retreat back to the safety of the attic. But curiosity clawed at my resolve, and I tiptoed down, my pulse quickening with each step.

As I reached the bottom, I found myself in the dimly lit backstage area, the heavy velvet curtains drawn tight. A shape flitted past, barely catching my eye—a blur of movement against the muted backdrop. "Lucas?" I called out, my voice trembling slightly, the name escaping my lips like a secret. Silence enveloped me, thick and suffocating, pressing against my chest.

Then, I heard it again—the voice, that mournful sound, now mingled with a soft giggle that danced through the air like a teasing ghost. My heart thudded violently as I followed the sound, deeper into the shadows where reality blurred and dreams twisted. "Show yourself!" I demanded, half-laughing, half-terrified, wondering if I had slipped into a scene from one of our more absurd rehearsals.

"Ah, but where's the fun in that?" came a lilting voice from the darkness, warm and familiar, yet tinged with something mischievous. The curtain fluttered, and then Lucas emerged, a wide grin plastered across his face. "You should see your face. I thought you'd scream."

"Very funny," I retorted, a laugh escaping my lips despite the lingering tension in the air. "You scared me half to death! What are you doing here?"

"I heard a crash, and it seemed like the perfect opportunity for a bit of fun." His eyes sparkled with mischief, and I couldn't help but roll my own in response. "But really, I came to check on you. You disappeared, and I thought I'd rescue you from your literary rabbit hole."

I couldn't help but smile at the thought of him playing the gallant hero. "I was busy unearthing secrets from the past, you know. There's an entire life trapped in that diary—an actress who vanished without a trace."

"Ah, the plot thickens!" He leaned closer, curiosity piqued. "What did she have to say?"

I hesitated, the weight of the diary pressing heavily on my thoughts. "It's... complicated. She spoke of her love for the stage, but there was an underlying sadness, a sense of being trapped. And there's something about the shadows she mentioned—how they hold secrets she wasn't ready to uncover."

His expression shifted, seriousness threading through the mirth in his eyes. "Sounds like she was haunted in more ways than one. But what about you? Are you uncovering your own secrets up here?"

I shrugged, biting my lip as I considered my next words. "Maybe. I feel like there's something more to this place, something waiting for us to discover. It's as if the theater itself is alive, holding onto stories and whispers from the past."

"Then let's dig a little deeper," Lucas suggested, his tone suddenly earnest, the humor of the moment shifting into something more profound. "You have to let me help you. Besides," he added with a wink, "I could use a bit of excitement. It's not every day you stumble upon a mystery in your own theater."

There was something invigorating in his words, a shared determination to unravel the threads of the past. We stood there, two figures cast in the glow of the dim lights, united by a common purpose that felt both thrilling and terrifying. It wasn't just the whispers of the actress that we were after; it was the very essence of the theater, the stories begging to be told, the secrets begging to be unearthed.

With a nod, I gestured toward the stairs leading back to the attic, our footsteps echoing in harmony as we ascended. "There's more to discover," I said, my heart racing with anticipation. "Let's see what other secrets the shadows are hiding."

We climbed back into the attic, a world suspended in time, where dust motes floated like tiny stars in a forgotten galaxy. The old diary lay open on the table, beckoning us to delve deeper into the life of the woman who had captured the stage and yet slipped away into silence. I could feel the gravity of her story pulling at us, weaving an invisible thread between her past and our present.

"Let's see what else she has to say," I murmured, flicking through the pages with a renewed sense of purpose. The air around us crackled with anticipation as I read aloud, my voice mingling with the whispers of the theater. "There was a time when the world was mine, when the applause of the audience was a warm embrace. But every performance has its cost, and in the end, I wonder if I gave too much."

Lucas leaned closer, his shoulder brushing against mine, a spark of electricity igniting in the small space between us. "You know," he said, his tone half-joking, half-serious, "that kind of talk always makes me think of the tragic endings in those old dramas. Do you think she was foreseeing her own fate?"

"Maybe she was just trying to cope with the pressure," I suggested, biting back a smile at his dramatic flair. "You know how intense it gets during rehearsals. We've all felt it—chasing perfection while trying to balance our sanity."

"Perfection is overrated," he replied, a teasing grin spreading across his face. "Besides, I prefer a good flub. It keeps the audience guessing."

We shared a laugh, the tension easing momentarily. Yet, beneath the humor, I sensed a darker thread woven into the fabric of the actress's life—a premonition of something not yet understood. I turned another page, eager to uncover more. The actress's handwriting danced across the paper, revealing snippets of her inner turmoil. "Tonight, I overheard whispers in the wings—words of jealousy, betrayal, and shadows lurking where they shouldn't. I must keep my heart guarded; the theater holds many secrets."

"What did I tell you?" Lucas interjected, his expression shifting to one of concern. "There's something going on here, and it sounds like she sensed it. Who was she worried about?"

"That's what I'm hoping to find out." I pressed my finger against the ink, feeling the heat of her emotions pulse through the words. "It's as if she could sense a storm brewing just beyond the curtain."

"Maybe we should look for clues," Lucas suggested, his eyes lighting up with intrigue. "There could be hidden messages in her belongings. Old love letters? Jealous notes from fellow actors? The makings of a perfect mystery."

His enthusiasm was contagious. Together, we began to sift through the artifacts piled in the attic: old costumes draped like specters over moth-eaten chairs, dusty playbills yellowed with age, and forgotten props that once sparkled under the spotlight. Each item held potential stories, remnants of laughter and tears, of triumphs and tragedies.

"What about this?" Lucas exclaimed, holding up a tattered silk scarf, its colors faded but still vibrant. "Looks like something from a leading lady's costume. Maybe it belonged to her."

"Or perhaps it was a piece of her heart," I replied, a thrill of excitement coursing through me as I imagined the lives intertwined within these walls. "Every actor leaves a bit of themselves behind when they perform."

As we explored further, I stumbled upon a dusty trunk hidden behind a stack of old crates. Its lock was rusted but appeared slightly ajar, as if inviting us to pry open its secrets. My heart raced as I exchanged a glance with Lucas. "Should we?"

"Definitely," he said, eyes wide with anticipation. With a nod, I pushed the lid open, the hinges creaking in protest, releasing a cloud of dust that swirled in the air like a spell. Inside, we discovered an assortment of forgotten mementos: faded photographs of the actress in various roles, handwritten notes, and a fragile, yellowed envelope sealed with wax.

"What's this?" I murmured, lifting the envelope gingerly. The wax seal was embossed with an intricate design, a symbol I couldn't quite place. "It looks important."

"Only one way to find out," Lucas urged, leaning closer, his breath warm against my skin.

With cautious fingers, I broke the seal, the crack echoing in the stillness. Inside, I found a letter, its contents sending a shiver down my spine as I read aloud. "To whomever finds this, I write with a heart heavy with fear. There are eyes watching me, and I fear for my safety. I've seen things, things I cannot explain. If I disappear, know that it was not by my own choice. Protect the truth."

The words hung in the air, each syllable tinged with an urgency that felt all too real. "This is it," I breathed, my heart pounding in my chest. "This is why she vanished."

Lucas's expression turned serious, the lighthearted banter giving way to a deeper concern. "We need to figure out who was watching her. Who wanted her gone."

"Maybe we should talk to some of the older cast members," I suggested, excitement mixed with trepidation. "They might know more about the drama behind the scenes."

"Good plan, Sherlock," he said, a hint of admiration in his voice that warmed my cheeks. "But we should tread carefully. It sounds like whatever happened wasn't just a simple disappearance."

I nodded, determination surging within me. We had stepped into a mystery that felt more significant than either of us had anticipated. As we tucked the letter back into the envelope, a sudden gust of wind swept through the attic, sending a chill down my spine and rattling the old windows. It was as if the theater itself was urging us to act, to uncover the truth that had lingered in the shadows for far too long.

And just as we gathered our thoughts, preparing to descend back to the stage, a shadow moved across the doorway, dark and foreboding. I froze, heart racing, and turned to Lucas, who was equally still, eyes wide with surprise.

"Did you see that?" he whispered, the playful bravado of moments before replaced by a sharp tension.

Before I could respond, the shadow coalesced into a figure, stepping forward into the dim light of the attic. My breath caught in my throat as recognition dawned—this was no mere figment of our imaginations.

The figure stood there, cloaked in the darkness, a haunting familiarity in their posture. "You shouldn't be here," they said, their voice low and chilling, echoing the very fears that had woven through the pages of the diary.

And with that, the weight of the past bore down on us like a thundercloud, the promise of secrets unveiled hovering just out of reach.

Chapter 10: The Unearthing

The moment I stepped into the dimly lit theater, the air crackled with an energy I couldn't quite place, a mix of anticipation and trepidation that sent shivers down my spine. Dust motes floated lazily in the narrow beams of light slicing through the velvet curtains, the remnants of an era long past. Each creak of the old wooden floorboards beneath my feet seemed to whisper secrets of forgotten performances and lost dreams. I held the diary tightly in my hands, its leather cover warm against my palm, the faint scent of aged paper wafting up to greet me like a ghostly embrace.

Lucas stood at the center of the stage, his silhouette framed by the brilliant backdrop, a contrast to the world outside. I marveled at how he seemed to belong here, every fiber of his being resonating with the spirit of the theater. His dark curls caught the light just right, and his expressive eyes reflected both curiosity and concern as he took in the weight of what I had just discovered. "What's that?" he asked, gesturing to the diary, his voice laced with intrigue.

"This," I began, my voice trembling slightly, "is a diary from one of the actresses who vanished years ago during a production of Macbeth." I stepped closer, the stage looming like a vast ocean around us, and handed him the book, a tremor of excitement running through me. "She wrote about her fears, Lucas. She mentions a dark presence, something that felt almost alive."

Lucas's brow furrowed as he opened the diary, the pages crackling like fallen leaves underfoot. He read aloud, the sound echoing through the empty rows of seats. "I feel it creeping in, a shadow among the lights, lurking behind every curtain. It feeds on our fears, drawing us closer to the edge of oblivion." His voice dropped as he glanced up, the weight of the words settling between us like a thick fog. "What if this isn't just a coincidence?"

I could almost hear my heart pounding, a relentless drumbeat echoing the rhythm of my thoughts. "We need to know more," I insisted, stepping closer, the warmth of his presence a grounding force amid the uncertainty. "What if we're not just uncovering her story, but protecting ourselves from the same fate?"

Lucas nodded, a fire igniting in his gaze, a determination that mirrored my own. "Then we dig deeper. There has to be something more, some connection we're missing." He closed the diary, a soft thud echoing in the silence, and the theater seemed to shiver in response.

We spent hours combing through the archives of the theater, our excitement blooming like wildflowers amid the dust and shadows. Each discovery felt like a thread unraveling a tapestry of secrets, each name we uncovered weaving into the fabric of the mystery. The deeper we dug, the more the theater revealed its dark underbelly—stories of jealousy, rivalry, and despair hidden behind the glamour of the spotlight.

Lucas found a clipping from an old newspaper, the ink faded but the words still sharp as daggers. "Here!" he exclaimed, his voice slicing through the haze of our research. "This actress, Margot Lane, was reported missing right after a performance. They claimed she'd gone mad, that she believed the theater was haunted."

"Haunted," I echoed, the word tasting bitter on my tongue. "But what if she wasn't mad? What if she uncovered something the others couldn't handle?"

With each passing moment, the atmosphere thickened, a palpable tension wrapping around us like a shroud. Shadows danced in the corners of my vision, the theater's secrets whispering to me in a language I struggled to understand. I felt the weight of the world pressing down, the very walls of the theater closing in, as though they were aware of our search, our trespass into the forbidden.

The following day, a rehearsal loomed over us, the performance drawing near. Lucas and I had agreed to share our findings with the cast, a decision steeped in both hope and fear. As we gathered on stage, the bright lights turned our familiar haven into an unfamiliar battleground of revelations. The actors, each vibrant and layered with their own ambitions and insecurities, fell silent as Lucas and I presented our discoveries.

"We think the theater may be haunted," I began, my voice firm but trembling. "Margot Lane's disappearance isn't just a cautionary tale. It's a warning."

Skepticism flickered across the faces of our peers, but the unease was tangible, a current running beneath the surface of their disbelief. "You can't be serious," scoffed Maria, our lead actress, her arms crossed defiantly. "Ghost stories are just that—stories. This is the theater, not a horror flick."

"Perhaps," Lucas countered, his tone measured. "But what if there's more at play? We owe it to Margot to find out."

"Margot?" she sneered, rolling her eyes. "You really think we're in danger?"

In that moment, I felt a rush of empathy for her. I understood the impulse to dismiss the dark, to banish the unknown, but I also recognized the flicker of fear beneath her bravado. "It's not about fear, Maria. It's about awareness," I replied, my voice steady. "What if we ignore the signs? What if we're tempting fate?"

The discussion swirled like a tempest, opinions clashing and merging, each voice a brushstroke on the canvas of uncertainty. Yet amid the heated exchanges, I caught Lucas's gaze—steady, unwavering, a lighthouse in the storm of our unraveling story. The bond between us deepened, forged in the shared pursuit of truth, tethering me to him even as the shadows threatened to swallow us whole.

As the rehearsal wound down, a chill swept through the theater, a sudden draft that carried whispers of the past. The lights flickered ominously, and for a brief moment, I felt the presence of those who had come before us, their spirits lingering in the folds of the curtains, watching, waiting. I glanced at Lucas, and the unspoken understanding passed between us like electricity. We were no longer just performers; we were part of a narrative larger than ourselves, and its twists and turns awaited us with bated breath.

The air hung thick with anticipation as we gathered around the table in the theater's dimly lit lounge, the scent of stale popcorn mingling with the faint tang of paint. The walls, adorned with posters of past productions, echoed our whispered conversations, as if the spirits of long-gone actors leaned in to listen. I glanced at Lucas, who was shuffling through the various notes and newspaper clippings we'd gathered. The vibrant energy of the cast, who now lounged in various states of disbelief or skepticism, created a charged atmosphere that felt electric.

"Okay, let's review what we know," I said, my voice steady despite the flutter of nerves in my stomach. "Margot Lane vanished after performing in a production that had a reputation for strange occurrences. The theater itself has a history—one we're only beginning to scratch the surface of."

"Are you trying to convince us this place is haunted?" Maria interjected, her tone half-joking but undercut by a flicker of genuine concern. She leaned back in her chair, arms crossed defiantly, her striking features reflecting a mix of skepticism and curiosity.

"Not haunted, per se," I replied, leaning forward to catch her eye. "More like... influenced by something darker. Something that thrives on fear. Just look at the headlines." I gestured to a yellowing newspaper clipping that detailed strange happenings: unexplained accidents, actors leaving mid-performance, a fire that had nearly consumed the theater decades ago.

"Honestly, who writes this stuff?" Ethan, our sarcastic stage manager, chimed in, his eyes rolling dramatically. "Sounds like a desperate attempt to drum up ticket sales."

"Or a cry for help," Lucas countered, his voice calm yet firm, causing the room to shift as all eyes turned to him. "Maybe these aren't just stories. Maybe there's truth hidden within."

The tension thickened as the group absorbed his words, the skepticism giving way to an unspoken agreement that perhaps we needed to be cautious. "How about we explore the theater tonight?" Lucas suggested, his gaze sweeping over the assembled cast. "If we're going to uncover whatever is lurking in the shadows, we need to do it together."

"Are you suggesting a sleepover in a potentially haunted theater?" Maria's laughter was bright, but it faltered under the weight of uncertainty. "Count me out unless there are marshmallows involved."

I couldn't help but smile at her jest. "I promise there will be snacks," I said, trying to lighten the mood, even as my heart raced at the thought of spending the night here. "But seriously, it's either we explore now or risk losing our chance to understand what happened to Margot."

After a moment of hesitation, one by one, nods of agreement spread through the group, fueled by a mix of intrigue and apprehension. As the sun dipped below the horizon, casting long shadows through the theater's high windows, we transformed our rehearsal space into a makeshift command center. Lucas had brought along flashlights and a portable speaker, while others scavenged the lounge for snacks—chocolate bars, gummy bears, and enough soda to fuel a small army.

"I think this is the real audition for our roles," Ethan joked, tossing a candy into his mouth as he leaned against a table piled high with our collected materials. "Survival of the fittest, or in our case, the most gullible."

As the night deepened, we settled into a pattern of playful banter, laughter punctuating the thickening air. Yet as the minutes ticked by, I sensed a shift; the laughter felt more nervous, more strained. The flickering lights overhead added to the unease, casting erratic shadows that danced along the walls like whispers from the past.

Finally, with everyone gathered on stage, Lucas led us through the plan. "Let's split into pairs. Explore the backstage area first—there's a storage room with props from past performances that might give us more insight. We can meet back here in an hour."

"Perfect. I'll take the haunted dolls," Maria said with a smirk, her bravado returning.

"Great! I'll take the creepy masks," I shot back, my heart racing with excitement and fear as I found myself paired with Lucas.

As we ventured backstage, the air grew cooler, the sounds of our footsteps swallowed by the darkness. The narrow hallways twisted like a labyrinth, each corner revealing shadows that lurked just beyond the reach of our flashlights. I felt an electric thrill at being alone with Lucas, the familiar tension between us crackling in the dim light.

"So, what do you think we'll find?" he asked, his voice low, almost conspiratorial as we turned down a particularly darkened corridor.

"Honestly? I don't know," I admitted, a shiver running down my spine. "But I can't shake this feeling that we're being watched. It's like the theater itself is alive."

"Maybe it is," Lucas replied, casting a sideways glance at me, his lips curving into a smile that made my heart skip. "Or maybe we're just letting our imaginations run wild. It's easy to get lost in the story, isn't it?"

Before I could respond, the temperature dropped noticeably, a chill that sunk into my bones. I glanced around, unease prickling the back of my neck. "Did you feel that?" I whispered, halting mid-step.

He nodded slowly, his expression shifting from playful to serious. "Yeah, I did. Like... something's here with us."

The tension crackled between us as we continued deeper into the darkness, our footsteps echoing in the silence. Shadows clung to the walls, and the ancient wood creaked ominously underfoot, an orchestra of whispers surrounding us. I felt as though we were being drawn toward something hidden, something that had been waiting for us to arrive.

As we reached the door to the storage room, the air thickened, and I hesitated, my heart pounding against my ribcage like a trapped bird. "Should we really open this?" I asked, my voice barely above a whisper.

"Together," Lucas replied, his determination anchoring me. "On three."

"One, two, three!" We pushed the door open, and it creaked ominously, revealing a trove of forgotten props and costumes stacked haphazardly, draped in dust and shadows.

"What the..." I breathed, stepping inside. The air felt heavy with the weight of the past, and as I shone my flashlight over the costumes, I noticed a familiar fabric—the deep crimson velvet of Margot's dress, its vibrant hue dulled with age.

"Is that...?" Lucas stepped closer, his voice trailing off as he reached out to touch the fabric, and as he did, an electric jolt ran through the air.

Before I could respond, the door slammed shut behind us with a resounding thud, and the darkness thickened around us, swallowing our light. Panic surged as I fumbled for the doorknob, but it wouldn't budge. "Lucas! It's locked!"

His eyes were wide, but there was something else—something thrilling about the danger we faced. "We'll find a way out. Just stay close," he said, his voice steady despite the panic bubbling in my chest.

In that moment, I realized we were no longer just investigating a mystery; we were entwined in it, pulled deeper into the theater's haunting embrace, with the shadows reaching for us as we stood at the precipice of a story that demanded to be told.

The air was thick with tension, our breaths forming ghostly clouds as we stood in the dimly lit storage room. The door, an impenetrable barrier behind us, left us trapped with only the flickering beam of our flashlight to pierce the oppressive darkness. The warmth of Lucas's body was a comfort beside me, a beacon of calm amid the encroaching unease.

"What now?" I asked, my voice barely above a whisper, the adrenaline coursing through my veins drowning out the rhythmic pulse of my heartbeat. I tugged at the doorknob again, a fruitless effort that made panic claw at my insides.

Lucas frowned, glancing around at the stacks of props, their dusty forms looming like specters in the shadows. "We should search for another exit. There has to be a way out of here."

His words brought a flicker of hope, and I nodded, pushing aside my fear. We began to sift through the clutter, each costume and prop a relic of stories past. A vibrant feather boa brushed against my arm, and I recoiled instinctively, the sudden touch startling me. "Maybe we should have brought some ghost-busting tools instead of snacks," I joked nervously, but Lucas remained focused, his brow furrowed in determination.

"Ghosts don't care about snacks," he replied with a half-smile, though his eyes betrayed his concern. "But they might care about a dramatic exit."

In that moment, a loud bang echoed through the storage room, causing us both to jump. The sound reverberated like a clap of thunder, and I turned to Lucas, my heart racing. "What was that?"

"Stay close," he said, his tone suddenly serious. He moved deeper into the shadows, and I followed, my flashlight beam trembling in the dark. The air felt charged, as if we were standing on the cusp of something monumental, something that had been waiting for us to arrive.

As we rounded a stack of props, we discovered an old trunk, its surface covered in dust and age, the wood weathered and cracked. "Look at this," Lucas said, kneeling beside it. "It could contain anything—old scripts, costumes, maybe even more clues about Margot."

"Or a hidden treasure," I added, a teasing lilt to my voice, though the nervous edge lingered. Together, we pried the trunk open, the hinges creaking in protest. Inside, we found a jumble of fabrics and forgotten memories: a faded photograph of a young actress with a captivating smile, a delicate beaded necklace, and a stack of brittle scripts, their ink faded with time.

"Who is she?" I asked, holding up the photograph, my curiosity piqued.

"Not sure, but she looks familiar," Lucas said, peering closer. "Maybe one of Margot's contemporaries?"

Just then, a low rumble echoed through the theater, causing the ground beneath us to tremble. The lights overhead flickered violently, and I felt the air grow heavy with tension. "This isn't good," I muttered, my heart racing as I clutched the photograph tightly.

"Let's move," Lucas urged, grabbing my hand and pulling me away from the trunk. The adrenaline surged through me as we raced toward the door, but when we reached it, it remained stubbornly shut. "It won't budge!" I cried, desperation creeping into my voice.

"Then we'll have to find another way." Lucas's grip on my hand tightened as he led me deeper into the storage area, his eyes scanning for any potential escape routes. We ducked behind a row of costumes hanging like ghosts in the dark, and I felt a chill ripple through me as the shadows danced menacingly.

"There has to be a back exit," he said, determination etched on his face. "Let's keep looking."

As we navigated the narrow aisles, I caught glimpses of strange props: a broken mirror with cracks spiderwebbing across its surface, a faded portrait of a woman who looked strikingly similar to Margot, her eyes dark and haunting. "Lucas, look at this," I said, stopping to study the portrait. "She feels... familiar."

"Maybe it's a clue," he replied, studying the artwork. "Something that connects all of this."

A sudden noise echoed from the entrance of the storage room—a whispering, almost melodic voice that sent a chill racing down my spine. "Help me..."

I exchanged a frantic glance with Lucas, my breath catching in my throat. "Did you hear that?" I whispered, my heart pounding.

He nodded, his expression a mix of fear and fascination. "We're not alone."

"Maybe we should leave," I suggested, backing away slowly, but the whisper came again, clearer this time, echoing through the darkness. "Help me..."

It was a plea, raw and desperate, and something in my chest tightened. "What if it's Margot?" I said, my voice trembling.

"Or something else entirely," Lucas murmured, his eyes darting around the room. "We need to find out where it's coming from."

The voice beckoned us forward, an eerie melody pulling me deeper into the shadows. Against my better judgment, I stepped closer, Lucas right beside me, our hands still clasped together. "Hello?" I called, my voice shaky. "Is someone there?"

The atmosphere shifted, a chill wrapping around us like a cocoon. The whispering intensified, swirling around us like a dark mist, beckoning and warning all at once. "Help me..."

"Let's check that door over there," Lucas said, pointing toward a dimly lit exit at the far end of the storage room. "It might lead to the backstage area."

As we approached the door, the whispers faded, replaced by an unsettling silence. We exchanged glances, a mix of determination and dread in our expressions. Lucas reached for the doorknob, his brow furrowed with concentration. "On three," he said, his voice firm. "One, two—"

Before he could finish, the door swung open with a force that sent us stumbling back. The light from the hallway poured in, illuminating the room and casting our shadows long against the wall. My heart raced as I glanced into the corridor, a flicker of movement catching my eye at the far end. "Did you see that?" I gasped, pointing into the hallway.

"What was it?" Lucas's voice dropped, his eyes narrowing as he squinted into the darkness.

"I don't know," I replied, stepping closer to him, my pulse quickening. "But I think someone's there."

We hesitated at the threshold, the weight of uncertainty pressing down upon us. "Should we go after them?" I asked, a mixture of fear and adrenaline coursing through me.

He looked at me, determination flickering in his gaze. "We have to. Whatever is happening, we need to know the truth."

Taking a deep breath, we stepped into the hallway, the door swinging shut behind us with a soft thud, sealing us off from the safety of the storage room. The corridor stretched ahead, dimly lit, and the shadows seemed to elongate as we ventured further into the unknown.

"Hello?" I called out, my voice echoing off the walls, the sound fading into the darkness.

But there was no response, only the distant sound of whispers weaving through the air, weaving a web of intrigue and terror. I felt a shiver race down my spine as we moved cautiously forward, each step echoing our resolve.

As we rounded a corner, the air grew colder, the whispers intensifying into a cacophony that drowned out my thoughts. "We're getting closer," Lucas said, his grip tightening around mine.

And then, just as we turned to face a door marked with peeling paint, the whispers abruptly stopped. An eerie silence enveloped us, and I felt the hairs on my arms stand on end.

"What just happened?" I whispered, my voice trembling.

Before Lucas could answer, the door creaked open slowly, revealing a room cloaked in shadows, and a figure stepped out from the darkness, their features obscured. "You shouldn't have come here..." they warned, their voice low and haunting, sending chills racing down my spine.

I froze, the weight of their words crashing over me like a wave, as I realized we were no longer just uncovering the past; we were staring into the depths of something far more sinister, and the night had only just begun to reveal its secrets.

Chapter 11: Ties That Bind

The scent of aged wood and musty velvet filled the air, wrapping around me like a warm blanket as I stepped back into the heart of the theater. Dim lights flickered above, casting long shadows that danced along the walls, reminiscent of the ghosts that haunted this place. Rehearsals had resumed, and the urgency in our voices echoed against the polished stage, every note sharp with a purpose that felt electric. Yet, beneath the surface, a different kind of tension simmered—a current that neither Lucas nor I could ignore.

He stood a few paces away, his brows furrowed in concentration as he rifled through a stack of old photographs. The glow from the single overhead light illuminated his features, emphasizing the strong lines of his jaw and the faint dusting of stubble that gave him an air of ruggedness. My heart fluttered uncomfortably in my chest, an unwelcome yet thrilling sensation that made it hard to concentrate on the task at hand. This was more than just a job for both of us; it had morphed into a mission, an investigation into the theater's mysterious past that seemed to bind us together in a way I hadn't anticipated.

"Look at this," Lucas said suddenly, pulling a faded photograph from the pile. His voice was low and slightly raspy, sending a shiver down my spine. I moved closer, drawn to him as if by an unseen force, my pulse quickening in time with the intensity of the moment.

The photo depicted a group of performers from decades past, their faces frozen in laughter, the fabric of their costumes vibrant against the sepia tone of the print. I could almost hear the echoes of their voices, feel the energy they radiated. "These people," Lucas mused, his eyes softening as he traced a finger over the image, "they had dreams just like us. They poured their souls into this theater."

I met his gaze, feeling a strange knot of emotion swell in my chest. "And what if their dreams turned into nightmares?" I asked, a hint of trepidation creeping into my voice. The shadows felt darker tonight, as if they were inching closer, whispering secrets that danced just beyond our reach.

Lucas's expression shifted, the warmth replaced by a shadow of concern. "That's why we're here, isn't it? To uncover the truth." His eyes locked onto mine, and in that shared silence, the weight of our unspoken fears hung thick between us, pulsating like the beat of a drum.

Before I could respond, he leaned in, the closeness igniting something within me, something wild and reckless. "Do you believe in ghosts?" he asked, a teasing lilt in his tone that was unmistakably charming.

I smirked, feigning nonchalance. "Only the ones that haunt my to-do list. They're particularly clingy." The banter felt effortless, the rhythm of our words entwining like the threads of a tapestry being woven. But as I spoke, I noticed a flicker in his eyes—an understanding, perhaps a shared acknowledgement of the deeper ghosts that loomed over us.

"Maybe we're all just a little haunted," Lucas replied, his voice lowering to a more serious timbre. The smile faded from his lips, replaced by an intensity that sent a rush of heat through my cheeks. "Especially with everything that's been happening."

The thought hung in the air, a fragile web woven with the strands of danger that loomed closer each day. My heart beat louder, thrumming against my ribs as I searched his face, looking for the clarity I desperately craved. Did he feel it too? The magnetic pull that had transformed our partnership into something more? I could sense it, a tangible energy crackling around us, sparking with every glance and fleeting touch. Yet, the fear of what lay ahead kept my heart in a vice grip, threatening to crush any burgeoning hope.

Our moment was interrupted by the sound of footsteps echoing in the hall, and I stepped back, the air between us shifting like a breeze had swept through. As the other cast members trickled in, laughter and chatter filled the space, shattering the intimacy that had cocooned us just moments before.

I forced a smile, banishing the heaviness that had settled on my shoulders. We moved through the rehearsal, the lines we recited punctuated by stolen glances and lingering touches. Every time Lucas brushed past me, I felt a jolt, a reminder that the connection we shared was both exhilarating and terrifying. It was a delicate balance, like walking a tightrope strung high above the ground.

Later, as we gathered around the table to review our lines, I caught Lucas's eye across the expanse of the room. There was something unspoken in that look, a question lingering between us that begged to be answered. The air buzzed with anticipation, thick with the uncharted territory we were navigating, and I could feel the heartbeat of the theater pulsating beneath our feet—a living entity that thrummed with life and secrets.

"Hey," Lucas whispered, leaning in as the others debated a scene. "After rehearsals, let's go back to the archives. I think there's more to uncover."

I hesitated, the weight of his words settling heavily on my chest. The thought of delving deeper into the shadows of this theater stirred a sense of dread, but I couldn't deny the thrill that accompanied the idea of being alone with him again. "Are you sure that's a good idea?" I murmured, glancing around to ensure we wouldn't be overheard.

He smiled, a wicked spark lighting his gaze. "When has a little danger ever stopped us?"

And just like that, the thrill of adventure rekindled within me, igniting a fire I had thought extinguished. With each passing moment, the ties that bound us grew stronger, and I realized that whatever we uncovered together would change everything—our lives, our dreams, and the fragile bond we were forming in the shadows of the theater.

The archives were a sanctuary of forgotten dreams, dust motes swirling in the shafts of moonlight that filtered through the grimy windows. I pushed the heavy door open, the creak echoing in the silence like an old friend calling me home. The familiar scent of old paper and leather bindings enveloped me, a nostalgic embrace that made my heart swell with the weight of history. Lucas followed closely behind, the warmth of his presence wrapping around me, igniting a flicker of anticipation that danced along my spine.

"Welcome to the land of the lost and found," he quipped, a playful grin breaking across his face. He stepped into the room, glancing around as if he expected the ghosts of the past to materialize at any moment. "If we find an ancient script for a tragedy about star-crossed lovers, I'm holding you responsible."

I laughed, unable to suppress the mirth bubbling up inside me. "Only if you promise to act it out dramatically. I can already picture the tearful monologues and the inevitable tragedy of love unrequited." My words hung between us, laced with layers of meaning as I looked into his eyes, sensing the tension that still lingered from our earlier conversation.

We began sifting through the boxes, each dusty photograph and crumpled letter a piece of the puzzle we were determined to solve. Lucas flipped through a box of old playbills, his fingers deftly maneuvering as he pulled one out. "This is from the 1950s," he remarked, holding it up for me to see. "Can you imagine the energy in this place back then?"

"Probably electric," I replied, a wistful smile creeping onto my face. "Everyone was filled with hope, chasing dreams that felt just within reach. Unlike us."

"Why not us?" he challenged, leaning closer, his breath warm against my ear. "We're in the theater, the stage is set. All we need is a little courage and a decent script."

"Courage? Check. Script? We'll have to see," I said, letting the teasing tone of our exchange linger in the air. I could feel his gaze on me, a weight that was both comforting and unnerving.

With each photograph we uncovered, I could sense the story of the theater unfurling like a tapestry, each thread colored with joy and sorrow. I held up an image of a woman in a feathered headdress, her smile bright and wild, a sparkle of mischief dancing in her eyes. "Who do you think she was?" I mused, imagining her in the spotlight, captivating an audience with her charm.

"Definitely the life of the party," Lucas said, his tone playful. "I can't decide if I want to be her best friend or her worst enemy. Probably both."

I chuckled, the lighthearted banter easing the tension. "I think you'd be her worst enemy," I replied. "She'd steal your spotlight without a second thought."

"Only if I let her," he countered, an edge of challenge in his voice. "But really, isn't that the point of this? To shine brighter together, not dim each other's light?"

His words struck a chord, reverberating within me as if they were the lyrics of a song I'd long forgotten. "You might be onto something," I admitted, my heart racing.

We continued our search, the air thickening with shared glances and unspoken feelings. The more we explored, the more our laughter faded, replaced by a quiet intensity that felt as palpable as the dust particles swirling in the light. Each moment stretched, teasing the line between friendship and something deeper, more dangerous.

As I reached for another photograph, my fingers brushed against his. A jolt of electricity shot through me, and I looked up, startled. Our eyes locked, and in that moment, the world around us faded away. The shadows crept closer, the specter of danger lurking just beyond our cozy sanctuary.

"What if," I started, my voice barely above a whisper, "the stories we uncover lead us into something we can't control?"

Lucas held my gaze, a flicker of uncertainty flashing across his features. "Then we face it together. It's better than facing it alone, right?"

"Is it?" I challenged, the weight of his words settling over me. I had always believed in facing my fears alone, relying on my own strength. But with Lucas, I was starting to question everything I thought I knew.

"Absolutely," he replied, a hint of seriousness creeping into his voice. "In this crazy world, it's all about connection. You can't unravel the threads of the past without a partner."

Before I could respond, a loud crash echoed from the far end of the room, startling both of us. We jumped apart, the tension snapping like a taut string. Heart pounding, I turned toward the sound, dread pooling in my stomach. "What was that?"

"Let's find out," Lucas said, his tone shifting from playful to resolute. He took a step forward, his protective instinct kicking in. The shift in his demeanor ignited something fierce within me. Together, we approached the source of the noise, our footsteps echoing in the stillness of the archive.

As we rounded the corner, the sight that met us made my breath catch. A heavy wooden shelf had toppled over, sending boxes tumbling to the floor like fallen soldiers. The dim light caught a glint of something shiny half-buried beneath the debris, an object that radiated an unsettling energy.

"Stay back," Lucas commanded softly, positioning himself between me and the mess. The protective instinct in him ignited a rush of warmth, but the sight of the fallen shelf set off alarm bells in my head.

"What if there's something valuable in there?" I urged, my curiosity battling with a sense of foreboding. "What if it's a clue?"

"It could also be dangerous. We don't know what's hidden in those boxes," he countered, his gaze sharp and focused.

A shiver raced down my spine as the implications settled over me. The theater was more than just a backdrop for our burgeoning romance; it was a labyrinth of secrets and shadows, every corner holding the weight of the past. I couldn't shake the feeling that whatever we were about to uncover would either bind us together or tear us apart.

As Lucas leaned down, carefully moving the debris aside, my heart raced with anticipation. The tension between us crackled in the air, thickening as we inched closer to the unknown. I could feel the very essence of the theater, alive with its stories, breathing around us, urging us forward into the depths of its tangled history. What lay ahead was uncertain, but with Lucas by my side, I felt an unwavering resolve to face whatever emerged from the darkness.

As the last box tumbled over, revealing a cascade of forgotten treasures, I couldn't shake the feeling that we had stumbled upon something both magical and ominous. Lucas knelt beside the wreckage, his brow furrowed in concentration, the light glinting off something that looked like a tarnished locket, partially buried beneath old scripts and faded photographs. My heart raced, a mix of excitement and apprehension swirling within me.

"Careful," I warned, the words slipping out before I could catch them. "That could be cursed."

Lucas shot me a sidelong glance, his lips curving into a smirk. "Cursed? Or just really, really old? I think we both know my track record with old things. They seem to have a habit of leading me into trouble."

"Trouble? Please. More like adventure," I shot back, a playful glint in my eyes. The truth was, the more time I spent with Lucas, the more I realized he thrived on chaos. His carefree attitude was infectious, igniting a part of me that I had long buried under layers of caution and practicality.

He brushed the debris aside, revealing the locket fully, its intricate design echoing stories from a time long past. "What do you think? Should we open it?" His eyes sparkled with mischief, the thrill of discovery palpable between us.

"Why not?" I replied, emboldened by his enthusiasm. "But I'm warning you, if it's filled with the ashes of a long-lost playwright, I'm out."

With a grin, he flipped the locket open, and we both leaned in, our faces close enough that I could see the flecks of gold in his dark eyes. Inside was a tiny photograph of a woman, her face familiar in a way that sent chills racing through me. Her gaze was fierce, full of passion and secrets, and I felt a sudden jolt of recognition.

"Do you know her?" Lucas asked, a mix of curiosity and concern creeping into his tone.

"I... I think I do," I stammered, my mind racing back to the stories I had heard as a child about the theater's legendary actress who vanished without a trace. "Her name was Vivienne Hart. They said she was as brilliant as she was beautiful, but she disappeared right before the opening of her last play. No one knew what happened."

Lucas leaned back on his heels, processing the revelation. "And here we are, in her old haunt, surrounded by whispers of the past," he mused. "Is it possible her spirit is still here, lingering among the shadows?"

"Or maybe she took a wrong turn and ended up in a very different story," I countered, a half-smile playing on my lips. "The kind that involves unsolved mysteries and lost loves."

He laughed softly, the sound reverberating in the dusty stillness. "Well, let's see what else this treasure trove holds. If we can find Vivienne's story, maybe we can piece together what happened to her."

The locket lay between us, a tangible link to the past, and I felt a sense of purpose solidifying in my chest. Together, we would unravel this mystery, and in doing so, perhaps we'd discover more about ourselves than we anticipated.

As we continued to sift through the remnants of bygone eras, the thrill of discovery pushed aside the creeping sense of danger that had followed us. With each photograph, each faded letter, we crafted a narrative, piecing together the story of the theater and its haunting legacy. The lines between history and our present began to blur, igniting a connection that crackled with an intensity that took my breath away.

Then, just as I pulled out another tattered letter, the atmosphere shifted. A chill swept through the room, causing the hairs on the back of my neck to stand on end. The shadows seemed to deepen, curling around us like a shroud. I turned to Lucas, who wore a frown, his earlier playfulness replaced by a seriousness that made my heart race anew.

"Did you feel that?" he asked, his voice dropping to a whisper.

"Yeah, it's like the air thickened," I replied, scanning the dim corners of the room, the sense of unease creeping back in. "Maybe we should wrap this up for tonight."

But before I could suggest we leave, the lights flickered ominously, casting the room in an eerie half-light. A low creak echoed from the far end of the archive, drawing our attention.

"Did you hear that?" I whispered, my pulse quickening. The atmosphere felt charged, electric, and I fought against the instinct to flee.

"Stay here," Lucas instructed, his eyes narrowing as he moved toward the sound. "I'll check it out."

"Are you serious? I'm not letting you go alone!" I protested, adrenaline surging through me.

He hesitated, glancing back with that confident smirk that made me both infuriated and oddly comforted. "You're brave enough to chase down ghosts in a haunted theater. Surely you can handle a little noise, right?"

His teasing tone coaxed a reluctant smile from my lips. "Fine, but I'm right behind you. If it's a ghost, I want to be the first to know."

As we approached the source of the noise, the tension crackled between us, igniting the air like a storm about to break. Lucas reached for the door leading to the back of the archives, pushing it open with a slow, deliberate motion. The hinges groaned, as if warning us of the secrets hidden beyond.

I took a deep breath, preparing for whatever lay ahead. But just as Lucas stepped through, the lights flickered again, plunging us into darkness for a heartbeat before they burst back to life, illuminating a figure standing just beyond the threshold. My breath caught in my throat.

"Who are you?" I managed to ask, my voice trembling with a mix of fear and fascination.

The figure remained shrouded in shadow, but I could make out the glint of something metallic in their hand. "I've been waiting for you," they said, their voice low and smooth, like silk stretched taut over a dagger.

Before I could react, a sharp crack echoed through the room as the figure stepped forward, and the world around me spiraled into chaos. The history of the theater was about to unfold, but at what cost?

Chapter 12: A Mysterious Benefactor

The warm glow of the stage lights illuminated the worn wooden floor of our theater, casting long shadows that danced with each flicker. A familiar scent of aged velvet and lingering popcorn filled the air, wrapping around me like a comforting embrace. I perched on the edge of the worn seat, my heart thrumming with a mixture of anticipation and anxiety. The production, which had consumed my life for months, was now merely days away from opening night. Yet, instead of reveling in the excitement of our imminent debut, I found myself tangled in a web of unease, a feeling that had been growing stronger ever since our unexpected benefactor had arrived.

Lucas, my steadfast partner in both production and life, leaned against the wall, arms crossed, a frown etched deep across his brow. "Something about him doesn't sit right with me," he muttered, his eyes fixed on the empty stage as if it might offer some explanation. His skepticism mirrored my own; a wealthy stranger showing up with an offer to fund our fledgling theater felt too good to be true, a plot twist straight out of a melodrama.

I nodded, glancing back at the opulent figure who had strode into our lives like a summer storm. His tailored suit was immaculate, the fabric shimmering in the light like a creature from another world. Despite the charm that dripped from his every word, there was an edge to his smile, a hint of something lurking just beneath the surface. "His generosity feels like a well-written script," I replied, feeling the weight of unease settle heavily in my stomach. "I just can't shake the feeling that there's more to this story."

"Let's dig a little," Lucas suggested, his eyes lighting up with the thrill of investigation. There was a fire in him that I adored, a sense of adventure that turned mundane days into daring escapades. Together, we made a formidable team—two misfits fighting against the odds in a world that seemed intent on burying our dreams beneath layers of skepticism and debt.

The moment we stepped outside, the crisp autumn air greeted us like an old friend, invigorating and refreshing. Leaves crunched underfoot, their colors a tapestry of fiery reds and golds, echoing the whirlwind of emotions stirring within me. As we wandered through the town, I couldn't help but feel the pulse of history around us, the ghosts of past performances whispering in the wind. Each corner held a memory, a tale of triumph or despair, and somewhere, buried in those stories, lay the secrets of our patron.

We decided to start at the library—a quaint, brick building with ivy crawling up its facade, as if nature itself was trying to reclaim the knowledge within. The librarian, an elderly woman with silver hair and an eagle-eyed gaze, welcomed us with a knowing smile. "Looking for something in particular?" she inquired, her voice smooth as honey, laced with the wisdom of countless tales.

"Research," Lucas replied, leaning over the counter, his curiosity igniting. "We need to know more about Robert Calloway."

At the mention of the name, the librarian's demeanor shifted, her eyes narrowing as if she had been handed a well-worn script that had long been tucked away. "Ah, Mr. Calloway. A name that carries a weight, indeed. There's history there."

With a wave of her hand, she beckoned us to follow her to the back of the library, where the air grew cooler and the scent of old paper enveloped us. Rows of dusty books lined the walls, the stories of a thousand lives waiting patiently for someone to uncover them. We settled into a cozy nook as she produced a stack of yellowed newspapers, their headlines screaming with intrigue.

"Here," she said, placing the top article before us. "A tragic fire in the theater nearly a century ago. The callous negligence of a wealthy benefactor left countless lives in shambles."

As I scanned the details, chills crept up my spine. The patron's name was not just linked to our theater; it was entwined in its darkest chapter. The whispers of a fiery disaster that had claimed lives and dreams echoed ominously through my mind. Lucas's expression mirrored my horror as we absorbed the implications. "What are the odds?" he mused, his voice barely above a whisper. "This could be a coincidence, or..."

"Or it could be a cycle," I finished for him, the weight of the revelation pressing against my chest. The thought lingered like a specter, the laughter and joy we had woven into our production now marred by a shadowy past.

We left the library, the air heavy with the ghosts of history, our resolve steeled. The streets felt different now, as if the very bricks beneath our feet were alive with the stories they had witnessed. A sense of urgency propelled us forward, our minds racing with possibilities and the desire to confront this patron with the truth we had unearthed.

Back at the theater, the energy had shifted. The cast, buzzing with excitement, filled the rehearsal space with their laughter, unaware of the storm brewing just beyond the wings. I caught sight of our benefactor, casually leaning against the wall, a confident smile plastered on his face. He exuded charisma, the kind that could charm the stars from the sky, yet now, all I could see were the shadows dancing around him, hiding secrets.

"Ready to have a little chat?" Lucas asked, his voice low, laced with determination.

"More than ready," I replied, drawing in a deep breath. We were on the cusp of unearthing something bigger than ourselves, something that could change the course of our production—and perhaps our lives—forever. As we approached the figure cloaked in mystery, I felt a shiver of anticipation. The show was about to begin, and this time, the stakes were higher than the curtain rise.

The moment we stepped toward our patron, a palpable tension crackled in the air like the static before a storm. Robert Calloway, draped in an air of affluence and mystery, turned to us with that same charming smile that had first captivated our attention. Yet now, it felt like a mask concealing something darker, a façade hiding a labyrinth of ambition and possibly deception. I felt the weight of our discovery pressing against my ribs, the reality of his connection to the theater's tragic past hanging unspoken between us.

"Ah, my creative partners," he declared, his voice smooth as silk but with an underlying note of steel. "How delightful to see you both. I trust you're ready to discuss the future of our grand production?"

Lucas stepped forward, his posture rigid, arms crossed defiantly. "We need to talk about your interest in our theater," he said, his tone a perfect blend of bravado and caution. "What's in it for you?"

Calloway's smile widened, but his eyes narrowed slightly, as if he appreciated the challenge but found it mildly amusing. "Ah, the ever-curious Lucas. I admire your tenacity. Let's just say, I have a passion for the arts, and I believe this theater has tremendous potential."

"Potential? Or ghosts?" I shot back, my heart racing at my own boldness. "We've uncovered quite a bit about you, Mr. Calloway. Your history with this place is... complicated."

The atmosphere shifted, the playful banter giving way to something much more serious. I could see a flicker of annoyance pass over his features before he masked it with an amused tilt of his head. "I appreciate your research. The past is indeed a curious beast, but it doesn't define my intentions today." His voice dropped, the casual tone slipping away. "However, it would be wise not to stir too much of the dust that has settled."

"Is that a threat?" Lucas challenged, his eyes dark with determination. "Because if it is, we won't be intimidated."

Calloway chuckled, a low, resonant sound that echoed off the walls. "Not a threat, my friend. A suggestion. The theater holds many secrets—some better left undiscovered." His gaze shifted to the stage, the glimmer of the lights reflecting in his eyes, hinting at a past intertwined with both beauty and tragedy.

"We're not afraid of secrets," I replied, the fire in my belly igniting. "But if you're truly invested in this production, you'll understand our need for transparency."

A pause stretched between us, heavy with unspoken words and unshared histories. Calloway finally broke it, his expression shifting to one of genuine interest. "Very well. Transparency it is. But let's not forget who holds the purse strings here."

I exchanged a glance with Lucas, our silent agreement echoing between us. "Then let's make a deal," I proposed, the adrenaline surging through my veins. "You share your intentions, and we'll give you a chance to prove your commitment."

The corner of Calloway's mouth twitched, his interest piqued. "A negotiation, I see. Very well, I'm intrigued." He gestured toward the seating area, a grand chair crafted from rich mahogany that seemed out of place in our humble theater. "Shall we sit?"

Settling into the plush seats, I felt a strange sense of foreboding wash over me. We were not merely discussing our show; we were entangled in a game of power and trust, the stakes higher than any opening night I'd ever faced. "So, what's your angle?" Lucas pressed, leaning forward, intensity radiating from him.

"I want to see this production succeed, and I have the means to ensure that happens," Calloway replied, his eyes glinting like polished stones. "But I also want to leave my mark, a legacy that transcends mere entertainment. This theater has a storied past, and I intend to weave that history into a narrative that captivates."

"Captivates or manipulates?" I interjected, my skepticism threading through the air like an invisible cord. "There's a fine line between honoring history and exploiting it."

Calloway leaned back, a satisfied smile curving his lips as if my challenge had pleased him. "A fair point. But consider this: what better way to confront the past than to bring it to the forefront? Imagine a production that intertwines the theater's legacy with fresh, vibrant storytelling. It would be a masterpiece."

"Or a disaster," Lucas countered, the shadows of doubt creeping back into the conversation. "You're playing with fire."

"And isn't that what theater is all about?" Calloway replied, his tone playful yet laced with an edge. "Drama, tension, and yes, the risk of burning. But without risk, what is art?"

My thoughts raced as I took in his words, a tantalizing mix of ambition and danger. Could we truly harness the shadows of the past, transforming them into something meaningful without being consumed by them? "What's your vision, exactly?" I asked, searching for clarity amidst the haze of his allure.

"An immersive experience, where the audience doesn't just watch—they feel, they become part of the story. I envision interactive elements, incorporating local history and perhaps even elements from that unfortunate event long ago." He leaned closer, his voice dropping to a conspiratorial whisper. "Imagine unveiling the ghosts, allowing the audience to confront their fears while celebrating the resilience of this theater."

"Sounds like a recipe for chaos," Lucas muttered, clearly uneasy with the idea.

"Or a chance for redemption," I countered, my mind whirling with the possibilities. "But we'll need more than just your funding. We need your commitment to preserve the integrity of the story, to ensure we don't exploit the tragedy for profit."

Calloway nodded, a gleam in his eye that hinted at something deeper—an understanding of the fine line we were dancing on. "Integrity is paramount, and I assure you, my interests align with yours. I want this production to be a testament, a reflection of our shared history. But I will not shy away from the darker elements that may arise."

The tension crackled as we considered his proposal, a precarious balance between ambition and ethics hanging delicately in the air. "What do you think, Lucas?" I asked, glancing at my partner, seeking his perspective amidst my own swirling emotions.

Lucas hesitated, his brow furrowing in contemplation. "It's risky, but maybe there's something to be gained here. If we play our cards right and keep our eyes wide open."

I could feel the thrill of potential unfurling in my chest, the promise of a new chapter just beyond our reach. Yet beneath it all lay the unsettling truth that the ghosts of the past were not just remnants of tragedy; they were living, breathing entities ready to intertwine with our lives once more. As we continued our conversation with Calloway, a sense of foreboding lingered, a reminder that this journey into the heart of our theater could lead us down paths we were not prepared to traverse.

The atmosphere in the theater was electric, charged with the anticipation of our unfolding drama. Robert Calloway's proposal lingered in the air like a whispered secret, thick and tantalizing, drawing us into a narrative that was becoming all too complex. I glanced at Lucas, who stood slightly apart, his jaw clenched and brows furrowed, the weight of our conversation clearly heavy on his mind. "So, we dive headfirst into the depths of history, do we?" he said, a hint of sarcasm coloring his tone.

"History can be a powerful storyteller," Calloway interjected, the gleam in his eye suggesting that he reveled in the chaotic dance we were partaking in. "This theater isn't just bricks and mortar; it's a living, breathing entity. It deserves to be celebrated, even if that means unearthing its past."

"Celebrated or exploited?" Lucas shot back, his skepticism a shield against the man's charisma. "You talk a big game, Calloway, but we need to ensure that whatever we unearth doesn't end up backfiring in our faces."

I felt a familiar flutter of anxiety settle in my chest, the disquiet of the unknown making my heart race. "Maybe we should draw up some ground rules," I suggested, trying to bridge the chasm of tension that had formed. "If we're going to go down this road, we need to protect the integrity of our story."

"Ground rules?" Calloway laughed, a rich sound that echoed through the empty seats. "Oh, darling, I love a spirited negotiation! But let's be clear—art requires freedom. And what is more freeing than the truth?"

Lucas scoffed. "You're talking about truth like it's some pretty little bauble, but it can also be a sledgehammer."

"Ah, but it's the sledgehammer that can build something new," Calloway countered smoothly, leaning forward with an intensity that was hard to ignore. "I can make this theater the talk of the town, a shining jewel in a crown of mundane productions. Think of the possibilities!"

A fleeting glance at the stage flickered through my mind, a vision of our show, infused with the essence of the theater's past. A chance to breathe life into forgotten tales and lost souls. I could see the lights dimming, the audience leaning forward, rapt with attention. "What if we told the story of the fire, but as a tale of resilience and hope?" I proposed, my imagination ignited by the very idea that had once terrified me. "What if we showed how the community rebuilt, how art can heal?"

Calloway's expression shifted, the sharp edge of intrigue softening into something more contemplative. "Now you're speaking my language. But remember, my dear, a little danger can spice up a narrative. Perhaps we incorporate some of those darker elements as well, entwining tragedy with triumph."

Lucas sighed, clearly torn between his protective instincts and the allure of the opportunity. "I'm in," he finally said, a reluctant agreement that hung in the air like a fragile truce. "But we'll do this on our terms. If we feel the narrative is shifting away from what we discussed, we pull the plug."

"Agreed," I chimed in, relieved that we were united in our commitment to safeguard the essence of our production. "And perhaps it's time to dig deeper into our research. There are layers to this story, and we need to uncover every last one of them."

As we solidified our plan, Calloway leaned back, an enigmatic smile playing at the corners of his lips. "Excellent. Let's meet tomorrow night. We can discuss our direction further and explore the old archives. There's much to reveal, and the night holds its own mysteries."

The thought sent a shiver down my spine, a mix of excitement and apprehension swirling together. I couldn't shake the feeling that the archives, those dusty corners of the theater that had lain dormant for too long, were hiding more than just old scripts and fading photographs.

The following evening, I arrived early, the theater cloaked in shadows and silence. The air felt charged, as if the walls were holding their breath, waiting for the stories we would unearth to breathe life back into their weary bones. I wandered through the dimly lit space, tracing my fingers along the edges of forgotten props, their surfaces rough and splintered from years of neglect. Each item seemed to hold a memory, a whisper of the performances that had once captivated audiences.

Lucas arrived a short while later, his brow furrowed in thought. "Ready for this?" he asked, glancing around as if he could sense the hidden weight of the theater's past.

"As ready as I'll ever be," I replied, trying to project confidence, though my heart pounded with uncertainty.

The archive room was a cavern of dust and shadows, filled with crates and boxes that contained the remnants of bygone eras. I shivered as I crossed the threshold, the air growing thicker, the history pressing in from all sides.

Calloway arrived moments later, the flickering overhead light casting a dramatic shadow across his sharp features. "Ah, the treasure hunters," he said, his voice rich with playful enthusiasm. "Shall we begin our excavation?"

Together, we began sifting through the contents, uncovering playbills and scripts, each piece of paper imbued with the spirit of those who had come before us. I felt like an archaeologist, carefully brushing away the dust of time, uncovering stories waiting to be told. Yet as we dug deeper, the unease inside me began to rise like a tide, relentless and cold.

"Look at this," Lucas said, pulling out a tattered old scrapbook that looked like it had been through the wars. Its pages were yellowed, and the spine creaked ominously as he opened it. "These are old reviews. And—wait a minute."

"What is it?" I asked, leaning closer, drawn in by the sudden gravity of his discovery.

He flipped through the pages, the silence stretching like a taut string, and then froze, his fingers hovering over one particular entry. "There was an eyewitness account of the fire," he said, his voice dropping to a whisper as if afraid the shadows might overhear. "Someone claimed to have seen a figure in the window the night it happened."

Calloway leaned in, the intensity in his gaze sharpening. "A figure? How intriguing. Perhaps we're onto something truly extraordinary."

I felt a chill dance along my spine, a shiver of foreboding weaving through my thoughts. "What if this figure isn't just a ghost of the past? What if they were someone who had a hand in what happened that night?"

Lucas's eyes darkened, the weight of our unearthing suddenly feeling more like a curse than a blessing. "We need to find out who this person is. If they were connected to the theater back then, they could shed light on the circumstances surrounding the fire."

Before I could respond, a sudden crash echoed from behind the stacks, a sound so jarring that it sent my heart racing. We turned to see a shadowy form retreating into the darkness, the flickering light barely illuminating the figure as it slipped away.

"What was that?" I gasped, my breath catching in my throat.

"Stay here," Lucas instructed, stepping cautiously toward the source of the noise, his instincts kicking in.

I wanted to follow, to understand, but something held me back, an invisible force rooted in primal fear. The shadows were alive, and whatever was lurking within them was not ready to reveal itself. As Lucas moved deeper into the shadows, I called after him, my voice trembling. "Be careful!"

The tension in the air thickened, and just as I was about to step forward, a sudden darkness enveloped the room, the overhead lights flickering violently before plunging us into an eerie blackness. The echo of Lucas's footsteps faded, swallowed by the silence, leaving me in a world of shadows, heart racing and uncertainty swirling around me like a tempest.

And in that stillness, I felt it—a presence, watching, waiting, lurking just beyond the reach of the light. The air grew heavy, filled with secrets, and as the shadows pressed closer, I realized that we were about to uncover something that would change everything.

Chapter 13: Confronting Demons

The theater was alive, a throbbing heart of emotion, wrapped in velvet and whispers. As the stage lights dimmed, the flickering glow cast an ethereal light across the sea of faces, each one a mix of expectation and excitement. The air was thick with the scent of fresh paint and the subtle musk of aged wood, a heady combination that filled me with both a thrill of anticipation and a gnawing anxiety that nestled in my stomach like a stone. The audience murmured in hushed tones, their anticipation tangible, and for a moment, I forgot the restless specter of worry hovering at the edges of my consciousness.

Tonight marked our second performance, and the atmosphere crackled with a strange energy that felt both exhilarating and foreboding. Lucas stood next to me, his dark curls tousled and eyes sparkling with a mix of confidence and mischief. "Ready to dazzle them again?" he asked, his voice low but buoyant, the perfect blend of encouragement and playful challenge. I smiled back, trying to mirror his enthusiasm, but inside, the familiar anxiety twisted like a coiled serpent.

The curtain rose with a flourish, unveiling the world we had crafted—a sun-drenched garden with oversized flowers, each petal painted with meticulous detail, hues of magenta and gold that danced under the lights. I stepped forward, feeling the warmth of the stage beneath my feet, and launched into my lines, allowing the rhythm of the dialogue to wash over me. As the words flowed, however, an unease gnawed at the edges of my focus. It was subtle at first—an offbeat glance from a stranger in the audience, a rustle in the wings where no one should be—but it simmered beneath the surface, relentless and insistent.

With each scene, my awareness sharpened, a hawk tracking the movement of its prey. Then came the first strange incident: a prop,

PHANTOM LINES

a heavy garden bench, suddenly teetered precariously as I turned to deliver a line, nearly crashing to the ground. Gasps echoed through the audience, but I managed to recover with a wry smile, hiding the thud of my heart. "Well, they say gardening can be hazardous," I quipped, the words slipping from my tongue before I had fully processed them. The audience laughed, tension easing, but the knot in my stomach tightened.

Lucas caught my eye as we finished the scene, his brow furrowing in concern. "Did you see that?" he murmured, stepping closer, our shared space pulsating with unspoken fears. "That wasn't supposed to happen."

"I know," I whispered back, the weight of his gaze anchoring me in the moment. The second act unfolded, but the oddities only intensified. A spotlight flickered, momentarily plunging us into darkness, and a crucial set piece—a towering trellis—swung dangerously close to my head. I dodged, barely keeping my composure. This was no longer an amusing mishap; it was something more sinister.

As the final act approached, the tension spiraled. The realization gripped me like a vice; someone was trying to sabotage our performance. Each incident felt like a taunt, a personal affront to our hard work and dreams. I exchanged glances with Lucas, each look a silent acknowledgment of the chaos swirling around us. The buzz of the audience became a distant hum, drowned out by the rapid beating of my heart.

After the curtain fell, I found myself backstage, pacing in the cramped space behind the set. The air was thick with the scent of sweat and anxiety, and the chatter of cast members faded into the background. "We need to confront our benefactor," I declared, my voice steady despite the tremor in my hands. Lucas nodded, the gravity of my words settling between us like a thick fog.

"I'll back you up," he said, determination etching lines across his face. We approached the back room, the sanctuary of our mysterious benefactor, a man cloaked in secrecy and promises. I felt a mix of excitement and dread, the anticipation of unveiling the truth battling with the fear of what we might discover.

The door creaked open, revealing him seated at a cluttered table, papers strewn about like fallen leaves in autumn. His eyes met mine, sharp and calculating, and I sensed the instant shift in the atmosphere. "You two look serious," he remarked, a smirk playing on his lips, as if he reveled in our discomfort.

"Cut the theatrics," I snapped, surprising even myself. "We know something's off. The accidents on stage—this isn't just bad luck. Are you behind this?"

The air crackled with tension as the room fell silent. His expression faltered for a moment, a flicker of something unnameable crossing his features. "You think it's me? How quaint."

"Quaint or not, it's the truth," Lucas interjected, his voice steady but fierce. "We deserve to know what's really happening."

A storm brewed behind the benefactor's eyes, and the atmosphere shifted. He leaned back in his chair, his expression inscrutable, and I felt the thrill of impending revelation dance in the air. "All right," he said finally, the tone of his voice lowering to a conspiratorial whisper. "But be careful what you wish for."

As he spoke, the pieces of the puzzle began to shift, unveiling a tapestry woven with threads of betrayal and hidden agendas. Secrets spilled forth, mingling with the shadows that danced across the walls, and I could feel the weight of the past pressing down upon us. What started as a journey of creativity and expression was morphing into a confrontation with our darkest fears, where nothing was as it seemed, and trust was a fragile thing.

And amid it all, I knew we were teetering on the brink of something monumental—an unraveling that could redefine everything we thought we knew about ourselves and each other.

The room felt electric, charged with an anticipation that was almost palpable as our benefactor leaned forward, fingers steepled beneath his chin, a figure woven from shadows and secrets. "You want the truth?" he asked, a hint of amusement dancing in his eyes, as if he were about to share a particularly juicy rumor rather than the fate of our fledgling production. "Truth can be a slippery concept, you know."

"Slippery or not, we deserve clarity," I shot back, the words bursting forth with more confidence than I felt. I could sense Lucas beside me, his silent support a steadying force against the rising tide of unease. The dim light from a single lamp illuminated the scattered papers around him, their edges curling slightly, as though they too were weary of the tension in the air.

"Let's not pretend this is about mere theatrics," Lucas added, his voice carrying an undertone of urgency. "We're talking about our lives here."

"Your lives?" he echoed, an eyebrow raised. "How dramatic. But let me assure you, my dear thespians, this is much more than a mere performance." His tone shifted, growing heavier with a gravity that made my pulse quicken. "You are entangled in something far more complex than you realize, and trust me, you don't want to know the full scope of it."

"Try us," I said, half-challenging, half-trembling. The room felt smaller, the shadows lengthening as if they were trying to swallow us whole. I could almost hear the pounding of my heart against the silence that followed, the air thickening with unspoken truths.

He studied us for a moment, his expression shifting from amused detachment to something more serious. "Very well, but don't say I didn't warn you." He leaned back, seemingly gathering his thoughts like a maestro orchestrating a symphony of chaos. "You see, the theater is not merely a place for art; it is a battleground for ambition, greed, and retribution. Your little production has attracted more than just an audience. It has drawn the eyes of those who do not take kindly to competition."

My stomach dropped as realization sank in, sharp and cold. "Are you saying someone wants to sabotage us? Why?"

He let out a low chuckle, shaking his head as if he were indulging in a child's naivety. "Because, my dear, not everyone appreciates the beauty of a rising star. Some prefer the darkness of the abyss."

Lucas shifted beside me, tension radiating from his body. "What exactly are you involved in? Are you saying our project threatens something bigger?"

"Bigger?" Our benefactor leaned forward, his eyes glinting with mischief. "I would say it threatens someone very powerful." He paused, allowing the weight of his words to settle. "You're not just performers; you're players in a game that you don't even know exists."

A chill coursed through me, the adrenaline of confrontation battling with dread. "And what do you get out of this? What's your stake?"

He smiled, a sly, enigmatic curve of his lips. "Oh, I'm simply the curator of chaos, ensuring that the right stories unfold, that the past doesn't remain buried."

"Then let's dig it up," I shot back, determination coursing through my veins like wildfire. "We need to know who's behind this before someone gets hurt."

The benefactor leaned back, the smirk fading slightly as he regarded us with newfound respect. "Very well. You may not like what you find, but I'll give you a name: Aria Caldwell. She's been watching you, manipulating the strings from the shadows."

The name hung in the air, heavy and foreign, like a dark cloud threatening to burst. I could feel Lucas stiffen beside me. "Who is she?"

"A former actress," he replied, "whose career fell apart in a spectacularly public manner. She's bitter, driven by vengeance, and she won't stop until she sees you fail."

"Why are you telling us this?" Lucas asked, his voice laced with skepticism. "You could easily stand aside and let it all unfold."

He waved a hand dismissively. "I have my own reasons for wanting to see this play succeed, but I'm not your fairy godfather. Be cautious; she is not the only one with a stake in this."

The weight of his warning settled around us like a thick fog, blurring the edges of our newfound reality. "We need to confront her," I declared, feeling a surge of determination mixed with trepidation.

"Oh, I wouldn't advise that," the benefactor cautioned, his tone suddenly serious. "She's dangerous, and she has connections that run deep in this industry."

"So we just sit back and wait for her to strike?" Lucas challenged, his voice rising with indignation.

"It's better than becoming a target," he said, his voice dripping with irony. "But if you truly wish to confront her, you must be prepared. She plays to win."

With that, the room fell silent, our minds racing with possibilities. "What do we do?" I asked, my voice barely above a whisper.

"Find her weaknesses. She may have eyes everywhere, but every performer has their cracks. Study her, learn her motivations."

"Great. So we become detectives now," Lucas said, sarcasm lacing his tone. "Why do I feel like we're in a noir film?"

"Because the world is often darker than the stories we tell," the benefactor replied, a flicker of admiration crossing his face. "But remember, in darkness, you can also find unexpected allies."

As we left the room, the weight of his words pressed down on me. The atmosphere of the theater had shifted; it felt like we were at the precipice of something vast and daunting. I could sense that every step we took now would lead us deeper into a tangled web of secrets, but the only way out was through.

"Do you really think we can face her?" Lucas asked, his voice a mixture of hope and fear as we stepped back into the buzzing world of the theater.

"I don't know," I admitted, feeling the rush of uncertainty wash over me. "But we can't let her win. Not now."

His eyes sparkled with an indomitable spirit that mirrored my own resolve. "Then let's make sure we're ready. After all, the best performances often come from the greatest conflicts."

And with that shared determination, we set forth into the vibrant chaos of our reality, each heartbeat echoing like the thunderous applause of an unseen audience, preparing for the battle ahead.

The backstage atmosphere felt charged with a sense of purpose as Lucas and I gathered our thoughts in a dimly lit corner, our breath mingling with the musty scent of old costumes and forgotten dreams. The vibrant colors of our set seemed muted under the weight of uncertainty, the looming threat of Aria Caldwell casting a shadow that felt all too real. I could hear the distant murmur of the audience filtering through the heavy curtains, their excitement mingling with my rising anxiety, a cacophony of hope and dread.

"Alright, so we need a plan," I said, forcing my voice to steady despite the churning in my stomach. "We can't just sit here waiting for her to make her move."

Lucas ran a hand through his curls, the gesture both exasperated and endearing. "I feel like I've stepped into a thriller novel. What's next? Stakeouts? Disguises?"

"Don't joke about that," I replied, half-laughing, half-serious. "If you can pull off a trench coat and a fedora, I'll buy the snacks."

"Perfect. Nothing says 'undercover' like popcorn and nachos." His lips curled into a smile, the warmth of his humor a necessary balm against the tension gripping my heart.

"Seriously, though. We should scout for her, maybe catch wind of her next move," I suggested, trying to piece together a strategy from the chaotic shards of fear and uncertainty. "If she's watching us, she'll slip up. Everyone has a weakness."

Lucas nodded, the flicker of determination in his eyes rekindling the fire within me. "Then let's make a list of our options. We could check out the usual haunts—local cafes, bars, maybe even the other theaters. She must have a favorite spot."

"Like the infamous 'You Can't Kill My Dreams' diner on Elm? I hear their pie is to die for."

"Ah yes, the perfect cover for a wannabe villain plotting her revenge. I can almost see her now, sipping on a latte and brainstorming her next dramatic act."

With a shared laugh, we stepped back into the theater's embrace, the audience's chatter now a backdrop to our resolve. The bright lights on stage felt like a lifeline, a reminder of why we were here—our passion for performance, our shared dreams woven into the fabric of the show. But as we settled into our roles for the next act, the gnawing uncertainty refused to let go.

The scene began seamlessly, my heart racing as I navigated the familiar lines, each word a tiny beacon of hope against the dark clouds looming above us. Lucas moved with a fluid grace, his energy infectious, but my thoughts drifted back to Aria. How could someone so intent on destruction exist in a space meant for creation?

My concentration wavered, and I stumbled over a line, a minor crack in our carefully constructed facade.

The audience's laughter rang out, a reminder of their presence, their joy. I forced a smile, but inside, I felt a restless urgency, a need to confront the chaos brewing beneath the surface. After the performance, as we stood in the wings, our adrenaline still coursing through us, I caught Lucas's gaze. "We have to act. Now."

"Right after the final curtain," he agreed, his expression turning serious. "Let's keep our eyes peeled. If she's here tonight, we need to know."

The finale brought a rush of energy, and as the applause filled the theater, a sense of camaraderie enveloped us. But as the curtain fell, the moment of triumph was short-lived. The lights dimmed, and an unsettling quiet settled over the theater, as if everyone was holding their breath, waiting for something to shatter the calm.

"Let's check the lobby," I whispered, my instincts kicking into high gear. "If she's here, she might be watching."

We slipped through the back exit and emerged into the bright lights of the lobby, where patrons milled about, laughter bubbling like champagne. I scanned the crowd, heart pounding, searching for any sign of the woman whose presence felt like a dark cloud threatening to eclipse our dreams.

"Over there," Lucas said, his voice low and urgent. He gestured subtly to a figure by the refreshments stand, a woman with striking auburn hair cascading over her shoulders. She wore a tailored jacket that hugged her frame and exuded an air of confidence, but there was something in the way she carried herself—an unmistakable tension that hinted at her true intentions.

"That's her," I breathed, my heart racing. "What's the plan?"

"Stay calm," he replied, his voice steady as he led me through the throng of bodies. "We can't approach her directly. We need to gather intel."

As we edged closer, I could hear snippets of her conversation, her voice smooth and seductive. "I appreciate your support, but I assure you, this play has no future without a little... interference." My blood ran cold. Was she orchestrating the very chaos that had plagued us?

"What if we recorded her?" I whispered, desperation creeping into my voice.

"Good idea. Let's get closer," Lucas urged, inching toward the nearby potted plant that offered some cover. We crouched low, our eyes fixed on her, my breath catching as she continued to speak with a man whose face was obscured by the crowd.

"Once they falter, the audience will see who they truly are—nothing more than amateurs playing at being stars," she said, her laughter slicing through the din of voices. "And when that happens, I'll be right there to pick up the pieces."

My heart raced, the weight of her words pressing down on me like a vice. "She's plotting to ruin us," I whispered, barely able to contain my panic.

"Let's get a clearer view," Lucas suggested, and as we shifted positions, a sudden commotion erupted on the other side of the lobby. A figure stumbled back, knocking over a tray of drinks, and in the chaos, I lost sight of Aria.

"Where did she go?" I asked, my pulse quickening as the crowd surged, drawn by the noise.

"Stay here," Lucas urged, his eyes darting through the shifting bodies. "I'll find her."

Before I could respond, he slipped into the throng, and I was left standing alone, my mind racing. Panic clawed at my throat as I strained to catch a glimpse of him, searching for any sign of his return amidst the swirling chaos.

Time seemed to stretch as I waited, each second heavy with dread. Just as I was about to turn back toward the theater, a sudden shout echoed from the far corner of the lobby.

"Hey! You!" The voice was familiar, but it sent a chill down my spine. I turned to see a security guard, eyes narrowed, marching toward me.

"Ma'am, you need to clear out of here!" he barked, pointing toward the exit.

"Wait, I'm just—"

Before I could finish, a loud crash reverberated through the lobby, and a wave of panic surged through the crowd. I spun around, dread pooling in my stomach as I searched for Lucas. Had Aria slipped away, or was she still here, weaving her web of chaos?

The guard advanced closer, his expression hardening. "Now!"

My heart pounded as I stumbled backward, torn between obeying him and the desperate need to find Lucas. Then, through the chaos, I spotted a flash of red hair. Aria, standing near the exit, an amused smile playing on her lips, as if she were watching a grand spectacle unfold.

Just as I took a step forward, the lobby doors swung open, and the cold night air rushed in, swirling around us like an unexpected storm. In that moment, everything shifted. The laughter, the shouts, the crashing sounds all melded into one cacophony, but above it all, Aria's gaze locked onto mine, fierce and unwavering.

And then, she turned, slipping out into the night with an unsettling grace, leaving behind a question that hung in the air like a lingering note from a dissonant chord. As I pushed through the crowd, desperation clawing at my chest, I realized one thing: whatever game Aria was playing, I was now a key player in a far more dangerous act than I had ever anticipated.

Chapter 14: An Unholy Alliance

The moon hung low in the sky, casting an eerie glow over the dimly lit backstage of the theater. Shadows flitted across the worn wooden floor, the scent of old velvet and stage dust mingling with the faint whiff of linseed oil from the recently painted set. The air was thick with tension, as palpable as the rustle of costumes being prepared for the evening's performance. I leaned against the cold brick wall, the coolness seeping into my skin, grounding me as the revelation about our benefactor, Martin Hale, washed over me like a cold wave.

Lucas stood a few paces away, his jaw clenched, eyes narrowed. The conflict with Hale had been electric, a confrontation charged with accusations and half-truths. His honey-brown hair fell into his eyes as he turned toward me, the flickering light above catching the worry etched into his handsome features. "Did you hear what he said?" His voice was low, barely more than a whisper, yet it resonated with the weight of a thousand unsaid things.

I swallowed hard, still grappling with the implications of Hale's words. "He knew her. He knew Vanessa," I said, letting the name roll off my tongue like a bitter pill. Vanessa was not just a name on a poster; she was a woman whose laughter had filled this very space, whose talent lit up the stage. And now, her absence left a gaping hole that swallowed light and warmth.

Lucas ran a hand through his hair, frustration radiating from him like heat from a flame. "And he just let her vanish?" His eyes glinted with indignation. "What kind of monster does that?"

"Someone with something to gain," I replied, recalling Hale's piercing gaze when he spoke of the actress. Beneath the charm and polished veneer, there lurked a darkness that sent shivers down my spine. "He didn't just lose a talent; he lost a ticket to success. And I have a feeling he'll do anything to keep that ticket from coming back."

Our eyes locked, and I felt the tremor of unspoken fears swirling between us, a storm waiting to break. "We need to dig deeper," I said, a mix of resolve and dread filling me. "This is bigger than we thought."

"I hate the idea of getting tangled up with him again," Lucas replied, fists clenching at his sides, his frustration morphing into determination. "But if it means finding out what happened to her..."

A silence enveloped us, thick with unspoken possibilities. It was strange how in that moment, with the world collapsing around us, I felt a flicker of warmth in my chest. The chaos was pulling us closer, revealing layers of vulnerability neither of us had dared to explore.

As the curtain rose on our first act, I found myself drifting through the motions, the lines blurring between reality and the play. The audience was a sea of faces, their laughter and applause ringing hollow in my ears. I was present, yet lost in thought, contemplating our unholy alliance. Lucas was at my side, every glance and shared smile igniting something deeper, an electric connection that pulsed with each fleeting moment we shared on stage.

Backstage, the chaos continued, the familiar sounds of rustling costumes and frantic whispers wrapping around us like a protective cloak. Between scenes, Lucas and I slipped into the cramped dressing room, a sanctuary amidst the turmoil. The mirror reflected our strained faces, but I noticed something more—a spark, an energy that sizzled in the air.

"Do you remember our first rehearsal?" he asked, a teasing smile breaking through the tension. "You were so nervous, you nearly tripped over your own feet."

I chuckled, the sound light against the heavy atmosphere. "And you were so focused on your character that you forgot to breathe. I thought you might faint."

Lucas laughed, the sound warming the cold edges of my heart. "I'd like to see you try to hold your breath for three hours while I recited Shakespeare."

The banter came easily, a balm for our frayed nerves, and for a moment, I allowed myself to imagine a world where the stakes weren't so high, where we weren't chasing shadows in the dark. But the reality of our situation loomed large, a shadow that could not be ignored.

As the curtain fell on the final act, our hands brushed against each other in a casual, electric touch. I glanced up, catching Lucas's gaze, and a silent understanding passed between us. The chase for answers had transformed us, forging an unspoken bond in the fires of uncertainty.

Outside the theater, the night air was cool, a sharp contrast to the stifling warmth we had left behind. I took a deep breath, the crispness invigorating my senses. "We should start looking into Hale's past," I suggested, the idea igniting a flicker of adrenaline.

"Agreed," Lucas replied, determination flooding his voice. "But we need to be careful. He's not just some shady businessman; he has connections, power. We can't afford to be careless."

"Trust me," I said, locking eyes with him, "I'm not going to let us get caught in his web. We'll stick to the shadows, gather intel, and expose him."

As we walked side by side into the night, the world felt both vast and intimate. Each step echoed with purpose, the streetlights casting our elongated shadows against the cobblestones. Lucas's presence felt grounding, a steady anchor amidst the swirling chaos.

With every secret we unearthed, every layer of betrayal peeled back, the stakes climbed higher. But so did the thrill of our unholy alliance, a bond forged in the fires of uncertainty. Our shared mission pushed us closer, revealing not just the darkness surrounding

Vanessa's disappearance but also the light we found in each other's company.

In the shadow of danger, a new passion ignited, swirling through the air like the smoke from the stage lights, captivating and intoxicating. And as we ventured into the unknown, I realized that amidst the turmoil, I was beginning to unravel my own desires—both for the truth and for the man who stood beside me, steadfast and resolute against the encroaching darkness.

The night was heavy with unsaid words and lingering questions as Lucas and I ventured deeper into our investigation. The streets shimmered under a veil of moonlight, casting ethereal shadows that danced around us like phantoms from the past. Each step echoed in the stillness, a reminder of the unseen eyes watching our every move. The air crackled with the thrill of pursuit, and for the first time in days, I felt alive with purpose.

"So, what's the plan?" Lucas asked, his tone laced with a mix of excitement and apprehension. He was leaning against a lamppost, the golden light framing him in a halo that made my heart skip a beat. I had grown accustomed to his easy charm, but tonight, there was a newfound intensity in his gaze that sent a ripple of anticipation through me.

"First, we need to figure out how far Hale's reach goes," I replied, allowing myself to enjoy the banter, even as our circumstances weighed heavily on my mind. "I think he's hiding something, something more than just a missing actress."

Lucas straightened, his brow furrowed in thought. "Right, but how do we even start? We can't just march up to him and ask for his diary." He smirked, a playful glint in his eyes. "Unless you think he keeps a list of all his nefarious activities right next to his cologne."

"Maybe we could pose as potential investors?" I suggested, raising an eyebrow. "I mean, if he's desperate for cash, he might spill his secrets if he thinks we could help his little empire."

He laughed, a rich sound that rang out against the night, dispelling some of the tension. "Ah yes, let's put on our best poker faces and charm the devil himself. What could possibly go wrong?"

"Nothing, except we'd probably end up in a dramatic showdown where we're outnumbered by his goons." I shrugged, feigning nonchalance, though my heart raced at the thought. "But at least we'd be in the right genre."

The banter continued, a welcome distraction from the darkness creeping closer. As we strolled through the quiet streets, a thought nagged at the back of my mind—Hale wasn't just a man of power; he was a master of manipulation, and every move he made was calculated. I couldn't shake the feeling that he had set us up as pawns in a much larger game.

"Maybe we should talk to some of the other actors," Lucas suggested, nudging me gently with his shoulder. "They might have heard something or noticed anything unusual about Hale's dealings with Vanessa."

"That's actually a brilliant idea," I replied, the wheels in my mind beginning to turn. "If we can get a few whispers about Hale's past, it might lead us to a crack we can pry open."

We decided to split up for the evening, each of us armed with our instincts and a determination that felt like a protective shield against the unknown. Lucas would head to a nearby café known for its late-night crowd of aspiring actors, while I would comb through the theater's archives, searching for any forgotten whispers caught in the dust of time.

The theater, usually a haven of creativity, felt ominous that night, the silence echoing in the empty halls. I slipped into the old archive room, where faded photographs and brittle scripts lay scattered like the remnants of dreams long gone. The dim light overhead flickered ominously as I began my search, sifting through the remnants of past productions.

Hours passed in a blur of yellowed paper and long-forgotten stories, but as I delved deeper, I stumbled upon something intriguing—a series of letters exchanged between Hale and a former actress, who had left the company under dubious circumstances. The letters were filled with longing and tension, words that hinted at a relationship fraught with manipulation and power struggles. My heart raced as I pieced together the fragments of a story that suggested Hale had a history of controlling those he deemed essential to his success.

A sudden noise startled me from my reverie—a creak of the floorboards echoed in the stillness, making my pulse quicken. I glanced around, straining to hear if someone else was lurking in the shadows. The weight of the silence felt oppressive, and just as I began to convince myself it was nothing, the door swung open.

"Found anything interesting?" Lucas stood in the doorway, his silhouette framed by the bright lights of the hallway behind him. He stepped into the room, and I could see the excitement sparking in his eyes.

"Actually, yes. You won't believe this." I handed him the letters, my fingers trembling slightly. "It looks like Hale had a... complicated relationship with one of the actresses. She left under mysterious circumstances, and I think there's more to it than we realized."

Lucas read through the letters, his expression shifting from curiosity to concern. "This doesn't look good. If he was involved with her, he might have more reason to want Vanessa out of the picture than we thought." He looked up, the gravity of our findings settling over us like a storm cloud. "This could be a direct link to her disappearance."

"Or it could be a distraction," I replied, chewing my lip. "He might be covering his tracks, trying to bury any connection. But it's a lead, nonetheless. We need to find out who this actress is and what happened to her."

With renewed determination, we began formulating a plan. The names and faces of those in the letters felt like a puzzle waiting to be pieced together. Lucas's presence was a comforting anchor amidst the whirlwind of uncertainty, and I could see the fire in his eyes—he was all in, just as I was.

"We should reach out to some of the old crew members," he suggested, his voice firm. "They might have insights into what happened behind the scenes."

"Agreed. But let's do it carefully." I leaned closer, the thrill of our collaboration igniting a spark between us. "If Hale's watching us, we can't let him see us coming."

The stakes felt higher than ever, but in that moment, I felt a flicker of hope. As we plotted our next move, I couldn't shake the feeling that we were finally getting closer to the truth, threading together the strands of a narrative that had long been obscured by darkness. Each step felt like a dance, a balance of danger and desire, pulling us ever closer to the heart of a mystery that might finally set us free—or trap us forever.

The days that followed unfolded like a tightly wound coil, each moment bursting with the tension of our secret investigation. Lucas and I became clandestine allies, navigating the treacherous waters of the theater world while keeping our discoveries cloaked in shadows. The stage felt both familiar and foreign, a battleground where the line between performance and reality blurred.

Our next move was to delve into the history of the actress whose letters had piqued our curiosity. Over coffee in a cozy café, the scent of freshly brewed espresso hung in the air, mingling with the chatter of patrons. Lucas leaned forward, his elbows resting on the table, a glimmer of excitement dancing in his eyes. "So, who do we need to talk to?"

I sifted through the notes I had compiled, the crisp pages filled with hurried scrawls and highlights. "I found out her name is Lila

Mercer. She was one of Hale's stars before she disappeared." I paused, gauging Lucas's reaction. "Her last known location was a small apartment not far from here. It was right before she left the production. I think we should start there."

"Sounds like a plan," he replied, a serious edge creeping into his tone. "But if Hale's involved, we need to be smart about it. One wrong move, and we could end up like a couple of bad actors in a tragedy."

"Right, but we're not going to let that happen," I shot back, feigning bravado. "Just a couple of intrepid detectives, stumbling through the dark, armed with nothing but charm and a questionable sense of direction."

Lucas laughed, the sound infectious and warm. "Charm? I thought we were relying on my boyish good looks." He tilted his head with a playful smirk, his confidence both endearing and disarming.

"Don't push it," I replied, rolling my eyes, though I couldn't hide my smile. "We need a solid plan. Let's check Lila's apartment, see if we can find any clues about her relationship with Hale. Maybe she left something behind that can give us insight into what's really going on."

With our mission set, we headed out, the streets a canvas of golden streetlights and cool evening air. The atmosphere crackled with an electric thrill, but underneath it all, a layer of anxiety lingered. As we approached Lila's apartment building, a nondescript structure nestled between more flamboyant neighbors, I felt a shiver run down my spine.

"This is it," I murmured, staring up at the peeling paint and cracked windows. "Home sweet home for a woman who vanished without a trace."

Lucas placed a reassuring hand on my back, and together we climbed the narrow stairs, the old wood creaking beneath our weight. Each step felt heavier than the last, laden with the weight of uncertainty. The hallways were dimly lit, the air thick with neglect and the scent of damp.

We reached the door, its surface marred with scratches and dents. "You ready?" Lucas asked, glancing at me with a mix of determination and concern.

"Let's do this," I said, my heart racing. He nodded and knocked, the sound echoing ominously in the empty corridor. When there was no answer, I turned the knob, surprised to find it unlocked.

The door swung open, revealing a small, cluttered apartment frozen in time. Dust motes floated lazily in the air, illuminated by the slivers of light peeking through the closed curtains. It felt like stepping into a forgotten dream, the remnants of a life lived echoing in the silence.

"Wow," Lucas breathed, surveying the scene. "Talk about a time capsule."

I stepped inside, careful not to disturb anything. "Let's look for anything that might give us a clue." The walls were adorned with fading photographs and posters from past productions, reminders of a vibrant spirit now shrouded in mystery.

As we moved through the space, I noticed a small desk piled high with papers and playbills. "Over here," I called, my heart quickening as I rummaged through the papers. Most were mundane—bills, receipts, and old scripts—but then I spotted a notebook tucked beneath a pile of faded letters.

I pulled it out, its cover worn and frayed. "This looks promising." I flipped it open, revealing a jumble of thoughts, sketches, and random notes. As I scanned the pages, snippets of Lila's life emerged—a vibrant soul filled with dreams, but also a woman clearly haunted by her decisions.

"Read this," I said, handing it to Lucas. "She mentions Hale a lot. It's like she was caught in his orbit."

Lucas's brow furrowed as he read. "This is... intense. She talks about wanting to break free, but there's also this fear that he might retaliate. It's almost as if she knew he was dangerous."

"What if she found out something she wasn't supposed to?" I suggested, piecing together the fragments of a life cut short. "Maybe she was trying to leave before it was too late."

Just then, a sound reverberated through the walls—a loud thud followed by an urgent knock at the door. My heart raced as Lucas and I exchanged a panicked glance. "We need to hide," he whispered, his voice urgent.

We darted into the adjoining room, crouching behind a faded armchair as the door swung open. Two figures entered the apartment, their voices low but clearly laced with tension.

"Did you check the other places?" one of them said, his voice a deep rumble. "We can't let her disappear like this. Hale won't be pleased."

"Relax," the second figure replied, his tone sharp. "I'm sure she's around here somewhere. We'll find her before Hale knows we're looking."

I held my breath, my pulse pounding in my ears. "Who are they?" I whispered, my eyes wide as Lucas leaned closer, his presence anchoring me amidst the storm of fear.

"I don't know, but it sounds like they're looking for Lila," he replied, his gaze fixed on the intruders. "We can't let them find us."

The men moved further into the apartment, rummaging through the clutter as our hearts raced in unison. "What if they're working for Hale?" I breathed, dread pooling in my stomach.

Lucas clenched his jaw, his determination sharpening. "If they find us here, we'll be in serious trouble. We have to get out, now."

As we quietly made our way toward the back exit, the weight of our discovery settled heavily on my shoulders. But just as we reached the door, one of the intruders paused, tilting his head as if sensing something was amiss.

"Did you hear that?" he asked, his voice suddenly alert.

"Just the wind," the other replied, though the uncertainty in his tone belied his bravado.

With adrenaline coursing through my veins, I exchanged one last look with Lucas, our unspoken understanding igniting a spark of courage. But before we could escape, the door swung open behind us, revealing a silhouette framed by the dim light of the hallway.

My heart dropped as I recognized the face. "Hale..." I whispered, my voice barely audible over the pounding in my chest.

"Looks like I found you," he said, a predatory smile curling at the edges of his lips. The tension in the room snapped, and in that moment, everything changed.

Chapter 15: Into the Abyss

The diner stood like a weary sentinel at the edge of town, its neon sign flickering desperately against the encroaching night. The once-vibrant hue of blue had dulled to a ghostly shimmer, casting long shadows that twisted across the cracked pavement. I stepped inside, the door creaking ominously as I entered. The air was thick with the scent of burnt coffee and stale grease, the remnants of a better time clinging stubbornly to the faded vinyl booths. I slid into a booth in the far corner, my fingers tracing the edge of the table, its surface sticky with a history of forgotten meals.

This was no ordinary meeting. I was here to meet Linda, an old friend of the missing actress, Clara, who had vanished under the spotlight's glare. Linda was a whisper of a memory, a figure from the fringes of Clara's life who now held a crucial piece of the puzzle. My heart raced with anticipation, the weight of desperation driving me forward. I had spent too many sleepless nights ruminating over Clara's fate, and each moment felt like sand slipping through my fingers.

As I waited, I glanced around the diner, noting the few patrons scattered about—an elderly couple sharing conspiratorial whispers over a plate of fries, a trucker hunched over his coffee, and a waitress moving with the weary grace of someone well-acquainted with hopelessness. Outside, the wind howled, rattling the windows as if echoing my own unease. I leaned back against the cracked vinyl, forcing myself to breathe deeply, to steady the frantic beat of my heart.

A flash of movement caught my eye. Linda entered, her silhouette framed against the diner's harsh fluorescent lights. She was a wisp of a woman, her hair a riot of curls that framed her face like a cloud of chaos. Her eyes were wide, darting around the room as if she were afraid of being seen, the light catching the edges of her skin and illuminating the tension there. I waved her over, my smile faltering as I took in the haunted look in her eyes.

"Sorry I'm late," she murmured, sliding into the booth opposite me. "I wasn't sure if I was being followed."

"Followed? By whom?" I asked, a knot tightening in my stomach. The unease that had settled in the diner deepened, wrapping around us like a heavy fog.

"I can't explain everything right now," she whispered, her voice barely above a breath. "You need to understand—Clara was involved in things… things that went deeper than we realized. I thought she was safe, but—" she hesitated, glancing toward the door.

"Safe? You mean to tell me that she wasn't?" The words slipped from my mouth, laced with disbelief.

Linda shook her head, biting her lip. "No, she was tangled up in something dangerous. The last time I saw her…" Her voice faltered, and I leaned in, urging her to continue. "She was frantic, pacing back and forth in her apartment. I was worried she might do something reckless. She was supposed to meet someone, but she didn't tell me who."

"Who?" I pressed, feeling the weight of my own impatience gnawing at me.

Linda looked down, her hands fidgeting with the hem of her sweater. "I don't know, but I overheard her talking about a party… something big. It was happening that night, right before she disappeared." She took a breath, steeling herself as if gathering courage from within. "I think she planned to confront someone there. Someone who could help her, or—"

"Or hurt her," I finished for her, the implications unfurling like a dark cloud above us. I glanced around the diner again, the shadows now feeling more like lurking figures. "What else do you know?"

Linda swallowed hard. "That's when I saw him. A man in a black coat, lurking outside her building. I thought he was just a passerby, but there was something in the way he watched her. It felt... predatory. And then I saw her leave with him."

I felt the chill creep down my spine. "Leave with him? You didn't try to stop her?"

"I didn't know what to do! Clara was so determined, and I felt powerless." Her voice cracked, and I reached out to comfort her, but my heart raced with the weight of this new revelation.

The diner's bell tinkled as the door swung open, a gust of wind carrying in a chill that made the hairs on my arms stand up. I glanced over, and my stomach dropped as I recognized the figure silhouetted in the doorway. A tall man with an angular jaw and a coat that swept like a shadow, his eyes scanning the room with an intensity that sent my instincts into overdrive.

"Linda, we need to go. Now," I said, urgency propelling my words.

"What? Why?" Her brow furrowed, confusion flickering across her features.

"He's here," I whispered, my voice barely audible above the whir of the ceiling fan.

Without waiting for a response, I grabbed her wrist and bolted for the back exit. The door swung open with a loud creak, and we slipped into the night, the cold air biting at our skin as we dashed into the alley behind the diner. Shadows danced menacingly in the flickering streetlights, but I couldn't let fear take hold. We raced through the maze of darkness, hearts pounding in unison, the sense of danger pressing down on us like the weight of the night itself.

"Where do we go?" Linda gasped, glancing over her shoulder as if the darkness itself might be chasing us.

"Anywhere but here," I replied, adrenaline coursing through my veins, urging me forward. The echo of footsteps behind us fueled my resolve. As the alley opened up into a narrow street, the sirens in my head screamed for us to move faster, to escape whatever chaos lay in wait behind us.

The alley swallowed us whole, the darkness a tangible blanket that pressed against our skin as we sprinted down its length. My mind raced alongside my feet, weaving through a tapestry of questions and fears. The sharp edges of bricks and the bitter scent of mildew painted a gritty picture of our escape, but I could barely focus on the surroundings as Linda's breathless panic clawed at my nerves.

"Do you even know where we're going?" she gasped, her voice strained as we rounded a corner, skidding to a halt beneath the glow of a flickering streetlamp. The beam cast an eerie light over us, illuminating the growing fear in her wide eyes.

"I'm working on that," I replied, scanning our surroundings for any sign of safety. I didn't have a plan, not really—just the instinct to put distance between us and whatever had lurked behind us in that diner. "We can't stay out here. Let's head to my place."

"Your place? Are you sure that's a good idea?"

"Honestly? No. But right now, it's the only idea I have that doesn't involve a police station or a waiting room full of angry, sharp-suited detectives."

Linda nodded, still catching her breath, and together we slipped out of the light, ducking into the deeper shadows of the alley. As we moved, the night felt alive with possibilities, each rustle of leaves or distant honk of a car sparking a jump in my chest. We threaded through the labyrinthine streets, my heart pounding not only from the exertion but from the escalating tension. With every step, I could feel the weight of the revelation that had erupted in that diner—the mystery of Clara's disappearance twisting around me like a noose.

By the time we reached my apartment, the world around us had quieted, leaving only the soft thrum of city life echoing in the distance. I fumbled with my keys, my hands shaking, as I glanced back over my shoulder. The night felt too still, too watchful. I swung the door open, pulling Linda inside and shutting it behind us with a decisive click. The small space was dimly lit, cluttered with stacks of books and half-finished art projects—my sanctuary, my chaos.

"Okay, we're in," I said, letting out a breath I hadn't realized I was holding. "We can talk here. Just... don't touch anything."

"Touch anything?" she echoed, a wry smile breaking through her worry. "You mean like the unidentifiable food on that plate over there? I thought it was a science experiment."

"It's a painting I'm working on," I replied, rolling my eyes playfully. "In theory, it's still edible."

"Good to know. You're quite the artist, aren't you?" she teased, but her gaze turned serious as she crossed her arms tightly. "What do we do now?"

"Now?" I echoed, pacing the small space, my thoughts colliding like pinballs in my head. "Now we figure out what Clara was involved in. Who was that guy she left with? And why did it look like he was waiting for her?"

Linda flinched at the mention of Clara's name, her eyes glistening with unshed tears. "I should have tried to stop her. I just... I didn't know what was at stake."

"You couldn't have known," I reassured her, softening my tone. "None of us did. But we're here now, and we can dig deeper. We can find out what really happened."

"Do you think she's okay?" The question hung heavy in the air, a fragile thread that tugged at my heart.

"I don't know," I admitted, the weight of uncertainty pressing down on me. "But I can't believe she's gone forever. Not without a fight."

Just then, a sharp knock rattled the door, making us both jump. My pulse quickened as I exchanged a glance with Linda, her eyes wide and fearful. "What if it's him?" she whispered, her voice trembling.

"Only one way to find out," I said, forcing myself to sound braver than I felt. I tiptoed toward the door, peering through the peephole. A familiar silhouette stood outside, one that sent a rush of relief through me. I pulled the door open cautiously.

"About time you let me in!" Jenna exclaimed, a whirlwind of energy as she strode inside. "I thought you were going to leave me out here to fend for myself. You know how dangerous it is in this neighborhood at night."

"Jenna! You scared me half to death," I replied, pulling her into a quick hug before glancing nervously at Linda. "What are you doing here?"

"I heard from one of the guys at the studio that Clara's been missing. I had to see if you were okay." She took in our disheveled appearance, the tension in the air palpable. "What's going on?"

"Everything," Linda blurted out, her voice trembling again. "Clara was last seen leaving with a man, and we think she was in trouble."

Jenna's expression shifted, the vibrant energy fading into a serious focus. "We need to find her. What do you know?"

I shared everything Linda had told me, the words spilling out in a rush. Jenna listened intently, her brow furrowing deeper with every detail. "We need to contact her friends, anyone who might know who this guy is," she finally said, her determination igniting the room.

"But what if it's too late?" Linda interjected, her voice shaking.

"It's never too late," Jenna replied fiercely, her eyes flashing with determination. "We can't sit around waiting for something to happen. We have to take action."

"Action? Like what?" I asked, my heart racing again. "We can't just go charging out there without a plan. That would be reckless."

Jenna grinned, a spark of mischief lighting her eyes. "Oh, don't worry. I have a plan. But first, we need to get some intel. I know a few people who might have seen something at that party Clara went to. Let's see if we can dig up some dirt."

Linda and I exchanged glances, a mix of hope and fear coursing through me. There was no way to know what lay ahead, but with Jenna's fierce spirit at our side, it felt like we might stand a chance against the darkness that had swallowed Clara whole. As we set our course, the thrill of the unknown pulled us forward, each heartbeat echoing with the promise of adventure, danger, and maybe—just maybe—some answers lurking in the shadows.

With Jenna's fierce resolve guiding us, the three of us crowded around the small kitchen table, its surface cluttered with remnants of my chaotic life: art supplies, old takeout containers, and a coffee-stained notebook brimming with half-baked ideas. I felt a rush of gratitude wash over me. Together, we might stand a chance against whatever darkness loomed over Clara's fate.

"First things first," Jenna said, her tone sharp as she leaned forward, her fingers steepled like a strategist plotting an ambush. "We need to identify the man Clara left with. That's the key."

Linda nodded, her expression shifting from fear to a flicker of determination. "I might remember more details about that night. The party she was supposed to attend—it was supposed to be exclusive. Maybe it wasn't just a social gathering."

"An exclusive party sounds perfect for a clandestine meeting," I said, biting my lip as I recalled the whispers that had drifted around the studio in the days leading up to Clara's disappearance. "I heard rumors about a producer who had been making a big splash lately. He was known for throwing extravagant parties. If Clara was there, she might have been involved with him somehow."

"Exactly!" Jenna exclaimed, her eyes lighting up. "If we can track down the guest list, we might be able to narrow it down to a few suspects. People who could have seen or heard something."

As we tossed ideas around, a flicker of hope ignited in the dim room. We spent the next hour brainstorming, Linda recounting details of her last conversation with Clara, while Jenna began rummaging through her phone for contacts who might have insights into the elusive producer and the night of the party.

"Let's try reaching out to some of the other actresses who were rumored to be on the guest list," Jenna suggested, her voice filled with a resolute energy. "They might know something we don't."

"Do you really think they'll talk to us?" I asked, uncertainty creeping back in.

"Why wouldn't they? We're not trying to ambush them. We're just looking for answers." Her confidence was contagious, pushing me past my hesitations.

Just as Jenna began texting a few names from her contacts, a sudden noise interrupted us—an ominous rattle of metal against metal, like the sound of a door slamming shut. My heart skipped, the sound sharp and intrusive against the silence that had settled over us. I turned to look at Linda, whose eyes mirrored my concern.

"Did you hear that?" I whispered, my breath hitching in my throat.

Jenna frowned, her fingers pausing over her phone. "It was probably just the wind."

"Or a cat," Linda offered, her attempt at humor falling flat in the tense atmosphere.

"Right, because a cat sounds like a metal door," I replied, forcing a lightness that barely masked my dread. "Let's check it out."

With the flickering overhead light casting erratic shadows, I cautiously approached the door, every nerve in my body on high alert. I peered through the peephole again, my pulse hammering in my ears. The hallway outside was empty, but I couldn't shake the feeling of being watched, of something just beyond my line of sight.

"Is anyone out there?" I called out, hoping for a reassuring response.

Silence enveloped us like a heavy fog.

Just as I turned back to the others, I spotted a shadow shift at the far end of the hallway. I barely had time to register my shock before a figure stepped into the dim light—a man with a chiseled jaw and dark hair that fell haphazardly over his forehead. He looked vaguely familiar, but the intense gaze of his green eyes set my heart racing.

"Who are you?" I demanded, my voice steadier than I felt.

The man stepped forward, raising his hands in a gesture of peace. "I'm not here to cause trouble. My name is Alex. I'm a friend of Clara's."

"Clara?" Linda's voice was barely above a whisper. "What do you know about her?"

"Enough to know she's in danger," he replied, his voice low and urgent. "We don't have much time. They're looking for her."

My stomach dropped, a wave of dread washing over me. "Who's looking for her? What do you mean she's in danger?"

He glanced around the room as if weighing the danger of being overheard. "There are people who don't want her to be found. They'll do anything to keep her quiet."

"Why?" Jenna interjected, crossing her arms defensively. "What could she possibly know?"

"More than you realize. Clara was involved in something—something bigger than any of us," he said, his voice dropping to a conspiratorial whisper. "And if they find out you're looking for her..." He trailed off, the implication hanging heavy in the air.

I exchanged worried glances with Jenna and Linda, the gravity of his words settling like a lead weight in my chest. "How do you know all this?" I pressed, desperation creeping into my tone.

"I was at the party the night she disappeared," Alex confessed, a flicker of shame crossing his face. "I saw her leave with him, the man in the black coat. I thought she was safe. But when I realized she was gone, I knew I had to find her. I can help you."

"Help us?" Linda echoed, skepticism etched across her features. "How do we know you're not part of this? You could be lying."

"I'm not," he insisted, his voice strained. "I've been trying to get to her for days. I came here hoping to find someone who could help me track her down. But you need to trust me."

Trust him? The word felt foreign on my tongue, especially given the precarious situation we were in. Yet there was something in his gaze that suggested sincerity, a hint of desperation that mirrored my own.

"Okay," I said, my voice barely above a whisper as I fought against my instinct to pull away. "But you need to tell us everything. We can't afford to waste any more time."

Alex nodded, his expression earnest. "I'll tell you what I know, but we have to move fast. They'll be searching for me soon too."

"What do you mean by that?" I asked, the anxiety in my gut tightening.

"Because I'm not the only one looking for Clara. And they'll do whatever it takes to find her first."

The atmosphere grew tense, the air crackling with the weight of unspoken dangers as Alex stepped closer, urgency emanating from him. "We need to find her before it's too late."

Just then, a loud crash echoed from the hallway, making us all jump. The sound of heavy footsteps pounded closer, the unmistakable thud of boots on the floor reverberating through the narrow corridor. My heart raced, adrenaline surging as I looked to Alex, fear mingling with determination.

"Go! We have to hide!" I shouted, and in that moment, as the footsteps approached, I knew we were out of time.

Chapter 16: Heartbeats and Hurdles

The stage was set, the theater darkened, but the world beyond the velvet curtains surged with chaos. The faint scent of popcorn mixed with the musty remnants of past performances hung in the air, a backdrop to the storm brewing in my heart. Lucas stood close, his silhouette etched against the dim glow of the emergency exit sign, tension radiating from him like heat waves. It was as if we had become two players caught in a scene neither of us had written, adrift in a narrative far too tangled for our liking.

"Can you believe this?" I asked, my voice barely above a whisper. I could feel the pulse of anxiety thrumming in my veins, each beat syncing with the staccato of my thoughts. "After everything, we're back here, ready to face whatever lurks in the shadows?"

Lucas turned to me, his eyes a stormy blue, swirling with emotions I couldn't quite decipher. "What choice do we have? We can't let them win." He leaned against the wall, arms crossed, and I felt a magnetic pull between us, thickening the air around us. It was the kind of chemistry that made you forget your worries, even if just for a moment.

"I know," I replied, biting my lip, uncertainty dancing in my chest. "But it's just so... exhausting. I thought once we uncovered the truth about the missing funds, it would all be over. I didn't expect more threats, more danger."

His gaze softened, and in that brief silence, I felt the world around us dissolve. The theater, with its peeling paint and dusty seats, faded away, and there was only Lucas and me. He stepped closer, the scent of cedarwood and something uniquely him enveloping me. I could see the worry etched on his brow, and it ignited a flame of protectiveness within me.

"It's okay to be scared, you know," he murmured, the huskiness of his voice wrapping around me like a comforting blanket. "I'm scared too. But together, we can handle anything."

"Together," I echoed, savoring the word as if it were a secret ingredient to a recipe I'd yet to discover. It was a promise and a challenge all at once, a tether that pulled me deeper into his orbit.

Just then, the distant echo of footsteps jolted me back to reality. I turned toward the noise, my heart thudding against my ribs like a caged bird. "We should get back," I suggested, reluctantly breaking the moment. "We can't let them see us falter."

As we slipped into the main auditorium, the atmosphere crackled with an unsettling energy. The theater was a realm of shadows and whispers, the flickering lights casting eerie shapes on the walls. I could feel the weight of our decision pressing down, a tangible force that threatened to crush me under its intensity.

The crew was gathered, their expressions a mix of determination and unease. The air thickened as we made our way to the center of the stage, the familiar wooden floor beneath my feet feeling like a fragile foundation for the tempest brewing around us.

"Glad you two are back," said Jenna, our stage manager, her voice a steady anchor in the tumult. "We need to talk. It's getting worse."

"What do you mean?" Lucas leaned forward, his posture tense as a drawn bowstring.

She glanced around, lowering her voice. "The messages have escalated. It's not just threats anymore—they've sent proof that they're watching us."

"What kind of proof?" I asked, a chill creeping up my spine.

"A video." Jenna's eyes darted nervously. "They showed footage of us rehearsing. It's clear they know more than we thought."

"Great," I muttered, crossing my arms over my chest. "Just what we needed. Now they're not just in our heads; they're in our lives."

Lucas's jaw clenched. "We have to push forward. We can't let them intimidate us into backing down." His gaze met mine, a spark of defiance igniting within those stormy depths.

"What's the plan, then?" I asked, a mix of adrenaline and apprehension coursing through me.

"Perform as scheduled," Jenna suggested, her voice steady. "But we'll set up additional security and stay alert. We can't let fear dictate our choices."

"Alright," I agreed, feeling a renewed sense of resolve surge within me. "Let's do it. But we need to make sure we're prepared for anything."

As we strategized, the energy in the room shifted, charged with a purpose that felt both exhilarating and terrifying. But beneath that pulse of determination lay an undercurrent of something deeper—a fear of what we might lose if the stakes became too high.

The rehearsal began, but the atmosphere was different. Each line spoken felt heavy with unspoken threats, every gesture infused with an urgency that made my skin prickle. I stole glances at Lucas, whose focus remained unwavering, yet I could see the storm brewing behind his eyes.

In the midst of the chaos, our chemistry simmered, each brush of our hands sending sparks flying. I could feel the heat radiating between us, a magnetic force that drew me closer, even as danger loomed just outside the theater doors.

It was a delicate dance—our hearts ached for connection, yet the world insisted on placing hurdles in our path. I could sense the tension, the anticipation that came before the storm, and I knew we were on the brink of something monumental.

Then, just as the final curtain call loomed on the horizon, a chill swept through the room as Lucas's phone buzzed. He glanced down, his expression morphing from concentration to dread in the blink of an eye.

"It's from an unknown number," he murmured, the color draining from his face.

"Read it," I urged, my heart racing in sync with the flickering lights above us.

As he read the message, the world around us fell away, and all I could hear was the pounding of my heart, a frantic rhythm that echoed the reality of our situation. The warning was clear: abandon the production, or the consequences would be dire.

In that moment, I realized the truth we had uncovered was merely the beginning. The real battle was only just beginning, and the stakes were higher than I had ever imagined. The pursuit of the truth had become a deadly game, and we were both unwilling players, our hearts entwined in a struggle that could cost us everything we had come to cherish.

As the tension hung thick in the air, I found myself navigating a precarious tightrope of emotions. The theater, once a sanctuary where creativity flourished, now felt like a stage for our darkest fears. The warning Lucas had received gnawed at the edges of my mind, relentless and taunting. Each tick of the clock echoed in my ears, a reminder that time was slipping away, and with it, our chances to uncover the truth that bound us together.

Lucas's hand brushed against mine, grounding me amidst the chaos. "We can't let this stop us," he said, his voice low and steady, as if uttering a sacred vow. "We need to dig deeper. Whatever they want, we have to find out why."

His determination was a flame against the backdrop of my own uncertainty, and it ignited a fierce resolve within me. "You're right," I replied, my voice firmer than I felt. "But we need a plan. We can't just charge in without knowing what we're up against."

The warmth of his gaze wrapped around me, a comfort amidst the storm. "Then let's strategize," he suggested, his eyes alight with purpose. "We have resources, people we can trust. If we can figure out who's behind this, maybe we can turn the tables."

I nodded, envisioning the cast and crew, each person a thread in this tangled web we'd found ourselves ensnared in. "We need to gather everyone. If we're going to fight back, we'll need all hands on deck."

As we moved to call an emergency meeting, the air hummed with anticipation. The crew gathered in the dim light of the backstage area, faces illuminated by the glow of cell phones, a motley assembly of worried expressions. I felt a swell of camaraderie; these were my people, my family, united in our shared love for the theater.

"Alright, everyone," I began, trying to project calm amidst the brewing storm. "As you know, we've received some troubling news. But instead of letting fear dictate our actions, we're going to turn this into our advantage."

The murmur of uncertainty rippled through the group, but I pressed on. "We're going to investigate who's behind these threats. We need to find out why they want us to stop and what we can do to protect ourselves."

Jenna stepped forward, arms crossed defiantly. "I'm in. We didn't come this far just to let someone bully us into submission."

Lucas nodded, his expression resolute. "Exactly. We're not backing down. Whatever it takes, we'll get to the bottom of this."

As the meeting continued, we pooled ideas and resources, a whirlwind of voices bouncing off the walls. My heart raced with a mix of fear and excitement, a pulse that matched the fervor of our discussions. There was strength in unity, and as we crafted our plan, I could feel the momentum building, lifting my spirits despite the looming threat.

When the meeting adjourned, Lucas lingered, his presence both a comfort and an invitation. "You really rallied them," he said, a hint of admiration threading through his words. "I knew you had it in you."

I shrugged, the compliment warming my cheeks. "I couldn't just stand by and watch them crumble. We've worked too hard for this."

"Exactly," he said, stepping closer, our shoulders nearly brushing. "And I'm glad I'm not doing this alone."

His gaze held mine, and in that moment, I felt the world outside the theater fade away. It was just us, two souls standing on the precipice of something both terrifying and exhilarating.

"What if we..." I hesitated, the words teetering on the edge of my tongue. "What if we used this as an opportunity to create something even more powerful? Something that speaks to what we're going through?"

His brow furrowed in thought. "You mean like turning our experience into part of the performance? To highlight the struggle?"

"Yes! Art has always been a reflection of life, right? We can weave our challenges into the production, show that we won't be silenced."

Lucas's expression shifted, a spark of enthusiasm igniting in his eyes. "That's brilliant. It could elevate our show to something transformative."

A grin crept onto my face, the idea taking root in my mind. "We could incorporate elements of suspense, danger, and resilience. It could resonate with the audience, show them the power of standing up against adversity."

The idea took on a life of its own, swirling around us as we plotted ways to infuse our production with our shared experience. Each suggestion felt like a brushstroke on a canvas, building towards a masterpiece that transcended mere performance.

"Let's start brainstorming scenes," I said, my heart racing with the thrill of creation. "We could use shadows, lighting effects, maybe even interactive elements to draw the audience into our world."

Lucas grinned, the tension between us momentarily forgotten as our excitement bloomed. "And we can use music to amplify the emotions. Imagine the crescendos during the climactic moments—"

Our ideas flowed like a river, and I was swept along, intoxicated by the synergy of our collaboration. The theater buzzed with energy, a sanctuary of creativity fighting back against the darkness threatening to engulf us.

As we worked, time slipped away, and before long, we found ourselves nestled in the worn seats of the auditorium, brainstorming in the soft glow of the dimmed stage lights. I leaned back, the fabric of the seat cool against my skin, the scent of wood and history wrapping around me like a comforting embrace.

"Do you think this will actually work?" I asked, glancing at him sideways.

He chuckled, a deep sound that rumbled in his chest. "If there's one thing I've learned, it's that you never underestimate the power of art. It can be a weapon and a shield, all in one."

"Wise words," I teased, a smile tugging at my lips. "You're turning into quite the philosopher."

Lucas's laughter echoed, and for a moment, it felt as if we were simply two friends sharing ideas, free from the weight of the threats looming outside. But that bliss was fleeting, overshadowed by the very real danger that lurked just beyond the theater doors.

Just as I began to lose myself in the dream of what our production could become, a sudden crash echoed from the backstage area, slicing through the lighthearted moment like a dagger. My heart leaped into my throat as I shot upright, adrenaline flooding my system.

"Did you hear that?" I whispered, the jovial atmosphere evaporating in an instant.

Lucas's expression darkened, and he nodded, tension crackling between us again. "Let's check it out. Stay close."

We rose, the thrill of fear igniting our senses. As we moved cautiously toward the backstage entrance, every creak of the floorboards beneath our feet felt amplified, each shadow lurking in the corners of the theater morphing into something sinister. The world we had begun to build together threatened to unravel, and I could feel the weight of uncertainty pressing heavily against my chest.

"On three," Lucas said, his voice a low murmur.

"Three," I echoed, bracing myself for whatever lay ahead, our hands instinctively finding each other, grounding me in the dark.

In that moment, as we ventured into the unknown, the line between fear and exhilaration blurred, and I knew that whatever awaited us, we would face it together.

The backstage area felt like a different world, an underbelly of the theater where shadows loomed larger than life. Lucas and I crept forward, every nerve ending tingling with a mix of trepidation and exhilaration. The crash echoed in my ears, a sharp reminder of the danger we faced, and my heart raced as we maneuvered past tangled cables and forgotten props, the smell of aged wood and dust enveloping us like an old friend.

"What if it's just the wind?" I whispered, though the tremor in my voice belied my uncertainty.

"Pretty sure the wind doesn't crash into things," he replied, his lips quirking into that familiar half-smile that sent warmth flooding through me. It was a fleeting comfort in a space that felt increasingly hostile.

As we reached the entrance to the storage room, I pushed the door slightly ajar, wincing at the loud creak that echoed through the dim corridor. The faint glow of a single bulb flickered overhead, casting erratic shadows that danced on the walls. I peered inside, the sight sending a chill creeping up my spine.

Amidst the haphazardly stacked boxes and forgotten costumes, I spotted something out of place—a dark figure hunched over, rummaging through our production materials. My breath caught, and I instinctively reached for Lucas's arm, gripping it tight.

"Who are you?" I shouted, the words tumbling from my lips in a mix of anger and fear.

The figure froze, its head snapping up to reveal a face partially obscured by shadows. "I—uh—" the voice stuttered, revealing a hint of panic.

Lucas stepped forward, a protective barrier between me and the unknown. "Step away from there," he commanded, his tone firm yet steady.

"Wait!" The figure raised its hands, stepping into the light, and recognition hit me like a freight train. "It's just me, Oliver!"

Oliver, our lighting technician, stood wide-eyed and flustered, his unruly hair sticking out in all directions. "I heard the crash and thought something was wrong. I came to check it out."

Relief washed over me, but it was short-lived, replaced by a new wave of tension. "What are you doing in here? We thought someone was trying to sabotage the show."

"I was looking for the new light gels we ordered," he explained, his voice earnest. "But then I heard the crash, and I freaked out. I thought maybe someone had broken in."

Lucas's shoulders relaxed slightly, but the tightness in his jaw remained. "Did you see anything? Anyone lurking around?"

Oliver shook his head, glancing nervously toward the shadows. "No, just me. But if you're feeling unsafe, we should tell everyone to be extra cautious. I don't want anything happening to the show."

"Exactly," I agreed, my pulse still racing. "This isn't just a normal rehearsal anymore. We need to stay vigilant."

As we emerged from the storage room, I felt the weight of the looming threat settle on my shoulders like a heavy cloak. Each face we encountered on our way back to the main stage wore a mask of concern, their eyes darting as if sensing an unseen predator lurking nearby.

"Okay, listen up!" I called out to the crew as we gathered back on stage, my voice cutting through the murmurs of uncertainty. "We need to be on high alert. There's someone watching us, and it's not just our imaginations."

The room fell silent, the gravity of my words hanging in the air like a thick fog. I glanced at Lucas, who stood beside me, his expression fierce, a fire kindled in his eyes that spurred me on. "We're turning this into something more than just a performance. We're going to use our experiences to fuel this production, to show that we won't be silenced."

Nods of agreement rippled through the crew, a palpable surge of determination building as we rallied together. "Let's brainstorm how we can incorporate this into our scenes," Jenna suggested, her voice steady and strong. "We need to show that we're united, that we won't back down."

The chatter began anew, ideas sparking like flint against stone. I caught snippets of dialogue, each suggestion igniting a flame of creativity. Suddenly, I felt as if we were all part of something greater than ourselves, a collective heartbeat driving us forward against the encroaching darkness.

But beneath the surface of enthusiasm lay a simmering anxiety that refused to be ignored. As we threw around ideas, I felt a creeping doubt: was it enough? Would this be enough to keep us safe?

The rehearsal progressed, and though we infused our scenes with layers of tension and urgency, a nagging feeling gnawed at me. I couldn't shake the sense that our enemy was still lurking, waiting for the perfect moment to strike.

During a break, I pulled Lucas aside, needing a moment to breathe away from the chaos. "What if they don't just want us to stop the show?" I asked, my voice barely above a whisper. "What if they want more? Something worse?"

Lucas studied me, his brow furrowed. "You're thinking they might be trying to intimidate us into quitting for good? That's possible. But we won't let that happen. We can't give them that power."

His confidence was reassuring, but it did little to quiet the storm in my mind. "I just feel like we're racing against a clock that's counting down to something we can't see."

"Then let's get ahead of it," he urged, his grip on my shoulders firm. "If we keep pushing forward, they'll see that they can't control us. And when they see us standing strong, it'll make them rethink their choices."

I wanted to believe him, to trust in our strength, but a part of me remained tethered to my fears. "And if it doesn't work? What if they retaliate?"

"Then we deal with it," he replied, his tone resolute. "We face it together. No matter what."

His words wrapped around me, bolstering my courage, but just as I was about to respond, a commotion erupted from the other side of the stage. Shouts and the sound of rushing feet sent adrenaline surging through my veins.

"What now?" I demanded, heart racing as we rushed back to the group.

A few crew members stood in a huddle, pointing toward the main entrance, their expressions a mix of confusion and alarm. I pushed my way through, Lucas at my side, and as we broke into the open, the sight before us froze me in my tracks.

A figure stood silhouetted in the doorway, framed by the harsh light spilling in from outside. The air shifted, the atmosphere thick with an unspoken tension, and I felt a chill creep down my spine.

"Who are you?" I shouted, my voice cutting through the chaos.

The figure stepped forward, revealing a face I never expected to see—an old acquaintance from my past, someone whose presence sent ripples of dread coursing through me. "I've come to deliver a message," the figure said, a smirk twisting across their lips.

And just like that, the air grew thick with foreboding, a palpable sense of impending doom looming over us, as the theater fell into a hush, our shared breath caught in the grip of uncertainty.

Chapter 17: The Final Performance

The theater loomed like a grand dame, its ornate facade whispering tales of glitz and glamour, yet shadowed by a weighty air of dread that seemed to cling to the velvet curtains. As I stood backstage, the faint scent of burnt popcorn mingled with the dust of a thousand performances. The nervous energy thrummed through the wooden beams and twisted ropes of the rigging, wrapping itself around my heart, tightening with every tick of the clock. My fingers brushed against the cool surface of the props, each one a silent companion in this unfolding drama, while the sound of my fellow cast members' hushed murmurs echoed in my ears.

"Did you hear about the missing spotlight?" Lucas asked, his brow furrowed as he adjusted the collar of his costume. He had a knack for finding trouble, a talent I both admired and wished would take a sabbatical. "They say it went dark during rehearsal yesterday. You think it's just bad luck or something more sinister?"

I met his gaze, the weight of his words settling over me like a shroud. "Let's hope it's just the usual theater quirks. We have enough to worry about without chasing shadows." But even as I said it, I could feel the chill of unease threading through my thoughts. I had learned in my time here that the theater had a way of revealing the darkest corners of human nature, and lately, those shadows had felt unusually close.

The chatter of the ensemble faded, replaced by the ominous hum of the audience settling into their seats. My heart thudded in response, each beat a reminder of what was at stake. With opening night here, the stakes were higher than ever. This performance had to be perfect, not just for the applause but to chase away the lingering threat that had crept into our rehearsals like a specter.

A gust of wind rattled the old windows, sending a shiver down my spine. "It's just the building settling," I whispered to Lucas, though my voice trembled slightly. "A little ghostly ambiance never hurt anyone, right?"

He shot me a quizzical look, amusement dancing in his eyes. "Not unless it's a ghost with a vendetta. Are we sure we're not in a horror play instead of a romance?"

I laughed, grateful for the brief distraction. "Only if you promise to scream like a banshee if something goes wrong. It'll be our new act—Scream and Dance."

"Only if you promise to be my backup dancer," he shot back, his grin infectious.

We shared a moment, the playful banter pushing the fear to the corners of my mind. But as the stage manager called for places, the lightheartedness faded, replaced by a tense silence that filled the air like smoke from a burnt-out candle.

I took my position at the edge of the stage, peering through the curtain into the vast darkness of the auditorium. The sea of unfamiliar faces blurred together, their anticipation palpable, like a living entity that buzzed with excitement. The glow of the stage lights warmed my skin, but it did little to thaw the ice forming in my stomach. My heart raced, fueled by a mixture of thrill and dread.

When the curtain finally rose, the world transformed. The theater shimmered with golden hues, the costumes vibrant against the backdrop of our setting. The audience leaned forward, their eager faces illuminated by the soft glow of the stage lights. I stepped into the spotlight, feeling its warmth envelop me as I delivered my first lines, my voice steady despite the chaos thrumming beneath the surface.

But as the story unfolded, weaving through laughter and poignant moments, I couldn't shake the sense that we were being scrutinized—not just by the audience but by something far more sinister lurking in the shadows. The haunting tales of the theater's past, of jealousy and sabotage, clawed at the edges of my consciousness, threatening to pull me into a web of paranoia.

Each scene shifted seamlessly, yet my instincts were on high alert, ready to react at the slightest flicker of the lights or an unexpected noise from the wings. Lucas and I moved through the choreography with precision, his energy a balm against the nagging anxiety swirling in my mind. "You're on fire tonight!" he whispered during a brief moment off-stage, his encouragement a flicker of light in the encroaching darkness.

"Let's just hope the fire doesn't turn into a blaze," I replied, half-joking, half-serious.

As we launched into a particularly emotional scene, my heart ached with the weight of our characters' struggles. I poured every ounce of my soul into the performance, the audience's rapt attention a balm to my fears. Yet, with every dramatic pause, every heartfelt glance exchanged, the feeling of being watched intensified. The hair on the back of my neck prickled as I caught a glimpse of a figure in the wings, lurking just beyond the reach of the stage lights.

It was just a trick of the light, I told myself, forcing my gaze back to the audience. But doubt crept in like an uninvited guest, and as the climax of the play approached, I felt a tremor of panic rising within me. The final moments loomed, and I could almost hear the whispers of the past brushing against my skin, urging me to tread carefully.

With the closing lines resonating in the air, I took a breath, grounding myself in the moment. We were on the cusp of triumph, the culmination of our hard work and passion. But as the applause thundered through the theater, a chill sliced through my resolve. The night wasn't over yet, and the shadows that loomed behind us held secrets waiting to be uncovered.

The final act of our performance unfolded with a rhythm that both exhilarated and terrified me. Each moment on stage was electric, the laughter and gasps from the audience wrapping around me like a warm shawl, yet an unseen weight pressed against my chest, stifling the thrill. The spotlight's glare felt like a lifebuoy in a tempest, illuminating our hard-earned artistry while casting the depths of our fears into shadow.

In one of the pivotal scenes, Lucas and I shared a poignant moment, a crescendo of raw emotion that demanded every ounce of vulnerability I had. I locked eyes with him, his intensity sparking a connection that transcended our characters, a shared understanding of the unspoken stakes. As I leaned in to deliver a line laced with longing, I saw it—the flicker of movement out of the corner of my eye, a shadow darting just beyond the stage. My heart skipped, a drumroll of unease echoing in my ears.

"Did you see that?" I murmured, the words barely escaping my lips as we stepped off stage for a breath, the rush of adrenaline still thrumming in my veins.

"See what?" Lucas replied, his brow furrowing as he reached for a towel to dab at the sweat glistening on his forehead. "You're not turning into one of those actors who thinks the ghosts are haunting them, are you?"

"No, I'm serious! I thought I saw someone." I leaned closer, my voice low. "In the wings. Just a flash of—something."

Lucas chuckled, shaking his head. "Probably just your imagination. Or maybe the ghost of some poor soul who couldn't get tickets." But his teasing smile didn't quite reach his eyes, and for a moment, a flicker of uncertainty passed between us.

Before I could respond, the stage manager's voice echoed through the cramped backstage, summoning us back into the spotlight. "Places! We're back in five!" The urgency in her tone pulled me from my spiraling thoughts. I took a deep breath, inhaling the familiar smell of greasepaint and adrenaline, and steeled myself for what was left of the night.

As the curtain rose again, the audience erupted into applause, a sound like waves crashing against the shore. I could feel the energy coursing through the theater, a living entity feeding off our performance. We plunged into the next scene, the dialogue flowing as we danced between laughter and tension, my focus narrowing to Lucas's every move, his expressions painting a vivid tapestry of the story we were weaving together.

The climax approached, and with it, the gravity of the night settled heavily on my shoulders. My character faced betrayal, a moment filled with heartbreak that required me to dig deep, to expose the tender places that I often kept hidden. As I delivered my lines, I poured my soul into the performance, my voice breaking just enough to catch the audience's attention.

But still, the shadow danced at the edge of my vision, a restless specter taunting me. I shook my head slightly, trying to dismiss it, to ground myself in the world we had created. "Focus," I chided myself internally. "You've got this."

The moment was electric, the tension palpable, when a sudden, jarring sound echoed through the theater, a crash that sent gasps rippling through the crowd. The lights flickered, casting eerie shadows across the stage, and for a heartbeat, everything hung in a delicate balance, suspended in time.

"What was that?" Lucas whispered, his eyes wide with concern as we froze in place, our characters momentarily forgotten.

"I don't know," I replied, my voice a mere whisper. "It sounded like something fell backstage."

The audience murmured, their unease palpable, and I could sense their collective heartbeat quickening, the thrill of the unknown pulsing through the air. Just as the chaos settled into an uneasy silence, the stage manager rushed on, a look of panic etched across her face.

"Keep going!" she hissed, urgency lining her words. "Just keep the show moving!"

With a shared glance, Lucas and I resumed our positions, the earlier tension still crackling in the air. We leaned into our characters once more, but the warmth had dissipated, replaced by an unsettling chill that clung to my skin. Every movement felt weighed down, as if the very fabric of the performance was being pulled taut by an unseen hand.

As the scene reached its peak, I suddenly felt a tremor beneath my feet, a subtle vibration that sent my heart racing. "Did you feel that?" I gasped, casting a quick look around, trying to discern the source of my mounting dread.

"Yeah, what the hell is happening?" Lucas replied, his voice a mix of concern and irritation, his attention split between our performance and the disturbance.

But there was no time for further discussion. As I prepared to deliver my character's final, heart-wrenching plea, the lights flickered again, and in that split second, I caught sight of a figure moving just outside the spotlight. It was only for an instant, a glimpse of dark fabric and a glint of something sharp—a knife? I shook my head, dispelling the thought. My imagination was clearly playing tricks on me.

With a deep breath, I launched into my lines, pouring everything I had into the moment. The audience hung on my every word, and for a fleeting heartbeat, the chaos of the theater melted away, leaving only the connection between my character and her lover—a lifeline that pulled me back from the brink of my mounting fears.

As I stepped into the final moments of the performance, the applause surged like a wave, crashing over us as we delivered our bows. But even as I smiled and accepted the appreciation of the crowd, the unease gnawed at me, a shadow lingering just beyond the light. The figure was gone, but the threat remained, hidden in the dim recesses of the theater.

As the curtain fell, I could feel the weight of the night settling into my bones. I turned to Lucas, his face alight with the exhilaration of our success, but in my heart, the unease festered, a dark undertow in the sea of our triumph. The night was far from over, and the real performance was just beginning.

As the applause faded into the hush of the theater, a lingering echo remained, heavy with unspoken fears. I glanced at Lucas, his exuberance infectious, yet my own heart thudded with a mixture of triumph and unease. The moment we had awaited for weeks was finally here, yet it felt like standing on the precipice of an abyss, the depths swirling with unseen dangers.

"Did you feel that?" I whispered, unable to shake the unsettling sensation that something—or someone—still lurked in the shadows.

Lucas brushed off my concern, a teasing smile playing at the corners of his mouth. "It's just the adrenaline talking. You know how dramatic we can get, right? It's like we're in one of those suspense thrillers where the killer is lurking right behind us."

"Very reassuring," I replied dryly, unable to entirely dismiss the weight of his words. The stage may have felt electric, but the atmosphere behind it was heavy with doubt, thick like fog that refused to lift.

We retreated backstage, the frenetic energy of the audience still buzzing in my veins. The sound of laughter and applause faded, replaced by the muted voices of our fellow cast members, their expressions shifting between exhilaration and anxiety. I caught snippets of their conversations—whispers about the backstage accident, rumors of mischief in the shadows.

"I heard someone was seen lurking around the prop room," one actress said, her voice trembling slightly. "Right before the lights flickered. Do you think it's true?"

"Probably just a prank," another chimed in, though the tremor in her tone betrayed her doubt.

I exchanged a look with Lucas, the playful banter fading as we both registered the tension in the air. The weight of the night pressed down on us, the fear that something sinister was brewing just beneath the surface.

As the next scene approached, I forced myself to focus on the performance, shaking off the nagging doubt clawing at my thoughts. The lights dimmed once more, and I took my position on stage, determined to lose myself in the character, to channel the raw emotion that had brought me this far. The lines flowed as easily as the wine in the bar downstairs, but each time I glanced toward the wings, the specter of unease clung to my senses like a stubborn stain.

We moved through the act with a seamlessness that felt almost magical, yet I couldn't escape the feeling that something was amiss. As the curtain fell on another scene, I stepped back into the shadows, my heart racing not from the thrill of performance but from the fear that had nestled itself deep within me.

"Okay, let's take a moment," I said to Lucas as we huddled near the props. "Something is definitely not right."

"Alright, detective, what's the plan?" he asked, raising an eyebrow, though I could see the concern brewing beneath his playful demeanor.

"We need to figure out who or what is messing with our show. I can't shake this feeling that there's more going on here than just an accident."

Before Lucas could respond, a sharp crash erupted from the prop room, followed by a series of thuds that sent adrenaline coursing through my veins. The sound cut through the air like a knife, silencing our banter and pulling the attention of our castmates.

"Is everyone alright?" the stage manager called out, her voice wavering slightly.

I exchanged a quick glance with Lucas, the unspoken agreement hanging between us like a taut string. We had to check it out. As we made our way toward the noise, the hairs on the back of my neck stood on end.

"Stay close," I urged, leading the way into the dimly lit corridor that wound behind the stage. The flickering overhead lights cast eerie shadows against the walls, making the space feel like a labyrinth of ghosts. Each step echoed ominously, a reminder of the uneasy quiet that had enveloped us since the beginning of the night.

The prop room door stood ajar, creaking slightly as I pushed it open. Inside, chaos reigned. Props lay scattered across the floor, overturned like discarded toys after a tempest. A few fellow cast members huddled near the far wall, their faces pale and taut with fear.

"What happened?" I asked, my heart racing.

"Something fell," one of them replied, shaking. "We think it was just a set piece, but…"

Lucas's eyes darted around the room, scanning for any signs of the culprit. "But what?"

"I swear I saw someone move," she said, her voice barely a whisper, as if speaking too loudly might summon the phantom back. "They were here, and then they were gone. Just like that."

"Great, now we're haunted by a dramatic ghost," I muttered, trying to inject humor into the situation, though the weight of dread hung heavy on my heart.

"Look," Lucas said, pointing toward the back of the room. "There's something over there."

I followed his gaze, my breath catching in my throat as I spotted a dark figure slumped against the wall, half-hidden behind a rack of costumes. The dim light barely illuminated the scene, but I could make out a shape, the silhouette unmistakably human.

"Hello?" I called out, my voice trembling. "Is someone there?"

Silence enveloped the room, thick and suffocating. I took a cautious step forward, every instinct screaming for me to retreat, but curiosity tugged at me like an unrelenting tide. "Show yourself!"

As if responding to my challenge, the figure stirred, and a glint of metal caught the light. My heart lurched, and I stumbled back, gasping as realization hit me like a slap.

It wasn't just a wayward actor. The knife glinting in the dim light held a promise of danger, and the figure—clad in dark clothing—rose slowly, an ominous shadow against the backdrop of chaos.

"Time for the show to take a darker turn," the figure said, their voice low and menacing, sending a chill racing down my spine.

Before I could react, they lunged forward, and the room erupted into chaos, screams echoing as the reality of our final performance came crashing down around us.

Chapter 18: Shattered Illusions

The stage lights dimmed to a soft glow, casting an ethereal light over the wooden boards that had felt the weight of countless performances before ours. The scent of greasepaint and fresh flowers filled the air, mingling with the palpable buzz of anticipation that crackled through the audience. I had spent months preparing for this moment, rehearsing lines until they flowed from my lips like water, and practicing movements until they became second nature. Yet as I stood there, the audience's faces blurred into a sea of eager smiles, a sinister presence lingered at the edges of my vision, a darkness that threatened to swallow the joy I had so carefully cultivated.

With every beat of the drum and the swell of the orchestra, my heart raced in tandem. The show began, and I threw myself into my character, my body responding to the rhythm of the narrative. I danced through the scenes, weaving in and out of light and shadow, drawing the audience into a world that sparkled with hope and romance. The applause that followed each act filled me with exhilaration, but even as I soared on the wings of my performance, an icy tendril of fear wrapped around my heart.

Then, there he was—the man who had haunted my thoughts like an unwelcome ghost. He stood in the back, partially obscured by the curtains that swayed gently in the draft, but his eyes were fixed on me with an intensity that sent chills skittering down my spine. Panic surged within me, a wild, uncontainable thing that threatened to consume everything I had worked for. My breath quickened, and for a moment, the stage felt unsteady beneath my feet. Just as I teetered on the edge of a full-blown collapse, a strong hand grasped my arm, pulling me back from the precipice.

"Hey, I've got you," Lucas murmured, his voice a warm balm against my frayed nerves. Our eyes locked, and in that brief moment, everything else faded away—the audience, the performance, the lurking threat in the shadows. It was just us, tethered together by an unspoken promise. He had always been my anchor, the one who reminded me to breathe when the world felt like it was closing in.

With a shaky breath, I regained my composure and forced myself to focus on the lines flowing from my lips. Yet even as I recited my lines, the man in the shadows remained a ghost at the edge of my awareness, a dark specter that pulled my attention away from the beauty unfolding on stage. The performance reached its climax, the characters entwined in a love story as rich and vibrant as the costumes that adorned us. Applause erupted like a thunderstorm, but my heart raced with a different kind of fear, one that clung to me like a second skin.

As the final curtain fell, I took a moment to bask in the collective joy radiating from the audience. Cheers and whistles surrounded me, a chorus of appreciation that momentarily drowned out my anxiety. But then reality crashed back in with all its brutal force. I could feel the weight of his gaze even as I turned to Lucas, a shared understanding passing between us like an electric current.

"We need to talk," he said, his brow furrowing with concern. The afterglow of success faded, replaced by a stark awareness of the danger we couldn't ignore any longer.

"Not here," I whispered, my eyes scanning the crowd, looking for the flicker of familiar faces amid the sea of strangers. I could feel the pulse of excitement in the air, yet I was drowning in a tidal wave of dread.

We slipped through the backstage door, the raucous applause still echoing in the distance. The theater's dimly lit corridors felt claustrophobic as we navigated our way toward the exit. "You saw him, didn't you?" Lucas asked, his voice low, threaded with concern.

"Of course I did. I can't escape him, Lucas. He's everywhere." My voice trembled, a mix of frustration and fear. The weight of my circumstances pressed heavily on my chest.

"We'll figure this out," he assured me, but the uncertainty in his eyes betrayed the confidence of his words. "Let's just get to my car."

The moment we stepped into the cool night air, a sigh of relief washed over me. The stars blinked down, indifferent to my plight, yet their twinkling felt like a fragile promise of hope. Lucas guided me to his car, a reliable old sedan that seemed to embody his steadfast nature. He opened the door for me, a chivalrous gesture that made my heart flutter, if only for a moment.

As we settled into the car, I felt the familiar contours of fear begin to settle in my stomach once again. "What do we do now?" I asked, breaking the silence that threatened to swallow us both.

Lucas started the engine, the hum of the car mingling with the rhythm of my thoughts. "We go to the police. We need to report this, and you need to take this seriously."

His words hung in the air, heavy with consequence. I nodded slowly, the thought of involving the authorities sending a shiver through me. What if it escalated? What if he retaliated?

The city lights blurred past as we drove, a kaleidoscope of color that mirrored the turmoil inside me. I was caught in a tempest of emotions—fear, anger, determination. I could no longer pretend that everything was fine. The illusion I had crafted around my life was shattered, and now I had to face the jagged edges of reality, ready or not.

"We're going to figure this out," Lucas said firmly, his voice a steadying presence amid the storm raging inside me. As I glanced at him, his jaw set with determination, I realized that together, we could face whatever darkness loomed ahead. The night was far from over, and in the depths of my heart, a flicker of hope began to ignite.

The weight of applause hung in the air like confetti, yet it felt more like shards of glass scattering through my mind. Each cheer was a reminder of the stark reality creeping around the edges of my consciousness, the man in the shadows morphing into a specter that haunted my every thought. The theater was alive with excitement, but my heart drummed a frantic tempo of fear that clashed with the celebratory atmosphere. I could see Lucas' brow furrowed as we navigated the throng of actors and audience members, a mass of joyful faces that blurred together, unaware of the dark undercurrent threatening to pull me under.

"Let's grab a drink," Lucas suggested, his voice low as he leaned closer, his breath warm against my ear, momentarily distracting me from my unease. "You need to unwind."

The idea of a drink sounded appealing, a temporary reprieve from the turmoil swirling inside me. "Sure, why not? Just one," I replied, forcing a smile that felt more like a grimace.

We slipped into a cozy little bar just around the corner from the theater, its dim lighting and vintage decor offering a welcome refuge from the chaos outside. The scent of aged wood and sweet, spiced cider filled the air, wrapping around us like a comforting embrace. Lucas ordered us drinks—something fruity and colorful that promised to mask the taste of my anxiety. As we settled into a booth, the world outside faded, leaving only the warmth of the dim-lit space and the steady thrum of conversation.

"Okay, spill," Lucas said, leaning forward, his blue eyes piercing through my facade. "What's really going on? I saw you freeze up there."

I fiddled with the napkin on the table, tearing it into tiny pieces, each shred mirroring my unraveling thoughts. "It's just... everything's been so overwhelming lately," I admitted, my voice a whisper. "I thought I was safe, that performing would be my escape. But he's still out there, and I don't know what he wants from me."

Lucas' expression shifted, a blend of concern and determination. "We'll figure it out. But first, let's focus on you. The show was incredible, and you have fans—people who admire you for your talent."

I couldn't help but chuckle at that, the sound light but laced with bitterness. "Fans? They don't know the half of it. They only see the perfect facade. They don't see the cracks."

"Cracks make things interesting," he said, his smile teasing, as he raised his glass to mine. "To imperfections."

"To imperfections," I echoed, clinking my glass against his. The sweet, fruity concoction was a welcome distraction, the first sip igniting a hint of warmth that spread through my chest, loosening the tension coiled there.

"Besides," Lucas continued, his voice playful, "who needs perfection when you can have drama? You're practically living in a soap opera."

"More like a horror show," I retorted, a grin breaking through my anxiety. "Complete with stalkers and ominous shadows."

"Okay, but you have to admit, it makes for a gripping storyline." He leaned back, the laughter fading into a more serious undertone. "We can take this to the police, but first, let's come up with a plan. There's no reason for you to feel unsafe."

The thought of involving the police sent a chill through me, the very idea making me feel vulnerable in ways I wasn't prepared to confront. "What if he retaliates? What if this gets worse?" My voice quivered, and I could feel the tremor echo in the spaces between us.

Lucas reached across the table, his hand warm and solid on mine. "I won't let anything happen to you, I promise. You're not alone in this."

As his words hung in the air, I felt a strange mix of comfort and fear. With him by my side, I felt slightly braver, yet the shadows of doubt loomed large. "What if it's all just a game for him? What if he enjoys playing with my mind?"

"Then let's turn the tables," he suggested, his eyes narrowing with fierce determination. "Let's make sure he knows you won't be his puppet. You're stronger than you think."

The fire in his voice sparked something deep within me, a flicker of defiance that pushed back against the waves of despair threatening to drown me. "Okay. But what if we mess this up?"

Lucas shrugged, his demeanor relaxed. "Then we'll just mess it up spectacularly. That's what makes life interesting."

Our laughter rang out, cutting through the heaviness in the air, and for a moment, I forgot the encroaching shadows. But as our drinks emptied, the reality of my situation seeped back in, heavy and unwelcome.

"Let's talk about something else," I said, desperately seeking to shift the mood. "What's your latest project? Anything exciting?"

He leaned back, a thoughtful expression crossing his face. "Oh, you know, just the usual drama in the life of a struggling playwright. Revisions, rewrites, and the occasional existential crisis."

"Ah, the trifecta of creativity. How's the existential crisis treating you?"

"Like an uninvited guest who shows up at the worst possible moment," he replied, his eyes sparkling with mischief. "But I've decided to embrace it. Who needs sanity anyway?"

I laughed, the sound lifting my spirits even as the shadows loomed just outside the bar's soft glow. "Maybe we should invite it to a drink. Sounds like it could use some company."

As the laughter faded, I looked around the bar, the flickering candles casting playful shadows against the walls. The world felt alive in that moment, vibrant and chaotic, just like my own life. But lurking beneath that lively facade was a lingering dread, one that I could no longer ignore.

"What if he comes after me again?" I asked, my voice trembling slightly. "What if he knows where I am?"

Lucas' expression turned serious, his hand tightening around mine. "Then we'll be ready. We'll take every precaution. I'll even have my sister help with a safe plan. She's got connections. But first, we need to keep your spirit high. If we're going to tackle this, you have to stay strong."

"Stay strong," I repeated, the phrase echoing like a mantra in my mind. "Okay. I can do that."

With a newfound determination bubbling within me, I raised my glass once more. "To staying strong, and to absurdly dramatic life plans."

"To absurdity!" Lucas echoed, his grin contagious as we clinked our glasses together, the sound ringing with hope amid the uncertainty. And as I sat there, surrounded by the flickering lights and the warmth of his presence, I felt a sense of belonging that wrapped around me like a cozy blanket. Together, we would confront the darkness waiting in the wings, ready to reclaim my story from the grip of fear.

The warmth of the bar lingered in my skin, but outside, the night was an inky darkness, pressing against the windows like a predator waiting for its moment. As I sipped the last of my drink, the vibrant flavors dulled by the weight of my fears, I stole a glance at Lucas, whose expression had turned thoughtful. He always seemed to know when my thoughts were veering into treacherous territory, and tonight was no exception.

"What's going on in that head of yours?" he asked, his tone light but his eyes probing. "You look like you've just bitten into a lemon."

"More like a grapefruit," I replied, letting out a small laugh that felt forced. "It's just... everything feels off. I've been running around in circles, trying to maintain this illusion of control. But now, the cracks are showing. It's exhausting."

"Maybe it's time to shatter the illusion entirely," he suggested, leaning closer, his elbows resting on the table. "You don't have to carry the weight of the world on your shoulders. We can do this together."

"Together," I echoed, tasting the word on my tongue like a sweet promise. "But what if we're not ready? What if this guy has a plan we can't see?"

"Then we'll outsmart him. We'll be the stars in our own story, and he'll be nothing but a plot twist we can dodge," Lucas said, his confidence igniting a flicker of hope within me.

Before I could respond, the bar door swung open, the bell tinkling as a gust of cold air swept in, ruffling the soft fabric of my dress. I turned, half-expecting to see a new customer stroll in, but my heart sank as I recognized a figure standing at the threshold—tall, menacing, the man from the shadows. My breath caught in my throat, panic clawing at my insides.

"Lucas," I hissed, my voice barely above a whisper as I gripped his hand tightly. "He's here."

In that split second, time seemed to stretch, the cacophony of laughter and music around us fading into a distant hum. I could see the man's eyes scanning the room, his expression cold and calculating. The realization struck me like a bolt of lightning; this was no coincidence. He had come for me.

"Stay calm," Lucas instructed, his voice steady, although I could feel the tension radiating off him like heat from a flame. "Let's get out of here."

"Where to? He's blocking the exit," I replied, my heart pounding in my chest, each beat a reminder of my vulnerability.

"Then we'll have to create a diversion," Lucas said, his eyes darting around the bar. "Are you ready to be a little reckless?"

"Reckless sounds good right about now," I said, the adrenaline pumping through me, spurring me into action.

Lucas stood, his hand still entwined with mine as we moved toward the bar. "Excuse me," he called out to the bartender, who was polishing glasses behind the counter. "Can we get a round of shots? On the house?"

The bartender blinked, confusion flitting across his face. "For you two? Now?"

"Trust me," Lucas urged, his voice low and persuasive, and the bartender, sensing the urgency, quickly complied, pouring two shots and sliding them across the counter.

"Just a little celebration," Lucas said, raising the glass. I followed suit, clinking my shot against his, a symbolic gesture that held more than just the thrill of liquor—it was a toast to our survival, to defiance.

"Now!" Lucas said suddenly, grabbing my arm and leading me toward a side door that I had almost overlooked. We slipped through it, the sharp cold of the outside air hitting me like a slap in the face.

"Where are we going?" I asked, my mind racing as I scanned our surroundings, searching for any sign of him.

"Backstage," Lucas said, his voice urgent as we ducked behind the dumpster at the rear of the bar. "There's an alley that leads to the next street over. We can lose him there."

Breathless, we crouched in the shadows, our hearts pounding in a frantic rhythm that echoed the urgency of our escape. "You think he saw us?" I whispered, peering around the dumpster's edge.

"I don't know, but we can't stay here," he replied, his eyes scanning the alleyway, alert and calculating.

Just as we prepared to make our move, a figure stepped into the alley—a silhouette that sent a wave of ice-cold fear washing over me. It wasn't just the man from the bar; it was two others, looming like phantoms, their faces obscured by the darkness. My heart sank as they began to approach, their intentions clear in the way they moved—predatory, relentless.

"We have to go now," Lucas urged, grabbing my hand again as we turned to slip deeper into the shadows. But just as we were about to dart into the adjacent street, a loud crash echoed behind us, and the familiar voice rang out like a death knell.

"There you are," he said, a smirk evident even in the dim light. "I've been looking for you."

Panic surged through me as I felt the heat of his gaze, and in that moment, everything came crashing down—the laughter, the drinks, the hopeful plans. All of it faded, leaving only the stark reality of our situation.

"Run!" Lucas shouted, his grip tightening on my hand as we tore down the alley, adrenaline propelling us forward, my heart racing with fear and resolve.

But before we could make it to safety, I felt a sudden jolt, like a trap springing closed. A hand grabbed my shoulder, yanking me back as Lucas continued to flee, unaware that I was being pulled away from him.

"Let her go!" I heard him shout, his voice raw with anger, but the sound began to fade, swallowed by the night as I was dragged into darkness, my world collapsing around me.

And in that instant, I knew this was just the beginning of a nightmare I couldn't escape.

Chapter 19: Descent into Chaos

The day dawned gray and heavy, as if the world outside the theater had taken on the same oppressive mood that hung within the walls of our beloved playhouse. I stood at the edge of the stage, the familiar wooden floor cool beneath my bare feet, a stark contrast to the heat swirling in my chest. The curtains, usually vibrant and alive with colors, seemed muted, their once-familiar fabric now an ominous curtain drawn over our lives.

An unsettling stillness hung in the air, broken only by the muffled sound of hurried whispers drifting through the wings. I felt it before I saw it—an electric tension that crackled in the silence, binding us all in a collective uncertainty. We were a family here, united by our shared passion for performance, and yet the sudden absence of one of our own had sent tremors through our foundation. Caroline, a vibrant spirit who had danced into our lives just a season ago, was missing.

"Have you seen her?" I asked Lucas, my voice barely rising above the low hum of concern surrounding us. He turned from his perch against the wall, his brow furrowed in thought, the way it always did when he was deep in contemplation. He had a knack for channeling his energy into curiosity, and right now, that was precisely what I needed.

"Not since yesterday's rehearsal," he replied, his voice smooth but laced with an edge of worry. "She left right after the final scene, and I thought she was just tired. She always seemed to have a lot on her mind." He shrugged, a gesture filled with frustration. "But no one has seen her since."

Lucas's green eyes darted toward the backstage area, scanning for any signs of life. The rest of the cast lingered close, huddled in small groups, exchanging worried glances as the theater director paced like a caged animal, trying to maintain some semblance of order. The mood was thick with fear; it enveloped us like a fog, whispering doubts that slithered through our thoughts.

"We should investigate," I suggested, a wild idea taking root in my mind. "Maybe we can find a clue, something that leads us to her." I could feel the fire of determination ignite within me, a flicker of resolve amidst the chaos.

Lucas's lips curled into a half-smile, a mixture of amusement and admiration. "I suppose we can play detective for a bit. Besides, who better to solve this mystery than the star-crossed lovers of the stage?"

With that, we embarked on our impromptu investigation, two reluctant sleuths wrapped in the cloaks of makeshift intrigue. Our first stop was the dressing room—a space bursting with the remnants of our performances: scattered costumes, crumpled scripts, and the lingering scent of hairspray mingling with the stale air. As we combed through her belongings, every object felt like a potential breadcrumb leading us closer to Caroline.

"Look at this," I said, holding up a frayed notebook filled with scribbles and doodles. It was a glimpse into her mind, a chaotic blend of thoughts and aspirations spilling onto the pages. I flipped through it, my heart racing at the possibility of uncovering something profound, something that could explain her absence.

"What does it say?" Lucas leaned in, his curiosity piqued, his shoulder brushing against mine—a fleeting but electrifying moment that sent my pulse racing.

"Just random notes about her character and the plot. But wait—here!" I pointed to a hasty sketch of a door with an arrow drawn beneath it, leading to a few cryptic lines about finding a secret. "This looks important."

"Or a side quest in a fantasy novel," he joked, his smile cutting through the tension, reminding me of the lighter moments we shared, those fleeting seconds where the chaos of our lives seemed to slip away.

As we discussed what the notes might mean, I noticed something glinting on the floor, half-hidden beneath her chair. A small silver locket, dulled with age but undeniably beautiful, caught the light as I reached down to pick it up. I opened it, revealing a faded photograph of Caroline, her eyes bright with mischief. The other side was empty, but there was an inscription etched into the metal, worn but legible: "For when you need a reminder of home."

Lucas raised an eyebrow, his expression shifting from playful to serious. "Do you think she felt out of place here?"

"Maybe." I ran my fingers over the locket, the weight of it heavy in my palm, as if it carried the very essence of her spirit. "Perhaps she was looking for a way out, a reason to escape."

The implications sent a shiver down my spine, the shadows around us growing longer as the afternoon light dimmed. There was an unspoken understanding between us, a sense that we had stumbled upon something larger than ourselves, an undercurrent of turmoil lurking just beneath the surface of our daily lives.

With newfound urgency, we resolved to talk to the others, piecing together fragments of conversations like puzzle pieces. The theater was a labyrinth of secrets, each corner hiding whispers of doubt, fear, and uncertainty. Every actor we approached seemed to carry their own burden of knowledge, a thread connecting them to Caroline, but every answer led us deeper into confusion.

Lucas and I pressed on, drawing closer together in our quest, the electric charge between us palpable in the charged air. The stakes were high, and with each passing moment, the threads of our investigation tightened around us, forming an intricate web of mystery that promised to unravel the truth—or ensnare us in its grasp.

The shadows had begun their slow encroachment on the theater, painting the once-vibrant backdrop with an ominous palette of deep blues and grays. Each creak of the old wooden floor echoed like a heartbeat in the silence, heightening the palpable tension that clung to the air. I found myself perched on a stool in the corner of the green room, tapping my fingers against the table, where a collection of uneaten snacks lay forgotten. The peanut M&Ms had turned stale, much like the mood hanging over our gathering.

Lucas leaned against the doorframe, arms crossed, his expression a cocktail of determination and concern. "You know," he said, breaking the silence, "I'd expected the drama of the stage to be more, well, theatrical. This feels more like a horror movie where the lead actress just goes missing."

"Maybe that's the twist," I replied, unable to resist a smile despite the gravity of the situation. "Everyone thought she was the star, but turns out she's just the first to go."

"Great. I'll be sure to avoid dark alleys and sudden noises," he shot back, rolling his eyes dramatically. "But really, we need to focus. What if Caroline left us a trail? Or maybe she just wanted to get out of this show?"

With that, we decided to retrace her last steps. We walked through the hallways lined with fading posters, each image capturing a moment frozen in time, a reminder of the laughter and applause that had once filled this space. It felt surreal, contrasting the empty air that now swirled around us, heavy with unspoken fears.

Our next stop was the props room, a veritable treasure trove of forgotten items, glittering in the dim light like lost dreams. It smelled of wood and paint, with an undercurrent of dust that hinted at neglect. "If I were a missing actress, where would I hide?" I mused, poking through the clutter with a sense of playfulness that belied the seriousness of our search.

"Probably not in a pile of dusty old costumes," Lucas replied, rummaging through a rack of garish outfits that would make even the most flamboyant peacock reconsider its choices. "But there's always a chance she could have found solace in the absurd."

He pulled out a sparkly dress adorned with feathers, and for a brief moment, the absurdity of the situation washed over us, and laughter bubbled up uncontrollably. "If she were here, she'd be rolling her eyes at us," I chuckled. "I can just hear her saying, 'Get a grip, you two.'"

The laughter was short-lived, though, as reality settled back in, heavy as a lead balloon. We continued searching through boxes filled with props, old scripts, and tattered curtains, piecing together remnants of our performances and, hopefully, clues to Caroline's whereabouts.

"What if she was trying to leave the production?" I speculated, my mind racing with possibilities. "Maybe she got cold feet and didn't want to face us."

"Or maybe she stumbled onto something she shouldn't have," Lucas countered, a hint of mischief dancing in his eyes. "You know how these things go. Someone always has a secret."

"Now you're starting to sound like one of those detective novels," I teased, nudging him lightly. "But you might be onto something. What if someone saw something? Or overheard a conversation?"

Our search led us to the common area where the cast often gathered to unwind. The room was strewn with empty coffee cups and crumpled paper towels, remnants of the rehearsals that had morphed into nervous chatter over the past few days. We approached Mark, a seasoned actor with a reputation for knowing everything that happened behind the scenes.

"Hey, Mark," Lucas called, gesturing for him to join us. "Do you have a minute?"

"Depends on what you need," Mark replied, eyeing us with a blend of skepticism and interest. "If this is about that missing girl, I've told everyone I know nothing."

"Just a few questions," I chimed in, leaning forward slightly. "You saw Caroline yesterday, right? Do you remember anything unusual?"

Mark rubbed his chin, a thoughtful look crossing his face. "Well, she was off in her own world lately. Kept mumbling about feeling trapped, but that's typical for a show like this. I figured she was just stressed about the performance."

"Trapped?" I echoed, intrigued. "Did she mention why?"

"Not really. Just something about needing to break free from the routine. But, you know how it is—one day you're here, the next, you're in a different headspace entirely," he shrugged, a glimmer of understanding in his eyes, perhaps from his own experiences.

As we continued to press him for details, I noticed the subtle shift in his demeanor. There was something lingering just below the surface, a hesitation that suggested he knew more than he let on.

"Mark, you know something, don't you?" I challenged gently, my tone coaxing him to open up.

He glanced around, as if checking for eavesdroppers, and then leaned closer. "Alright, but I can't be held responsible for what I say. Just remember, it's a rumor."

"Spill it," Lucas urged, his intensity matching the atmosphere.

"I overheard a conversation a few days ago—Caroline was talking to someone about leaving, and there was a mention of a 'better opportunity.' But I don't know the details; I only caught snippets."

"Who was she talking to?" I pressed, feeling a knot tighten in my stomach.

Mark hesitated, the wheels turning in his head. "I'm not sure, but it was someone from outside the cast. A friend, maybe? They seemed close."

With that, we felt another thread of tension unfurl. Caroline's motivations began to intertwine with a web of relationships that hinted at complications we hadn't anticipated. The layers of our investigation were thickening, wrapping around us like the very fabric of the costumes we wore on stage.

"Thanks, Mark," Lucas said, giving him a nod of appreciation. As we walked away, I couldn't shake the feeling that we were dancing dangerously close to a truth that might unravel everything we thought we knew about Caroline.

The longer we searched, the more I felt like we were peeling back layers of a fragile façade, revealing the chaotic, beautiful mess that lay beneath. I glanced sideways at Lucas, whose brow was furrowed in concentration, and I felt an unexpected warmth bloom in my chest. In this moment of uncertainty, he was my anchor, his presence both grounding and exhilarating, and I realized how much I needed him by my side.

"Do you think we're getting closer?" I asked, my voice steady despite the turmoil swirling within.

"Closer to the truth, or closer to trouble?" he quipped, a smirk dancing on his lips, but his eyes held a seriousness that mirrored my own.

"Both, I suspect," I replied, the gravity of our situation pulling us deeper into the unknown. We stepped back into the gathering of the cast, our hearts pounding in sync with the rhythm of the unfolding mystery, determined to uncover whatever lay hidden in the shadows.

The air hung thick with unresolved tension as we returned to the dimly lit main stage, the sense of foreboding swirling around us like the dust motes illuminated by the fading afternoon light. I could hear the distant murmur of actors rehearsing their lines, their voices a backdrop to the chaos that had seeped into our lives. It felt as if the theater itself had taken on a life of its own, each creak and groan echoing the anxiety of the missing cast member. Caroline's absence was a gaping hole in our world, and I was determined to fill it with answers, however elusive they might be.

Lucas and I exchanged glances, a silent agreement forming between us to delve deeper. The shadows cast by the old chandeliers seemed to dance mockingly, whispering secrets we were yet to uncover. "We need to talk to the others again, maybe get more details from those who were closest to her," I suggested, my voice barely above a whisper.

"Right, like a round of 'who's the biggest drama queen?'" Lucas quipped, his trademark sarcasm surfacing like a life raft in stormy seas. "But seriously, let's start with Julie. She was practically glued to Caroline's side."

We made our way to the rehearsal space, where Julie was hunched over a stack of scripts, her fingers nervously flipping through the pages as if they held the key to our questions. When she looked up, her eyes were wide, as though she had been expecting us. "You heard about Caroline?"

"Yeah, we're just trying to piece together what might have happened," I replied, my heart racing. "Do you know anything?"

Her voice trembled slightly as she spoke. "I haven't seen her since yesterday. But I did hear her talking about… well, things weren't great. She felt like she was being watched."

"Watched?" Lucas interjected, leaning closer. "What do you mean?"

"I don't know! It was just a feeling she had. Something about the backstage area feeling… off." Julie shook her head, her brows furrowed in confusion. "And she mentioned a strange guy who kept appearing at rehearsals. She thought he was taking an interest in her."

A cold shiver crept up my spine, the kind that whispered of danger lurking just outside the safety of our theater walls. "Did she say who he was?" I pressed, my mind racing with possibilities.

"Not really. Just some guy with a hoodie. I figured she was being dramatic; you know how she can get."

Lucas's gaze turned thoughtful, the cogs in his mind clearly spinning. "Dramatic can sometimes mean perceptive. If she sensed something, there might be a reason for it. We should find out who this guy is."

"Maybe we can ask around the nearby cafes or bars," I suggested, my mind already spinning tales of shadowy figures and secret rendezvous. "Someone must have seen him."

Julie nodded, but her expression was clouded with uncertainty. "Just be careful. If Caroline was scared, then maybe there's more to this than just a casual observer."

With a newfound sense of purpose, we headed out into the bustling streets, leaving the somber ambiance of the theater behind. The cool evening air felt refreshing against my skin, a stark contrast to the oppressive atmosphere we'd just escaped. As we made our way to a nearby café that Caroline frequented, I couldn't help but feel that we were treading dangerously close to a reality we might not be ready to face.

The café was a cozy little place, its interior a blend of warm colors and eclectic décor, but the energy inside was muted. Patrons sipped their coffees in hushed tones, casting furtive glances at the door as if expecting a storm to sweep in at any moment. Lucas approached the counter while I scanned the room, my instincts on high alert.

"Excuse me," Lucas said to the barista, a young woman with a friendly smile that faltered as she sensed the tension in the air. "We're looking for a friend of ours—Caroline. She used to come here often. Have you seen her recently?"

The barista's brow furrowed, and I could almost see the gears turning in her head. "I think I saw her a couple of days ago. She seemed... a bit off. Kind of nervous, you know? She kept looking out the window, like she was waiting for someone."

"Did she mention anyone?" I pressed, feeling a knot tighten in my stomach.

"She mentioned a guy," the barista said slowly, her eyes darting toward the door. "But I didn't catch his name. Just that he was watching her. I thought it was a bit odd, but you never know with people these days."

"Do you have a description?" Lucas asked, leaning forward as if trying to will the answer into existence.

She shrugged. "Just a hoodie and jeans. That's all I remember. But honestly, she seemed scared. Maybe you should talk to the owner. He might know more."

As we turned to leave, the barista's voice followed us. "Just be careful, okay? There's something weird going on."

Lucas and I shared a glance, the weight of her warning settling heavily between us. "We need to find this guy," I said, my resolve solidifying. "If Caroline was scared enough to talk about it, then we can't ignore it."

"I agree," Lucas replied, the flicker of determination igniting in his eyes. "Let's check out the theater again. Maybe someone saw him around there."

The streets blurred around us as we rushed back, the growing darkness casting elongated shadows that seemed to mimic our anxiety. Each step felt heavier, as if the very air was thickening with anticipation. The theater loomed ahead, its familiar façade now a fortress guarding secrets we were desperate to unveil.

As we entered, the buzz of activity continued unabated, actors moving through their routines, blissfully unaware of the storm brewing just beneath the surface. We slipped backstage, and my heart raced as I scanned the area, searching for anything that might give us a clue.

"Let's check the security footage," Lucas suggested, his voice low but urgent. "There has to be a camera in the lobby or outside."

We hurried to the small office where the security system was housed. The screens flickered with the mundane—the entryway, the ticket booth, and the various halls of the theater. My heart sank as I sat in front of the array of monitors, each displaying innocuous scenes from our daily lives.

"There!" Lucas pointed suddenly, his finger jabbing at the screen. "Rewind that footage."

I did, and we watched as the camera captured a glimpse of Caroline just before she left the theater, her eyes darting around as if she sensed something lurking just beyond the door. Moments later, a figure appeared—a tall man in a dark hoodie, blending into the shadows. He stood outside, watching her, his posture tense, as if he were waiting for her to make a move.

"Who is he?" I murmured, feeling a shiver of dread as I noted the way he loomed, an ominous presence in a place that had once felt safe.

"I don't know," Lucas replied, his expression grave. "But we're going to find out."

We continued to watch, our eyes glued to the screen, when suddenly, the footage flickered and went static, a jarring interruption that sent a wave of frustration coursing through me. "What the hell? It just... stopped?"

Lucas leaned closer, furrowing his brow. "This isn't just a coincidence."

The screens flickered back to life, but the image had changed. The man in the hoodie was gone, replaced by an empty street illuminated by the eerie glow of the streetlights. My stomach dropped, and I felt the weight of the unknown bearing down on me.

"We need to get out there," Lucas urged, his voice urgent. "We can't just sit here."

I nodded, adrenaline surging as we raced out of the office. The theater buzzed with life, but we were oblivious to it now. We had to confront the shadows, the fears that had taken root in our minds. We pushed through the backstage door, stepping out into the night, ready to hunt for answers.

As we navigated the streets, a sense of urgency propelled us forward, our breaths mingling with the cool night air. But as we rounded a corner, we stumbled into an unsettling scene—a group of people gathered in hushed conversation. The whispers hushed as we approached, and the air turned heavy with unspoken words.

"What's going on?" I asked, my heart racing.

One of the actors stepped forward, his face pale, his eyes wide with fear. "It's Caroline... we found something. You need to see this."

A chill ran down my spine as I exchanged a look with Lucas. We rushed forward, our minds racing with possibilities, the shadows of uncertainty looming ever closer.

Chapter 20: Confronting the Darkness

The musty scent of aged paper filled the cramped room, wrapping around us like an unwanted embrace. I squinted against the dim light filtering through the high windows, casting long shadows across the wooden floor, which creaked beneath our weight as if echoing the voices of the past. Lucas sat cross-legged on the floor, surrounded by a chaotic array of newspaper clippings and faded photographs, his brow furrowed in concentration. Every so often, he would glance up at me, his deep-set eyes searching mine, silently asking whether we were truly ready to unravel the threads of history woven into the very fabric of this theater.

"I can't believe how much we've unearthed," I said, my voice a hushed whisper, reverberating in the quiet stillness. "It's like the past is clawing its way back to the surface." I picked up a brittle newspaper clipping from the 1930s, the yellowed paper crackling under my fingers. The headline screamed of scandal, of a brilliant starlet who had disappeared without a trace, leaving behind only speculation and heartbreak.

Lucas leaned closer, the weight of the moment heavy between us. "Evelyn Carter," he murmured, the name lingering in the air like a ghost haunting the stage. "She was supposed to be the next big thing. They say she was beautiful, talented... and cursed." He brushed his fingers over the grain of the wood beneath him, as if trying to find a connection to her spirit. "It's like everyone who steps onto this stage is destined for tragedy."

I let the name wash over me, feeling a chill crawl down my spine. It was almost too easy to imagine her, a fiery talent with dreams of stardom, now reduced to mere whispers in the annals of this theater's dark history. My heart raced as I imagined the glittering lights, the sound of applause, and then the silence that followed her abrupt departure. "What if the rumors are true?" I asked, half-joking, half-serious. "What if she really is haunting this place?"

Lucas snorted, a smile breaking through the gravity of our task. "You're not seriously suggesting we hold a séance, are you?"

"Only if you promise to bring snacks. Spirits can be very demanding." I couldn't help but grin, the tension in the air momentarily dissipating.

But as quickly as it came, the smile faded. I turned my attention back to the scattered documents, trying to shake off the looming sense of dread. The deeper we delved into the theater's history, the more palpable the atmosphere became, thickening with each revelation. It was as if the very walls were closing in, urging us to either flee or confront whatever darkness lay within.

I found myself drawn to a worn ledger, its cover cracked and faded. Flipping it open revealed a meticulously penned list of cast members, their roles, and the dates of their performances. A shiver traced my spine as I scanned the names—some crossed out with a thick black line, others adorned with ominous annotations. I felt Lucas lean in, his breath warm against my cheek as he peered over my shoulder.

"Look at this," he said, his voice barely above a whisper. "They all met with misfortune shortly after their performances." His finger traced the name of an actress, a line marking her next to a note that read "accident" in a spidery hand. "It's like a curse."

"It can't be," I argued, but even as I said it, the weight of history pressed down on me, squeezing the air from my lungs.

A sudden crash echoed from the stage, reverberating through the dusty auditorium, and we both jumped, hearts racing. Lucas shot me a look, eyes wide, and we exchanged a silent agreement before tiptoeing toward the open archway leading into the main theater. The stage was cloaked in shadows, the remnants of old props cast in disarray, as if a tempest had raged through the space, tossing everything into disarray.

"Do you see that?" Lucas whispered, his voice trembling with a mix of excitement and fear.

The soft glow of a solitary light bulb flickered above, illuminating a figure standing at the edge of the stage. My breath caught in my throat as the shape slowly turned, revealing a woman cloaked in flowing white fabric, her hair cascading like silken threads around her shoulders. She stood there, ethereal and haunting, an apparition of the past reborn.

"Evelyn?" I breathed, half-convinced I had slipped into some fever dream.

"Who are you?" The voice that floated toward us was soft, almost melodic, yet laced with an undercurrent of sorrow that tugged at my heart.

I glanced at Lucas, who was frozen in place, a mixture of awe and terror painted across his face. "We're... we're just researching," I stammered, my voice steadier than I felt. "Trying to understand what happened to you."

Her laughter, light yet tinged with melancholy, filled the air, swirling around us like the softest breeze. "Understand?" she repeated, her eyes piercing through the shadows. "Some truths are best left buried."

Suddenly, the room felt alive, the temperature dropping as if the very essence of the theater were reacting to her presence. I stepped forward, unable to resist the pull of her sorrowful gaze. "What do you mean?"

"Every story has a price," she replied, her voice dropping to a whisper, "and every actor pays it."

The words hung between us like a thin veil, and I sensed that beneath her haunting beauty lay a depth of pain that echoed through the ages. In that moment, I understood: we were not just seekers of the past; we were entwined in it, bound to uncover the darkness that had claimed so many souls before us. And as I stood on the precipice of revelation, I felt a stirring of resolve within me—a determination to confront whatever shadows lay ahead, even if it meant unearthing the theater's deepest, darkest secrets.

Evelyn's presence hung in the air like an unfinished symphony, reverberating through the very marrow of the theater. Her ethereal form shimmered under the flickering light, casting an otherworldly glow that illuminated the room in shades of ghostly white. It was as if the fabric of reality had thinned, allowing a glimpse into a realm where time stood still, and the echoes of forgotten voices whispered secrets to those brave enough to listen.

"Did you just come from the other side, or are you simply too lazy to take the stage?" I quipped, half-joking, trying to mask the tremor in my voice. Lucas's eyes widened, and I felt a rush of warmth from his silent plea for sanity.

"Careful," he murmured, inching back as though retreating might somehow shield him from the surreal encounter. "She might actually be offended."

Evelyn's lips curled into a slight smile, a mix of amusement and sadness playing across her delicate features. "It's been ages since anyone dared to joke here," she said, her voice like a soft breeze. "But don't let the dust settle on your wit just yet. Humor can be a lifeline in a sea of sorrow."

"Well, if that's the case, I should stock up on punchlines," I replied, buoyed by her playful spirit. "We've got a lot to wade through in this sea."

"Wade through? More like drown," Lucas interjected, his tone half-serious, half-sarcastic as he shifted his weight. "You realize we're talking to a ghost, right?"

"Just because you can't see beyond the veil doesn't mean I can't," Evelyn said, her eyes sparkling with mischief. "Besides, the truth is more haunting than any specter. Why not seek it out?"

Her words settled over me, igniting a fire of curiosity deep within. "We want to help," I said, stepping forward, drawn by the gravity of her story. "What happened to you, Evelyn? Why did you vanish?"

The room grew still, and for a moment, I feared she might fade away like smoke on the breeze. But she held her ground, the intensity in her gaze sharpening. "In this place, the shadows have always danced with the light. My departure was but a ripple in a much darker tide. There were forces at work here, unseen and unfathomable. They claimed my spirit, and they may yet claim others."

"Great," Lucas muttered, crossing his arms defensively. "More ominous prophecies. Just what we need."

"Not prophecies," Evelyn corrected, a flicker of annoyance breaking through her calm demeanor. "Warnings. There are those who seek to protect the legacy of this theater at any cost, even if it means silencing those who dare speak the truth. I wasn't the first, and I certainly won't be the last."

My heart raced. "You mean others have disappeared too? Why didn't we find this in the archives?"

"Because some stories are buried beneath layers of deceit. Only those willing to dig will find them." Her gaze shifted toward the stage, where dust motes danced like tiny stars. "You must look deeper."

"Look deeper? Is that a euphemism for 'don't go in the prop room'? Because I have a strong suspicion that the only thing in there is a closet of nightmares." I tried to lighten the atmosphere, but my pulse quickened.

"The prop room is merely a manifestation of your fears," she replied, her tone playful yet heavy with meaning. "Fear is what keeps you from unraveling the truth, from confronting the darkness that lies within these walls."

"Wow, talk about dramatic," Lucas muttered under his breath, but I caught the flicker of intrigue in his eyes.

"What if we found what you're hiding?" I pressed, urgency rising in my chest. "What if we could set you free?"

Evelyn's expression softened, and for a moment, I saw a flicker of hope behind her sorrow. "You would do that? You would risk yourselves for a ghost's peace?"

"Risk? No, we're merely curious," Lucas interjected dryly, shooting me a sideways glance. "I'm sure the exit signs will guide us back to safety."

"Curiosity can be a dangerous game," she said, tilting her head. "But if you truly seek the truth, it lies beneath the stage. The past lingers in the darkness, waiting for those brave enough to confront it."

As the weight of her words settled over us, an unyielding pull began to form in my chest, urging me to explore the secrets buried below. "Let's go then," I said, my voice steady despite the storm of apprehension swirling inside. "We can't turn back now."

Evelyn nodded, a flicker of approval in her gaze. "Follow the sound of your heart, and it will guide you to the truth. But beware—the shadows are alive, and they don't take kindly to intruders."

With that, she began to dissolve into the shadows, the light around her dimming like the final curtain of a once-grand performance. "Wait!" I called out, desperation clawing at my throat. "How do we find you again?"

"Listen for the whispers of the past," she replied, her voice drifting like a haunting melody. "They will lead you."

The moment she vanished, the air felt charged with electricity, and an unsettling quiet enveloped us. Lucas and I exchanged glances, and I could see the mix of trepidation and resolve reflected in his eyes.

"Alright, let's get this over with," he said, the bravado in his tone at odds with the unease beneath. "Lead the way, fearless ghost hunters."

We made our way toward the stage, my heart pounding with each step. I could feel the weight of the theater's history pressing against us, the stories of those who had come before lingering in the air. As we reached the edge of the stage, I spotted a narrow trapdoor, nearly hidden beneath a curtain of cobwebs and dust.

"This must be it," I said, brushing the dust aside to reveal an iron ring.

"Or it could just be a trap," Lucas said, half-joking but glancing around as if expecting a horde of spirits to emerge at any moment.

"Only one way to find out," I replied, my pulse racing with anticipation and a tinge of fear. With a determined grip, I yanked the door open, revealing a steep, dark staircase leading into the depths below.

"Ladies first?" Lucas suggested, his voice dripping with sarcasm.

"Why, thank you. I'll make sure to leave the lights on for you," I shot back, my heart thundering in my chest as I descended into the unknown, the air growing colder with each step. The theater, once a place of light and laughter, now felt like a portal to another world—a realm where the past and present intertwined, waiting for us to uncover the truths hidden in the shadows.

The stairs creaked ominously underfoot as I descended, each step a reminder of the weight of history pressing down on us. The air grew colder, thick with an earthy scent that spoke of damp stone and secrets long hidden. Lucas followed closely behind, his presence a steadying force against the encroaching darkness, though I could sense his unease mirroring my own. The dim light from the stage above faded quickly, swallowed by the blackness below, leaving us reliant on the flickering beam of my flashlight.

"Who knew the theater was equipped with its own personal dungeon?" he quipped, his attempt at humor a thin veil over the tension thrumming between us.

"Better than a dungeon with no exit," I shot back, trying to maintain a brave front. "At least we're not about to be sacrificed to a vengeful spirit... I hope."

"Sacrificed?" he repeated, mock-seriousness edging his tone. "Great. Just what I wanted—an afterlife that involves group therapy with ghosts."

The light from my flashlight danced along the rough stone walls, revealing an assortment of props and discarded sets that had been left to gather dust over the years. I could almost hear the echoes of laughter and applause, ghosts of performances long gone reverberating through the dank corridor. But beneath that nostalgia lay something darker, something raw and unresolved.

"Look at this," I called, gesturing to a large trunk half-buried under a tattered velvet curtain. The chest was old, the hinges rusted, but a sense of urgency propelled me to reach for it. "What do you think we'll find? Forgotten costumes or more skeletons?"

"Let's hope it's the former. Though I'm not sure I'm ready for a costume party with ghosts," Lucas replied, peering over my shoulder with a mix of intrigue and apprehension.

With a heave, I lifted the lid, wincing as the hinges protested loudly, as if warning us to turn back. Inside lay a jumble of moth-eaten costumes, shimmering sequins dulled by time, and a few crumbling playbills, their ink faded but the names still legible. One of the bills caught my eye—a production of "The Phantom's Embrace," starring Evelyn Carter.

"Here we go again," I said, holding the bill aloft. "This looks like a treasure trove of bad decisions and worse hairstyles."

"More like a map to disaster," Lucas replied, his voice dropping as he scanned the trunk's contents. "Do you think these costumes are tied to the disappearances?"

"Wouldn't be the first time an ill-fated outfit led to tragedy," I mused, rifling through the garments. One particularly gaudy gown shimmered with an eerie luminescence in the flashlight's glow, its deep red fabric draping elegantly, yet ominously. "It's beautiful, in a 'please don't murder me' sort of way."

As I held the gown up to the light, a chill raced through the air, and suddenly, the trunk seemed to shudder, a deep, resonant sound echoing from somewhere beyond our reach. Lucas shot me a wide-eyed glance, the humor drained from his expression.

"What was that?" he whispered, tension tightening his voice.

"Your guess is as good as mine," I replied, heart hammering in my chest. "Maybe the theater is tired of us snooping around."

"Or maybe it just wants us to leave the trunk alone," he suggested, glancing nervously at the darkness creeping in around us.

Before I could respond, the sound came again—a low rumble, as if the very walls were groaning in protest. The trunk shook violently, sending a cascade of dusty costumes tumbling to the floor, and my breath caught in my throat as a thin, pale light flickered beneath the trunk, illuminating strange symbols etched into the stone beneath.

"What in the world...?" I murmured, kneeling to inspect the markings. They twisted and curled, resembling an intricate language I couldn't comprehend, and a shiver of recognition coursed through me. "Lucas, these look like they could be linked to some sort of ritual."

"Ritual?" His voice was a mix of intrigue and alarm. "You mean like summoning the spirits of actors past? Because I think I've seen enough horror movies to know how this ends."

"Maybe we're supposed to do something," I mused, running my fingers along the cool stone. "Like... activate it? What if these symbols are a key to understanding what happened to Evelyn?"

"Or a key to our doom," he countered, but I could see the spark of curiosity in his eyes.

I stood, determination rising within me as I faced the trunk once more. "We can't turn back now. Evelyn guided us here for a reason. We have to see this through."

Before Lucas could respond, the air around us crackled, a palpable energy swirling, lifting the hair on the back of my neck. I could feel the weight of the theater pressing down, urging us onward. I took a deep breath and began to recite the words I had found on the playbill, words that felt ancient and charged with power, flowing from my lips before I even realized what I was doing.

As I spoke, the symbols beneath the trunk began to glow, illuminating the darkness with an eerie light. Lucas's eyes widened in horror, but a rush of exhilaration surged through me, the thrill of uncovering a mystery overtaking my fear. "What is happening?" he asked, his voice rising.

"Something is awakening," I said, my heart racing. "Just keep reading."

With every word, the air thickened, and the ground trembled beneath us. Suddenly, the trunk burst open, and a whirlwind of energy erupted from within, swirling around us like a tempest. I barely had time to register the flash of vivid colors and shadowy forms before a blinding light enveloped the room, and I was forced to shield my eyes.

Then came silence—deafening, absolute silence. The light faded, leaving us in the dim, musty basement once more. I blinked, trying to adjust my vision, and as the shadows settled back into place, I realized we were no longer alone.

Standing before us was a figure, shrouded in darkness, its features obscured but undeniably present, its eyes glowing like embers in the night. The air crackled with tension, and my heart raced as I met its gaze.

"Who dares disturb my slumber?" the voice echoed, low and resonant, sending chills racing down my spine.

I grasped Lucas's arm, my mind racing. "We were just trying to help," I stammered, but even as the words left my mouth, I could sense the danger lurking in the air.

The figure stepped forward, its presence overwhelming, and I knew in that instant that we had crossed a line, stepping deeper into the theater's dark legacy than we ever intended. My heart thundered in my chest as I braced myself for the confrontation that lay ahead, the weight of the theater's history hanging heavy in the air, and the realization dawning that some truths may be better left undiscovered.

Chapter 21: The Truth Revealed

The theater stood before us, a hulking shadow against the pale evening sky, its once-grand facade marred by the ravages of time and neglect. A tangle of ivy clung desperately to the walls, as if the building itself were trying to hold onto some semblance of its former glory. Lucas and I approached, the air thick with tension, the scent of damp wood and rust lingering like ghosts of performances past. The dim glow of the streetlights cast flickering shadows, creating a surreal atmosphere where every creak of the floorboards seemed to whisper secrets.

"Are you ready?" Lucas asked, his voice low, but I could hear the steel beneath it. I nodded, though my heart drummed a frantic rhythm against my ribcage. This was it—the moment we'd been waiting for. Our last encounter with the mysterious benefactor had left me with more questions than answers, a churning confusion of intrigue and dread. The man had appeared out of nowhere, like a specter from the theater's haunted past, and now he beckoned us once again.

As we stepped inside, the scent of musty velvet and aged paper enveloped us, and the darkness seemed to pulse with anticipation. The theater was alive in its stillness, each shadow a reminder of the vibrant life that once filled its seats, laughter and applause echoing through the hallowed halls. I could almost hear the whispers of actors rehearsing lines, the shuffling of feet on the stage, but the silence now was a heavy weight, pressing down on us.

"Lucas," I said, my voice barely above a whisper, "what if he's waiting for us? What if this is a trap?" Doubt coiled in my stomach like a serpent, its fangs poised to strike. But Lucas's grip tightened around my hand, reassuring and steadfast. "We're not backing down now. We need to know what he's hiding." His determination sparked something within me, a flicker of courage amidst the encroaching shadows.

As we ventured deeper into the theater, we found ourselves in the grand foyer, its chandeliers dripping with dust, casting a ghostly glow over the forgotten elegance. "It's beautiful," I murmured, almost to myself. "It was beautiful." The remnants of luxury lingered in the intricate moldings and the faded opulence of the carpets, a stark contrast to the decay surrounding us.

Then, a door creaked open, and there he stood—the benefactor, a figure cloaked in mystery and mischief, with a grin that didn't quite reach his eyes. "Ah, my dear friends, welcome back!" His voice dripped with feigned warmth, but I could see the glint of something darker behind his facade. "I've been expecting you."

Lucas stepped forward, the protector I had come to rely on. "Enough with the games. We want answers." His words were like ice, and I felt the temperature in the room drop as the benefactor's smile faltered, if only for a moment.

"Answers? Such a curious notion," he said, tilting his head, eyes glinting with mischief. "What is it you wish to know? The secrets of the theater? The disappearance of our lovely leading lady?" His tone was mocking, and I could feel my heart race at the mention of the actress.

"Cut the theatrics," I snapped, emboldened by Lucas's presence. "Why did you orchestrate all this? What do you want from us?" I stepped forward, driven by an urgency that surged through my veins.

With a flourish, he gestured to the empty stage behind him, the shadows curling like smoke. "Ah, the stage is set for a grand reveal, isn't it? But it seems you're missing the larger picture." His eyes sparkled with a malevolent delight, and I felt a chill skitter up my spine. "I did this for a purpose, you see. The theater, its history, the actress—she was the key to reclaiming what was stolen from me."

"Stolen?" Lucas echoed incredulously. "You mean the theater? You think you can just waltz in and take back what you believe is yours?"

"Yes, exactly!" he exclaimed, an unsettling enthusiasm coloring his words. "This theater has been in my family for generations, and when they sold it—when it was allowed to fall into the hands of the unworthy—it was an affront to my bloodline. The actress? She's merely a pawn in my grand design."

My stomach twisted in knots as the realization hit me like a punch to the gut. "You were behind her disappearance," I breathed, horror dawning on me. "You used us to get what you wanted."

"Used? Oh no, my dear. You've been quite entertaining," he purred, stepping closer, his voice dripping with condescension. "But make no mistake, I need that actress. She is the final piece of the puzzle."

Lucas's protective instincts surged, and he stepped in front of me, a wall of strength. "You're not going to hurt her," he growled, his body tense, ready for whatever might come next.

"Oh, but you see," the benefactor sneered, "the beauty of this game is that you've already played your part. Now, all that's left is to decide how the curtain falls."

The atmosphere thickened, the air crackling with tension. The stakes had risen, and the shadows danced around us as if eagerly awaiting the outcome of this confrontation. My heart raced, not just from fear, but from the fiery spark of rebellion igniting within me. I was done being a pawn in this twisted game.

"Lucas," I whispered, my voice steadying, "we need to end this." I felt a surge of determination, buoyed by the love that had blossomed between us amidst the chaos. I wasn't just fighting for answers; I was fighting for our future, for the light we could bring back into this theater, and for the truth buried beneath the layers of lies.

The benefactor chuckled, but the sound was hollow, devoid of the joy he sought to portray. "Bravery is a lovely trait, but I assure you, it won't save you."

"No," Lucas interjected fiercely, "but love will." In that moment, I knew we would face whatever came next together, and no dark secret could extinguish the light we had found in each other. The theater might have its ghosts, but so did we, and together, we were ready to unveil the truth, no matter the cost.

The benefactor's laughter echoed through the theater like a distant thunderclap, reverberating off the faded velvet curtains that hung like forlorn memories. I glanced at Lucas, his jaw set and eyes blazing, a fierce determination radiating from him that made my heart swell with an unexpected mixture of admiration and dread. "What's it going to be then?" he challenged, his voice low and steady, cutting through the thick air of uncertainty. "You think you can just take her and walk away?"

"Why not?" The benefactor shrugged with an almost theatrical nonchalance, an unsettling smile playing on his lips. "In my experience, it's easier to reclaim what was once mine than to let the unworthy ruin it." His words dripped with arrogance, each syllable laced with the bitterness of lost legacy.

I stepped forward, fueled by a blend of fear and defiance. "You can't just manipulate people to get what you want. This isn't a play, and we're not your actors to command." My voice shook slightly, but I pushed against it, channeling the fire I felt bubbling inside. "This is real life, and we won't let you take her."

"Ah, but you see, that's where you're mistaken," he replied, his tone almost patronizing. "You're already entangled in my plot. You've danced to my tune, and now you're simply left to choose your exit." He gestured grandly, and I caught the hint of madness in his eyes—an obsession that threatened to unravel everything we had worked for.

"What's the point of all this?" Lucas asked, his tone measured yet edged with urgency. "You can't possibly believe that dragging this theater back into your twisted vision is going to fix anything."

"It's about legacy," the benefactor shot back, eyes narrowing. "The theater was meant to be a beacon of excellence, a monument to artistry. Instead, it's become a playground for amateurs, run by those who don't appreciate its true value. And the actress? She holds the key to restoring that legacy."

"Restoring?" I scoffed, incredulous. "You mean holding it hostage. You think you can just pull her back and expect everything to revert to some idealized past? That's not how life works."

"Life?" he echoed, a sardonic twist to his mouth. "Ah, how quaint. But tell me, what is life without passion, without drama? The world thrives on the stories we tell, and this theater—this beautiful, crumbling shell—is my stage. I will reclaim my birthright."

Lucas stepped closer, his eyes sharp and calculating. "And what do you think will happen if you succeed? You think you'll magically revive this place? The truth is, it's already fading, just like your grip on reality. You can't force it to be what it once was."

"Ah, but I can certainly try," he snapped, frustration sparking in his voice. "You think you're here to save the day, but you're merely pawns in a game much larger than yourselves. Your love story? A trivial distraction. The theater deserves its rightful heir."

The air between us crackled with the heat of our confrontation, and I could feel my heart racing, a wild drumbeat of adrenaline urging me forward. "No one is going to be a pawn any longer," I declared, feeling a rush of courage swell within me. "If we want to save this theater, we'll do it together. You think you can control everything, but you don't understand what real love and sacrifice can accomplish."

The benefactor's smile faltered, replaced by a flash of something darker. "Love? Sacrifice? Those are mere illusions, my dear. You'll find that in this world, power and control reign supreme. You're standing in the ruins of my legacy. You're nothing but dust."

"Dust that can rise again," Lucas interjected, his voice ringing with conviction. "You underestimate us. This theater was built on the passion of people who believed in its magic, and we won't let you extinguish that flame."

With a swift motion, the benefactor turned, moving toward the stage, where shadows lurked like ghosts waiting to be summoned. I exchanged a glance with Lucas, and in that fleeting moment, we shared a silent understanding. We couldn't let him manipulate the story any longer. We had to take control of our narrative, to write the ending we desired.

As the benefactor began to pace, his gestures animated, I felt an urgency grip me. "What if we could help you?" I blurted out, surprising even myself. The words tumbled from my lips, a desperate gamble. "What if we helped you find a way to honor this theater's legacy without all this destruction?"

He paused, curiosity flickering in his eyes. "And why would you propose such a ludicrous idea? You think I'm just going to walk away and embrace the kindness of strangers?"

"Because," I said, my voice steadying, "perhaps you're not as lost as you think. You're holding onto the past like it's a lifeline, but you don't have to destroy everything to reclaim it. We can work together, salvage what's left, and breathe new life into this place."

His expression shifted, a mixture of skepticism and intrigue. "Interesting," he mused, stepping closer, his voice dropping to a conspiratorial whisper. "You really believe you can turn this around? That I would entertain such an alliance?"

"Why not?" Lucas stepped forward, ready to back me up. "If your goal is to restore the theater, we can offer fresh ideas, a new vision that honors its history but isn't shackled by it. You've let bitterness consume you. It doesn't have to end this way."

The benefactor studied us, his brow furrowing as he weighed our words. I felt the air thicken around us, the possibility of change swirling like a tempest, a fragile hope threading through the darkness. But then, in the heartbeat of a moment, he laughed again—a chilling sound that sent shivers down my spine.

"You really think you can change me?" he sneered, but there was a glint of uncertainty beneath his bravado. "You're young and naive. The theater is built on tradition, not some fanciful dream of collaboration."

"Maybe it's time to redefine that tradition," I retorted, my voice stronger now. "This theater deserves a future, not just a past. It deserves a chance to evolve, just like we have. If you can't see that, then you really are lost."

The tension hung in the air, taut and electric, as we stared at him, refusing to back down. For a brief moment, doubt flickered across his features, and I could almost believe he was reconsidering, contemplating the possibility of redemption instead of revenge. But then, a shadow crossed his face, and the moment evaporated, leaving behind only the chill of uncertainty.

"Time will tell if you're right," he declared, voice laced with danger. "But know this—if you fail, the consequences will be dire."

I swallowed hard, feeling the weight of his warning settle over us. But I wasn't ready to let fear dictate our path. "We won't fail," I asserted, clenching my fists at my sides. "We'll make this work. Together."

As we locked eyes, I felt a fire ignite within me, fueled by love and defiance, ready to face whatever storm lay ahead. The theater may have been shrouded in shadows, but together, we would unearth its light, reclaiming not just the building but the stories that breathed life into it.

The benefactor's laughter hung in the air, a sinister echo that sent a chill down my spine. He stood there, arms crossed, the shadows swirling around him as if they were a cloak of secrets waiting to be revealed. "You think you can just redefine a legacy that's centuries in the making? How charming," he scoffed, his tone dripping with condescension.

Lucas stepped forward, his presence as solid as the crumbling walls of the theater. "We're not redefining it—we're revitalizing it. You may see it as a relic, but it still has the power to enchant, to inspire. That's what makes it worth saving." His voice was steady, a beacon of determination amidst the chaos.

"Revitalizing?" The benefactor mocked, tilting his head, a smirk playing at the corners of his mouth. "What makes you think you two—mere dreamers—can accomplish what others before you could not? This isn't a community theater production, my friends. This is the grandest stage of all, and I will not let you tarnish its legacy."

I felt the heat of anger rising in my chest. "What legacy? The one you've twisted into a weapon to scare people into submission? This theater deserves better. It deserves voices that sing, not threats that silence."

He stepped closer, the atmosphere thick with tension. "You speak of voices, but all I hear is a cacophony of ignorance. You don't understand what's at stake here." His eyes narrowed, the amusement fading to something far darker. "You don't know what I'm capable of."

"Then show us," Lucas challenged, his tone unwavering. "If you really believe in your cause, let's hear it. Let's see what you plan to do."

The benefactor's gaze flickered, something akin to respect—or perhaps curiosity—dancing behind his steely façade. "You're both rather bold, aren't you? But don't mistake that for courage. This theater has seen horrors that would make your skin crawl."

"I'm not afraid of your shadows," I retorted, feeling a surge of resolve wash over me. "I'm ready to face whatever demons you think you can unleash. You may have the history, but we have the heart."

He seemed to consider my words, the shadow of a smirk reappearing. "Ah, heart. The Achilles' heel of many an idealist. Tell me, what will you do when your heart fails you? When you face the truth of what this place truly holds?"

"Whatever it takes," Lucas said firmly, stepping beside me, his presence a comfort against the darkness. "We'll fight for it. For its past, for its future."

The benefactor leaned back, eyes sparkling with a mixture of delight and derision. "Very well. Then let's make this interesting. You wish to uncover the truth? Then let's take a walk down memory lane."

With a wave of his hand, the shadows shifted, parting like a curtain to reveal a hidden door I had never noticed before. It was slightly ajar, the hinges creaking in protest as if waking from a long slumber. A chill wind whispered through, carrying the scent of dust and decay, but also something more—a hint of the stories long buried within the theater's walls.

"After you," he said, gesturing with an exaggerated flourish, a glint of malice dancing in his eyes.

"Are you sure we want to follow him?" I whispered to Lucas, my heart pounding.

"Do we have a choice?" he replied, voice low. "We need to know what he knows. This could be our chance to find the truth about the actress and this theater's dark history."

With a deep breath, I took a step forward, crossing the threshold into the unknown, with Lucas right behind me. The narrow corridor beyond was dimly lit, the flickering light casting ominous shadows that seemed to reach for us. The air was thick with the weight of untold stories, and I felt an overwhelming urge to turn back, to escape the grasp of whatever darkness lay ahead.

As we ventured deeper, the walls closed in, lined with faded photographs and posters from long-ago performances. Each one told a story of passion and tragedy, of dreams woven into the very fabric of the theater. "Look at this," I said, pointing to a black-and-white photo of the leading lady from decades past, her radiant smile a stark contrast to the dusty gloom surrounding us. "She looks so alive."

"Alive and yet..." Lucas murmured, his eyes scanning the walls, "there's something haunting about it. Like they're all trapped in this place."

"Exactly. They've been forgotten," I said, my heart heavy. "Just like the actress we're trying to find. This theater holds so many secrets."

The benefactor moved ahead, his back to us, and I caught a glimpse of his expression—a mixture of nostalgia and something darker, something twisted. "Do you see what this place once was? Its magic? Its allure?"

"It was everything," I breathed, my fingers brushing against the frame of one poster. "And it can be again."

"Perhaps," he mused, "but only if you understand the cost of such magic." He stopped abruptly, turning to face us, the shadows casting deep lines across his face. "Are you prepared to sacrifice for it? This theater demands loyalty, and it will not suffer the weak."

"Sacrifice?" Lucas echoed, a flicker of uncertainty crossing his features. "What do you mean?"

"Nothing comes without a price," the benefactor said, eyes glinting with malevolent glee. "Not the theater. Not the actress. And certainly not you."

As the last word left his mouth, the ground beneath us trembled, a low rumble that sent vibrations through the walls. Dust cascaded from the ceiling, and I instinctively reached for Lucas's hand, the connection grounding me amid the chaos. "What have you done?" I shouted, panic rising in my chest.

"Only what must be done," he replied, an eerie calm settling over him. "This is the reckoning. The theater demands its tribute, and I am merely its messenger."

Before I could respond, the floor beneath us cracked open, a gaping maw of darkness yawning wider, threatening to swallow us whole. I felt the pull of gravity shift, as if the very theater were alive and determined to reclaim its secrets.

"Lucas!" I cried, gripping his hand tightly as we stumbled backward, the world around us spinning. "What's happening?"

"This is it! We need to get out of here!" he shouted, tugging me toward the dim light at the end of the corridor. The walls quaked, and I could hear the distant echo of laughter, mingling with cries of despair—a cacophony that resonated through the air, pulling at the very fabric of reality.

But before we could reach safety, a loud crash reverberated through the space, and the benefactor laughed, a sound filled with both triumph and madness. "You see? This is what happens when you disturb the past. Now, the theater will reclaim what it lost!"

With a final, desperate push, Lucas and I lunged for the exit, but the ground was giving way beneath us, the darkness reaching up like claws. I could feel the heat of desperation clawing at my throat, and as I turned back one last time, the benefactor stood amidst the chaos, a silhouette against the swirling shadows, a smirk etched across his face.

In that heartbeat, everything blurred into a whirlwind of fear and determination. We were on the brink of something monumental, and I could feel the fabric of the theater shifting, bending to the will of its past. And then, just as we thought we had escaped the grip of the darkness, the ground beneath us collapsed, plunging us into an abyss where secrets lay waiting to be unearthed.

Chapter 22: Breaking Free

The stage felt electric, a palpable energy coursing through the air as we gathered in the dimly lit theater. Shadows danced along the walls, flickering in time with the whispers of uncertainty that floated among us. It was as if the very building was holding its breath, waiting for the next act to unfold, one that none of us had anticipated. My heart raced in my chest, not just from the thrill of performance but from the weight of the revelation that had unraveled in our midst. The malignant force threatening our sanctuary was no longer a mere figment of imagination; it was a specter looming over us, cloaked in deceit and dark intentions.

"Can you believe it?" Maya's voice was a mixture of disbelief and simmering anger, her vibrant red curls bouncing as she paced like a caged lion. "All this time, we've been played like puppets, and the strings lead back to him."

"Calm down, Maya," I urged, though my own voice trembled. "We need to think clearly. This isn't just about us anymore. It's about the theater—our home." I gestured around the room, my gaze lingering on the grand chandelier overhead, its crystals catching the faint light, sending shards of brilliance across the worn wooden floor. Memories of countless rehearsals flooded my mind, laughter echoing in the corridors, the scent of fresh paint mingling with the lingering aroma of old popcorn. This place was a part of me, as much as my own heart and soul.

Lucas stepped forward, his expression a blend of determination and warmth. "We can't let him win," he said, his voice steady despite the turmoil swirling within us. "We've fought too hard to let our dreams die here." He turned to the group, locking eyes with each of us, his blue gaze intense and unwavering. "Together, we're stronger. We need to confront him—expose him for who he really is."

"Right," I added, feeling the weight of responsibility settle on my shoulders. "We need a plan. Something that will catch him off guard. He thinks we're scared, that we'll back down. But he doesn't know us." The adrenaline surged through me, igniting a fire of resolve that drowned out the creeping doubt. "He doesn't know what we're capable of."

The crew rallied, voices rising in a chorus of ideas and strategies, each one more audacious than the last. It was a beautiful chaos, the kind that felt like a dance—a symphony of thoughts and emotions intertwining in perfect harmony. I couldn't help but smile amidst the tension, feeling a sense of belonging that filled the empty spaces within me. This was my family, my tribe, and we would fight for our home.

As we hammered out the details, a hush fell over the group, the air thick with anticipation. It was then that I realized the stakes were not merely about saving a theater; it was about reclaiming our lives, our dreams, and—most importantly—our courage. I glanced at Lucas, our eyes meeting across the crowded room, and in that fleeting moment, the chaos faded into a quiet understanding. We had both been through our own battles, but now, we faced this one together.

"Are we really going to confront him?" Maya asked, her voice breaking the silence that had enveloped us. "What if he retaliates? What if he's more powerful than we think?"

"He's not invincible," Lucas replied, his conviction unwavering. "He thrives on fear, and if we stand together, we can take that away from him. We've faced obstacles before; this is just another act in our story."

"I just want my theater back," I said softly, the words a raw confession, an echo of my heart's deepest desire. "I want to feel the magic again, the joy of creating something beautiful with all of you."

As the tension melted into a shared resolve, we gathered our resources, laying out our plan like an intricate map leading to an uncertain destination. Every detail was scrutinized, every potential risk discussed. The theater transformed from a place of dread into a battleground where we would reclaim our narrative. The scent of fresh paint and varnish mingled with the musty air, revitalizing our spirits with every breath we took.

With each passing hour, the reality of what lay ahead became clearer. The confrontation was inevitable, and as we moved deeper into the night, a sense of purpose wrapped around us like a shroud. The flickering lights above seemed to pulse in rhythm with our collective heartbeat, a reminder that we were not alone. The echoes of past performances whispered encouragement, and I felt the strength of those who had walked the stage before us urging us on.

Finally, as the clock struck midnight, the moment arrived. We assembled backstage, our breaths hitching in unison as we prepared to face our adversary. Lucas stood beside me, his presence a comforting anchor in the whirlwind of emotions swirling around us. "Are you ready?" he asked, his voice barely above a whisper, but I could hear the intensity behind it.

I nodded, squeezing his hand tightly. "Ready as I'll ever be."

Together, we stepped into the spotlight, the weight of our fears and hopes bearing down on us. In the cavernous silence of the theater, I could almost hear the heartbeat of the place—the dreams, the laughter, the stories waiting to be told. As we faced the darkness that threatened to consume us, I felt a surge of hope rise within me, igniting a fire that would guide us through the impending storm.

And as the curtains began to part, revealing the shadows lurking beyond, I knew we would confront the truth, not just about our foe but about ourselves. This was our moment, and we would seize it, not just for the theater, but for the love that had bloomed amidst the chaos—a love that would give us the strength to break free.

The stage was set, not just for a performance but for the culmination of all our struggles. The atmosphere hummed with a mix of anticipation and fear, every creak of the wooden floorboards echoing like a heartbeat in the silence. Lucas and I exchanged glances, his eyes a stormy blue, brimming with an unspoken understanding. This was our moment to unveil the truth, to confront the puppet master who had cast shadows over our dreams. The theater, once a sanctuary, now felt like a battlefield, but it was one we were ready to fight on.

"Do you think he's already here?" Maya whispered, her voice barely audible over the soft rustle of fabric and the faint ticking of the wall clock. She fiddled with the edge of her costume, a vibrant gown that mirrored the fire in her spirit. Her nerves were palpable, and I felt a twinge of sympathy. It was strange how we could all wear our emotions like costumes, layering them thick to shield ourselves from the harshness of reality.

"He wouldn't miss this for the world," Lucas replied, his tone light but his eyes sharp, scanning the shadows that seemed to stretch endlessly across the stage. "He's like a moth to a flame, always drawn to the chaos."

"I'd say he's more like a cockroach," I muttered, trying to lighten the mood. "Always lurking in the dark, and you just can't get rid of him." The laughter that followed was a brief respite, a momentary balm to the anxiety coiling in our chests. We needed that release; it reminded us of our purpose and the camaraderie that fueled our resolve.

As the clock chimed the hour, the atmosphere shifted. A heavy silence descended, swallowing our laughter and replacing it with an oppressive tension. I felt the hairs on my arms stand on end, a shiver racing down my spine. It was time to confront the darkness, to draw the curtain back on the deception that had threatened to consume us.

The plan had been sketched out in frantic scribbles, a loose tapestry of strategies woven together by our desperation. Lucas took the lead, stepping onto the stage with an air of confidence that belied the turmoil beneath. He gestured for me to join him, and as I walked toward him, the spotlight felt like a warm embrace, a promise that we were not alone in this fight.

"Ladies and gentlemen," Lucas began, his voice strong and clear, echoing through the theater like a siren's call. "Thank you for joining us tonight. We have something important to share—something that concerns us all." He paused, letting the weight of his words settle over the audience like a thick fog. "We've discovered that our benefactor, who has been so generous to us, may not have our best interests at heart."

Maya stepped forward, her passion igniting the room. "That's right! We've been misled, manipulated into believing we were safe when, in fact, we were being set up for failure." Her words hung in the air, charged with emotion, and I could see the gears turning in the audience's minds. Some shifted uneasily in their seats, while others leaned forward, curiosity piqued.

I could almost hear the cogs of their thoughts grinding. "How could this be?" they wondered, their expressions a blend of disbelief and intrigue. It was the opening we needed, the crack in the facade that would allow the truth to pour through.

As the tension thickened, the lights dimmed momentarily, casting eerie shadows across the stage. I took a breath, summoning every ounce of courage I had. "We're not just here to expose the truth about our benefactor. We're here to take back what is rightfully ours," I declared, my voice trembling but resolute. "This theater is our home, a sanctuary where dreams are born and stories come to life. We refuse to let it be snatched away from us."

A ripple of applause broke the tension, a flicker of solidarity igniting among the audience members. I could see them stirring, their belief in us bolstering our resolve. It was as if the spirit of the theater itself was rising, urging us forward.

"Let's show them what we're made of," Lucas said, and his enthusiasm was infectious. I felt the heat of his determination radiating beside me, a reminder that we were in this together.

Just as we were gaining momentum, a figure emerged from the shadows. The air turned electric as the audience collectively gasped, recognition dawning upon them. Our benefactor, slicked back hair and a smug grin plastered across his face, stepped into the spotlight as if he owned it. "What a delightful gathering! I had no idea you were putting on such a riveting show," he sneered, his voice dripping with mockery. "But I must say, it's a bit unbecoming for you all to air your grievances in public."

Maya bristled, stepping protectively closer to me. "You think you can intimidate us? We know the truth now. We know what you've been doing."

His laughter rang out, sharp and derisive, cutting through our resolve. "Truth? What truth? The only truth here is that you're all in way over your heads." He leaned casually against the edge of the stage, his demeanor smug, as if he relished the chaos he had created.

But instead of backing down, the warmth of my anger ignited. "We're not afraid of you anymore," I said, surprising even myself with the steadiness of my voice. "Your control over us ends tonight."

His smile faltered for a fraction of a second, and I seized that moment, my pulse quickening with newfound bravery. "We've built a community here, one that thrives on creativity, passion, and unity. You can't extinguish that flame, no matter how hard you try."

He straightened, his demeanor shifting from mockery to irritation. "You really think you can rally these people against me? They'll see you for the failures you are, the theater that's crumbling around you."

"We may be down, but we're far from out," Lucas interjected, his voice unwavering. "And we're willing to fight for what we believe in. This theater isn't just a building; it's our legacy. We will not let you take it from us."

In that moment, a wave of emotion surged through the room, binding us together in a collective defiance. The audience, now roused, began to clap and shout encouragement, the sound rising like a tempest, drowning out the arrogance of our foe. The tide had turned, and for the first time, I felt the weight of fear begin to lift.

"Join us," I implored, my voice rising above the cacophony. "Together, we can reclaim our stage and drive out the darkness that threatens us. We can rewrite this story!"

As the clamor reached a fever pitch, I caught Lucas's gaze again. In that moment, I knew we would face whatever came next, not just as performers, but as a family united against a common enemy. And in that fierce, defiant spirit, I realized we were no longer just acting; we were living our truth, and it was a truth powerful enough to shatter the shadows surrounding us.

The roar of the audience surged around us like an unstoppable tide, their energy pulsating with determination and hope. The theater, once a cradle for our dreams, had become a battleground, and we stood at the forefront, ready to reclaim it. The benefactor, with his smug expression, shifted his weight as the clapping and shouting intensified. It was as if the walls themselves were vibrating with the collective force of our resistance.

"Isn't this just adorable?" he mocked, a feigned smile plastered across his face. "You really think you can rally these folks against me? They'll see your incompetence for what it is—a pathetic attempt to hold onto a dying theater." He leaned forward, his gaze sweeping over the audience, trying to gauge their resolve. "They want entertainment, not a lecture on loyalty."

A ripple of outrage spread through the crowd, and I could see the flicker of uncertainty in his eyes. It was my turn to respond. "You underestimate their spirit," I said, my voice steady, gaining strength with every word. "This theater is alive because of the people who love it. You may think you hold the strings, but the truth is, we're the ones with the power. We create the magic that draws them here. You're nothing without us."

"Ah, the age-old story of the little artist against the big bad businessman," he sneered, but I could sense the edge of desperation creeping into his tone. "But let's be honest—your little rebellion isn't going to change the reality of your situation. You're just delaying the inevitable."

Before I could respond, Maya stepped up beside me, her fierce expression radiating confidence. "You think we'll just roll over? You don't know us at all! We'll take this fight to every corner of this theater, every empty seat. You may think we're broken, but we're ready to rise, and we'll do it without you."

The audience erupted into cheers, the sound echoing off the walls, and I could see their faces lighting up with a shared purpose. This was more than just a performance; it was a revival, a reclamation of everything we had fought for. I glanced at Lucas, who nodded at me, his smile a beacon of encouragement. Together, we were a force, our hearts beating in unison.

Suddenly, the lights flickered, a surreal dance of shadows that made the benefactor recoil slightly, the bravado faltering for just a heartbeat. "What's wrong?" I taunted. "Afraid of the dark?"

"Enough of this nonsense!" he shouted, trying to regain control. "This is a waste of time. I'll simply buy you out, tear this place down, and build something worthwhile—something that doesn't involve your melodrama."

The gasps of the crowd rippled through the air, a collective intake of breath. My heart raced at the thought of losing everything we had worked for. "You think you can silence our voices with money? That our dreams are for sale? You're gravely mistaken."

With a newfound determination, I stepped closer to the edge of the stage, feeling the warmth of the spotlight enveloping me. "This theater has stood the test of time because of us—its actors, its crew, and its audience. We have woven our stories into its very fabric, and you can't buy that."

"Enough!" he bellowed, his voice booming across the theater. "You're delusional if you think a few impassioned speeches will save your precious little stage."

Just then, the heavy wooden doors at the back of the theater burst open, and in rushed a throng of former cast members, alumni of our productions, all clad in their old costumes. It was a flood of nostalgia—a wave of solidarity that washed over us. They had come to lend their voices to our cause, their history intertwining with ours in a beautiful tapestry of loyalty and love for this place.

"Looks like you underestimated us again," Lucas said, a grin spreading across his face as he stepped back, letting the crowd take center stage.

The benefactor's expression morphed from smug confidence to bewildered rage. "You think they will make a difference? They're nothing but memories!"

But the memories had weight, and as they filled the aisles, the very air crackled with their shared history. "We're not just memories," one of them shouted, a familiar face from my first production, now a seasoned actress. "We're the heartbeat of this theater, and we will not be silenced."

Emboldened by their presence, I turned to the benefactor, ready to drive the point home. "You don't understand the essence of what we create here. It's not just a theater; it's a community—a family. And families protect one another."

His composure was slipping, anger twisting his features. "You'll regret this. You're making a terrible mistake. I will make sure you pay for this defiance!"

As he began to step forward, Lucas moved to stand in front of me, a protective barrier against the wrath that radiated from the benefactor. "We're not afraid of your threats. You've manipulated us long enough, but this time, you're the one who's in danger of losing everything."

"Is that so?" The benefactor's voice dripped with sarcasm, but there was an underlying tremor that betrayed his unease. He glanced around the theater, surveying the sea of defiant faces, and for a moment, I could almost see the wheels turning in his mind. Perhaps he was calculating the cost of crossing us—both financially and in terms of reputation.

Just as I thought we had gained the upper hand, he sneered, and in one swift motion, he pulled out a small device from his pocket, pressing a button. The lights flickered again, plunging the theater into darkness for a heartbeat before emergency lights flickered to life. The air thickened, and a low rumble echoed through the building, like the growl of a beast waking from slumber.

"What did you just do?" I yelled, my heart pounding in my chest. Panic surged through the audience, and I could see faces turning pale as the reality of the situation sank in.

"This theater is mine, and I won't let you take it from me without a fight. Welcome to the final act," he taunted, his voice now low and dangerous.

The emergency lights flickered again, casting eerie shadows, and I felt a sense of dread wash over me as the ground beneath us vibrated ominously. "Everyone, we need to get out of here!" Maya shouted, panic rising in her voice, but we were frozen, caught in the web of uncertainty and fear.

As the vibrations intensified, the lights flickered one last time before plunging us into complete darkness. The air was thick with tension, a suffocating blanket that threatened to smother our resolve. My heart raced, pounding in sync with the chaos that erupted around us. It was impossible to see, impossible to know what lay ahead. All I could hear were frantic breaths, the shuffling of feet, and the ominous rumble that signaled the unraveling of everything we had fought for.

And then, just as suddenly, the lights flared back to life—but something was wrong. The benefactor stood at the edge of the stage, grinning wickedly, while shadows twisted around him like dark tendrils reaching out, ready to strike.

"Let's see how far you're willing to go to save your precious theater," he taunted, and with a flick of his wrist, the ground beneath us shook violently, threatening to swallow us whole.

In that moment of chaos, as screams filled the air and the theater threatened to collapse around us, I knew one thing for certain: this battle was far from over, and we were about to face the darkness head-on.

Chapter 23: The Echoes of Yesterday

The theater's façade shimmered like a jewel under the golden rays of late afternoon sun, its once-muted colors now vibrant, as if to celebrate our hard-won victory. I stepped inside, breathing in the familiar scent of aged wood mingled with a hint of stage dust—a sensory reminder of every laugh, every tear, and the fiery passion that had ignited within these walls. Lucas stood beside me, his presence as comforting as the soft velvet of the theater seats that awaited eager patrons. The past had nearly consumed us, but today, it felt like a fresh start.

"Can you believe we're actually here?" I asked, my voice barely above a whisper. I leaned against the cool marble of the lobby's counter, where our hopes had once teetered on the brink of destruction, now sturdy under the weight of renewal.

Lucas turned to me, his eyes sparkling with the same mischief that had drawn me to him from the beginning. "Believe it? I can hardly contain my excitement. It feels like we've turned the page on a rather dramatic chapter of our lives, and I'd say this one's more of a rom-com." He grinned, his playful demeanor cutting through the tension of the past weeks.

"Rom-com?" I scoffed lightly, raising an eyebrow. "More like a tragedy with a hint of dark comedy and a dash of suspense. But hey, as long as we're laughing, I suppose it's a step in the right direction."

He chuckled, the sound rolling through the air like a warm breeze, effortlessly brightening my mood. "You do know how to paint a vivid picture, don't you? But I'd argue that we're past the tragedy now." He stepped closer, the warmth of his body radiating against mine, grounding me in this moment of clarity. "It's time for our encore."

As we strolled deeper into the theater, the flickering light of the chandelier overhead caught my eye, casting playful shadows that danced across the walls. Each beam of light felt like a metaphor for our journey—fragile, beautiful, yet powerful enough to illuminate even the darkest corners. We paused in front of the stage, where our dreams had flickered to life amid the chaos, and I couldn't help but remember the nights we'd spent rehearsing lines, pouring our souls into characters that resonated with our deepest fears and desires.

"Look at that," I said, nodding toward the spot where our final performance had ignited a spark of hope in the audience. "It's almost hard to believe we were once paralyzed by fear and uncertainty. Now, it's like the past has reshaped into something we can build on."

Lucas's expression turned serious, the playful glint in his eyes fading slightly. "Yeah, but the echoes of yesterday aren't easy to drown out, are they? It's going to take time to silence those shadows." He ran a hand through his tousled hair, the gesture both endearing and revealing his vulnerabilities.

"I know," I replied softly, stepping closer to him. "But we're not alone anymore. We've built something together, and as long as we hold onto each other, I believe we can turn those echoes into something harmonious."

His gaze held mine, and in that moment, the world around us faded. It was just the two of us standing on the precipice of a future we'd fought so hard to reclaim. "You're right," he said finally, his voice steadying. "Together, we're stronger. We'll turn this place into a sanctuary for those who've lost their way—just like we did."

A smile broke across my face, pulling at the corners of my mouth. "You're going to be the best theater director ever, Lucas. I can already see it—the passionate speeches, the inspirational memos." I punctuated my teasing with a playful nudge.

"Right, because that's exactly how I envisioned my career," he replied, his eyes twinkling with humor again. "But really, I want to create a space where everyone feels welcome, like they can escape their troubles even if just for a moment. That's what this theater is meant for."

As he spoke, I envisioned the possibilities unfurling before us like the curtains on opening night. A community outreach program, workshops for aspiring actors, evenings filled with laughter and stories shared over coffee in the lobby. I could see families gathering, friendships blossoming, and lives intertwining within the very walls that had witnessed our struggles.

"Maybe we could host a few open-mic nights?" I suggested, my mind racing with ideas. "Or a 'write your own play' contest? We could give local writers a platform to showcase their talents."

His enthusiasm matched mine, and the energy between us crackled with potential. "That's brilliant! We can start with small productions and grow from there. The theater can become a hub for creativity and inspiration."

Excitement bubbled in my chest as we delved into our visions, our imaginations running wild, weaving plans for the future with the threads of our experiences. It was thrilling, this act of rebuilding—not just the theater but our lives, our love, and our dreams.

But as the day wore on, shadows from the past lingered in the corners, whispering reminders of the battles we'd fought. I couldn't shake the feeling that while we had defeated the immediate threat, the remnants of fear still clung to the edges of our aspirations.

"Do you ever think about what happens next?" I asked, my tone shifting from playful to contemplative. "I mean, we've overcome so much, but there's still so much at stake."

Lucas paused, his smile faltering slightly as he considered my words. "Every day. But I've learned something important through all of this. It's okay to be scared, as long as we don't let it hold us back."

I nodded, appreciating his wisdom, but uncertainty loomed like a distant storm cloud. We had emerged from the chaos stronger, but how long would the peace last?

With those thoughts swirling, I glanced back at the stage, the spotlight illuminating the space where we'd once fought to reclaim our dreams. There was still work to be done, layers to peel back, and stories to tell. I felt the weight of the past on my shoulders but also the exhilarating thrill of potential. Together, we would step into the future, ready to embrace whatever it held for us—come what may.

The theater buzzed with energy, each corner filled with whispers of new beginnings and the soft thud of excited footsteps. Lucas and I had invited our closest friends to help us prepare for the grand reopening, an event that felt as monumental as the first time we had taken the stage together. Today, the air was thick with possibility, and I could almost taste the sweetness of success mingling with the scent of fresh paint and newly polished wood.

"Do you think the ghosts of last season's cast will show up to haunt us?" I asked, smirking as I brushed some dust from the ornate railing, the remnants of our previous struggles still clinging to the old theater's bones.

"Only if you promise to perform an exorcism in a sequined dress," Lucas replied with a laugh, his eyes glinting as he set down a box filled with props. He leaned against the stage, arms crossed, his posture relaxed yet confident. "I'd pay to see that."

"Oh, trust me, I've got the sequins ready. It's the exorcism that's going to be tricky," I shot back, trying to suppress a grin.

As we decorated the stage, each item had a story—a pair of old shoes from a performance that had been a triumph and a heartache rolled into one, a backdrop painted with vibrant colors that had once filled the audience with wonder. It felt cathartic to arrange them, transforming reminders of our struggles into symbols of hope. Each piece became a part of a narrative that was no longer defined by fear but by resilience and creativity.

The chatter of our friends mingled with the sound of laughter, creating a warm symphony that resonated throughout the hall. They were excited, their energy palpable as they shared their ideas for our upcoming show. I caught snippets of conversations, each suggestion adding layers to the collective vision we were weaving together.

"Okay, how about we add a mystery element? Like a hidden treasure on stage!" A friend shouted, her enthusiasm infectious as she gestured animatedly.

"Or a surprise twist at the end!" another chimed in, eyes wide with the thrill of creativity.

Their ideas flowed like a river, each twist and turn sparking new conversations, laughter, and occasionally a few mock dramatic gasps. It was intoxicating, the way the theater seemed to pulse with life again, as if it had been waiting patiently for this moment to emerge from the shadows.

"Maybe we should turn it into a comedy," Lucas suggested, a devilish grin on his face. "After all, if we can survive a benefactor's threats, what can possibly faze us?"

"Spoken like a true optimist," I said, nudging him playfully. "But are we ready for that kind of pressure?"

"Ready? Darling, we've been ready since the moment we decided to take this theater back." He paused, his expression softening as he looked at me. "And look where we are now. We're reclaiming our story."

His words struck a chord deep within me. We were, indeed, reclaiming our story—not just the theater's, but our own. The laughter we shared today was a reminder of how far we'd come and how much we'd fought to create this new chapter. I felt a surge of determination as I surveyed the theater filled with my friends, each one an integral part of our journey. Together, we were stitching the frayed edges of our past into a tapestry of hope.

As the afternoon waned, the sunlight streamed through the grand windows, casting a golden hue over everything. The energy was electric, and the thought of the upcoming show made my heart race with anticipation. I wanted to encapsulate all we had endured, the love we had forged, and the community we had built into something tangible—something that would resonate with our audience and perhaps even heal them, just as this place had healed us.

"Let's brainstorm some more ideas for the theme," I proposed, my eyes lighting up. "What about something that reflects our journey? We could weave in elements of our past while looking to the future."

Lucas nodded, excitement sparking in his gaze. "I love that idea. It could serve as a reminder that while we can't change what happened, we can shape how we respond. And we can make it fun!"

"Fun and profound—like life itself," I added, tapping my chin thoughtfully. "It's a delicate balance, but I think we're up for the challenge."

As we continued to brainstorm, the room filled with more laughter and lively discussions, each voice adding to the creative frenzy. It felt like a celebration, not just of the theater's reopening but of every hurdle we had overcome together. We were a family, united by our love for the arts and the journey that had brought us here.

Suddenly, a loud crash interrupted our revelry. Everyone paused, eyes darting toward the sound that echoed ominously through the theater. My heart raced as I turned to see a stack of props tumbling from a table, sending papers and costumes flying across the floor.

"Okay, who was that?" I called out, trying to mask my panic with humor.

Lucas chuckled, easing the tension. "I'd wager it's just the ghosts of the last production making their dramatic exit."

With a sigh of relief, I joined in the laughter, but I couldn't shake the feeling that our past was lurking in the corners, waiting to remind us of its presence.

As we collected the scattered items, I caught Lucas's eye, a silent agreement passing between us. We would face whatever challenges lay ahead—together.

The evening stretched on, filled with more ideas, laughter, and a few more mishaps that only added to the chaotic charm of our gathering. As the last of the sunlight dipped below the horizon, I took a moment to step outside, seeking solace in the cool evening air. The stars began to twinkle above, scattered like glitter across a velvet sky.

"Hey," Lucas's voice broke through my reverie as he joined me, his hands shoved deep in his pockets. "You okay?"

I nodded, leaning against the cool brick wall, the rough surface grounding me. "Just taking it all in. It's amazing, isn't it? Everything we've built, everything we've overcome?"

"It really is." He moved closer, our shoulders brushing as we both gazed at the stars. "And to think, there was a time when we thought we'd lose it all. But look at us now—stronger than ever."

His words hung in the air, heavy with meaning, and I felt a swell of gratitude for everything we had shared. But with that gratitude came an undercurrent of apprehension; the echoes of yesterday still whispered warnings that we couldn't ignore. The threat may have been neutralized for now, but shadows lingered, a reminder that peace was often fleeting.

"Let's promise to keep moving forward, no matter what," I said, turning to meet his gaze, my heart racing with the weight of my commitment.

Lucas nodded solemnly, determination etched on his face. "No looking back. We'll face whatever comes next, side by side."

With our pact sealed under the vast expanse of the night sky, I felt a renewed sense of purpose. Together, we would continue to write our story, chapter by chapter, determined to create a future filled with laughter, love, and the occasional twist that life threw our way. As we turned back to the theater, I knew that whatever lay ahead, we would face it together, hand in hand, heart to heart.

The anticipation was palpable as the day of the grand reopening arrived, transforming the theater into a vibrant canvas of colors and emotions. Streamers adorned the entrance, and laughter floated through the air, mixing with the smell of freshly popped popcorn and the sweet scent of cotton candy. I stood at the door, a living, breathing bundle of nerves and excitement, greeting guests with a smile that I hoped masked my inner turmoil.

"Are we ready for this?" Lucas asked, his voice cutting through the chatter as he appeared at my side, his presence both grounding and invigorating. He was dressed sharply, his tailored jacket hugging his shoulders just right, and his eyes sparkled with a mix of mischief and determination.

"Ready? No. But we're going to pretend we are, right?" I replied, my heart racing as I scanned the crowd. Friends and patrons mingled, their faces illuminated with joy. It felt like a family reunion where everyone had come to celebrate not just the theater but the spirit of perseverance that had brought us all together.

"Pretending is half the battle. The other half is the actual performance." Lucas grinned, nudging my side gently. "You're going to be amazing."

"Don't you mean we're going to be amazing?" I corrected him, my voice light but with a touch of sincerity. We were in this together, and that notion brought me comfort.

The evening progressed with all the charm of a bustling production. Lively conversations swirled around us, and the buzz of excitement grew louder as the moment drew near. As I moved through the crowd, sharing laughter and stories, I couldn't help but feel a deep sense of belonging. This was my world—a tapestry woven with threads of community, creativity, and a fierce love for the stage.

As the lights dimmed, an electric hush fell over the audience. The anticipation hung thick in the air, and I took my place at the front of the stage, heart pounding with every heartbeat echoing through the silence. Lucas stood behind the curtain, ready to cue the start of our first act, his support like a beacon guiding me through the uncertainty.

"Ladies and gentlemen," I began, my voice steady despite the whirlwind of emotions swirling within me. "Welcome to our theater, a place that has seen laughter, tears, and dreams. Tonight, we celebrate not only a performance but the journey we've taken to get here."

Applause erupted, the sound warm and welcoming, and I felt a swell of gratitude as I looked out at the faces illuminated by the soft glow of the stage lights. Each person represented a part of our story, a reminder that we were no longer defined by our struggles but by our resilience.

The first act unfolded seamlessly, a tapestry of laughter and poignant moments that captured the audience's hearts. I reveled in the familiar rhythms of the performance, the dialogue flowing like a dance. My heart soared with every laugh and every heartfelt reaction from the crowd, a symbiotic connection that filled the theater with energy.

But just as the curtain fell on the first act, a sudden crash reverberated through the building, causing everyone to jump in their seats. My stomach dropped as the spotlight flickered erratically, casting shadows that danced menacingly across the stage.

"Lucas!" I shouted, panic rising as I hurried backstage. My heart raced with fear of what had gone wrong, images of our hard-earned triumph shattering in an instant flashing through my mind.

"Stay calm!" he urged, his voice cutting through the chaos. He was already assessing the situation, his brow furrowed in concentration as he moved swiftly toward the source of the disturbance. A piece of the set had fallen, narrowly missing one of our friends who was huddled on the ground, eyes wide with shock.

"Is everyone okay?" I asked, my voice rising with urgency as I knelt beside our friend, concern flooding my senses.

"Just shaken up," she replied, breathless but unharmed. I breathed a sigh of relief, though the tension hung in the air like a storm cloud.

"Who did this?" Lucas demanded, his voice low and fierce as he scanned the room, searching for answers. "This was no accident."

My heart raced at the implication. Had someone deliberately sabotaged our moment of glory? A knot of unease twisted in my stomach as I considered the possibility. The benefactor had been dealt with, but could there still be remnants of his threat lurking in the shadows?

Lucas turned to me, his expression a mix of determination and concern. "We need to ensure everyone is safe. I'll check the backstage area; you keep everyone calm out front."

"Be careful," I urged, gripping his arm for a moment. "This isn't over."

He nodded, the gravity of our situation sinking in. I watched him disappear into the darkness, my heart racing with anxiety. I took a deep breath and returned to the front of the stage, forcing a smile onto my face to reassure our audience, even though my insides churned with dread.

"Just a slight hiccup, folks!" I announced, my voice steady despite the storm of thoughts racing through my mind. "We'll resume shortly."

The crowd murmured, concern written on their faces, but I could see the glimmer of trust in their eyes. They believed in us, and I wasn't going to let them down.

As I made my way back to the center of the stage, I heard the low murmurs of conversations behind me, the sound of footsteps echoing in the hallway. My heart sank further. What if someone was lurking, waiting for another moment to strike?

Just then, a figure emerged from the shadows, silhouetted against the dim light. My breath caught in my throat as I strained to see who it was.

"Lucas!" I shouted, my voice rising above the growing tension in the theater.

He didn't respond, and an icy dread settled in my chest. The figure stepped into the light, and a gasp escaped my lips as recognition washed over me. It was someone I never expected to see again, someone whose presence brought back a flood of painful memories.

"Surprise," the figure said with a smirk, the coldness of their voice cutting through the air like ice.

My heart raced as I processed the implication of their appearance, the tension thickening like fog rolling in from the ocean. This wasn't over—not by a long shot.

Chapter 24: A New Dawn

The old theater loomed before me, its weathered façade kissed by the golden light of a late afternoon sun. Cracked bricks whispered secrets of the past, while the polished marquee gleamed with anticipation, the letters proclaiming the grand reopening in an elegant dance of luminescence. I stood there, my hand firmly clasped in Lucas's, the warmth of his palm sending a delightful shiver up my spine. The air hummed with the scent of fresh paint, mingling with the remnants of old popcorn and memories of raucous laughter that once filled the space. It was a vibrant tapestry of hope and nostalgia, and I felt every thread weaving into the fabric of our lives as we prepared for the performance that would define our future.

"Are you ready for this?" Lucas asked, his eyes sparkling with mischief and an undercurrent of nerves. His dark hair, tousled by the breeze, framed his face perfectly, accentuating the soft curve of his jaw. I loved how he could shift so easily from the serious director to the charming goofball who would launch into an impromptu dance routine just to coax a smile from me.

"Ready? Darling, I was born ready," I replied, my voice dripping with playful bravado. "But maybe not ready for your version of 'The Robot' at the after-party."

Lucas laughed, the sound rich and warm, instantly erasing any lingering worries that had taken root in my chest. The truth was, this moment felt monumental. After years of toil and sweat, we were finally standing on the precipice of our dreams, poised to leap into the unknown with nothing but each other's unwavering support. The audience would soon arrive, eager for distraction from their own lives, and I was determined to deliver.

As the sun began to dip lower in the sky, casting long shadows across the cobblestone street, I took a deep breath, inhaling the possibility that crackled in the air. It was intoxicating, like the first sip of champagne—bubbly and effervescent. The past may have shaped us, yes, but today, we were sculptors of our own destiny, chiseling out a new narrative with each rehearsal and each late-night brainstorming session filled with half-baked ideas and laughter.

"Can you believe how far we've come?" I said, my voice softening as I gazed into the distance, where the faint outline of the city skyline melded into a cotton-candy horizon. "There were times I thought we'd never see this day."

"Believe me, I have the dramatic emails to prove it." He grinned, that trademark smirk of his pulling at the corners of his mouth. "But here we are. You and me against the world, ready to shake the dust off this place."

I turned to him, our eyes locking with a sense of shared history and an undeniable bond forged in the crucible of theater. There had been heartbreak, uncertainty, and the ever-looming threat of failure, yet we had chosen to face it together. This was more than just a show; it was a celebration of resilience, a testament to the strength of our partnership, both on and off the stage.

The theater doors swung open, and the eager chatter of our guests spilled out like confetti. Each laugh and gasp echoed against the walls, mingling with the anticipation that hung heavy in the air. A group of friends pushed through the threshold, their faces bright with excitement, ready to witness the fruits of our labor.

"Look at that," Lucas said, gesturing toward the crowd. "They came for us. Can you believe it?"

My heart swelled at the sight. These were not just patrons; they were our allies, our support system, and I cherished each of them for believing in our vision. "And they'll leave transformed," I added, my spirit buoyed by the thought.

Moments later, as the first notes of the orchestra swelled from the pit below, I took my place on the stage. The spotlight warmed my skin, and I felt the electric pulse of the audience's energy surrounding me like an invisible cloak. It was exhilarating and terrifying, an alchemy of emotions swirling within me as I looked out at the sea of expectant faces.

With Lucas beside me, our hearts in sync, we stepped forward, ready to pour our souls into every line and melody. As we launched into our first scene, the world outside faded away, leaving only the intoxicating allure of the story unfolding in front of us. Words flowed like water, laughter bubbled forth effortlessly, and the music wrapped around us, a living entity breathing life into our creation.

The night wore on, and each act unfolded with a rhythm and grace I had almost forgotten could exist. It was a tapestry woven from the very essence of who we were, the struggles we had endured, and the triumphs we had celebrated. Each scene was a love letter to the passion we shared for the stage, a celebration of the resilience that had brought us to this moment.

The audience laughed, cried, and cheered as we navigated the twists and turns of our story. Each applause resonated through the theater, a symphony of encouragement that reminded us why we had fought so hard to bring this vision to life. And in those moments, I felt a profound connection with Lucas, the kind that spoke of shared dreams and a future waiting to be embraced.

As the final curtain fell and the audience erupted in applause, I turned to Lucas, breathless and exhilarated. The light danced in his eyes, reflecting the magic of the night. Together, we had not only resurrected the theater but had also resurrected our hopes and dreams. The journey had just begun, and I couldn't wait to see where it would lead us next.

The applause echoed in my ears like a thunderous wave, reverberating through the hallowed halls of the theater, drowning out the last notes of our final song. I blinked against the bright stage lights, the warmth of the spotlight fading as the cool air of the backstage enveloped me. The cacophony of excitement from the audience filled the space, a palpable reminder that we had achieved what many deemed impossible. The theater was alive again, and it pulsed with the vibrant energy of hope and rebirth.

Lucas was at my side, his grin as wide as the crescent moon outside, and I felt an exhilarating rush of gratitude wash over me. "We did it!" he shouted, his voice barely rising above the chatter and laughter spilling from the audience. "I mean, I always knew we would, but still! Did you see their faces?"

"Of course I saw them! They were like kids on Christmas morning," I replied, unable to keep the smile from stretching across my face. "And you—your dramatic flair in the last act was positively Oscar-worthy."

"Oh, please. I'm simply preparing for my one-man show," he quipped, winking at me. "You know, a gripping tale of one director's journey through the tangled webs of love, loss, and the occasional misplaced prop."

I laughed, the sound bubbling up from deep within me, releasing the last remnants of tension that had built up over the weeks of preparation. "Just promise me you'll hire a decent stage manager to keep track of your props. I can't have you throwing a vase again and expecting it to land gracefully."

As we walked through the dimly lit backstage area, the remnants of our performance—the scattered scripts, the half-drained water bottles, and the faint scent of makeup—told the stories of countless hours spent perfecting every detail. We had invested ourselves entirely, pouring not just our time but our hearts into this production. I glanced around, catching sight of our cast members embracing one another, celebrating the triumph we had all shared.

But in the midst of the joyful chaos, a flicker of unease darted through me. What came next? With the grand reopening behind us, we stood at a crossroads, where possibilities branched out like the limbs of a mighty tree. Would we ride this wave of success into another production, or would the pressures of expectations loom larger than life, casting shadows on our newfound joy?

Just as I began to spiral into that uncertainty, a familiar voice cut through the excitement. "Congratulations, darling!" My heart skipped a beat at the sight of my mother, her smile as bright as the stage lights that had just illuminated our performances. Her presence was a comforting anchor, but I knew it also came with a flood of opinions and expectations.

"Thanks, Mom! I'm so glad you could make it," I said, wrapping her in a warm embrace that momentarily shielded me from the pressures of reality. "What did you think?"

"Oh, it was absolutely delightful! You and Lucas were positively charming," she exclaimed, her eyes twinkling with enthusiasm. "But tell me, when are you going to settle down and give me some grandbabies? I can't wait forever, you know!"

"Mom!" I protested, pulling back to look her in the eye, my cheeks flushing. "Can't we just enjoy the moment without diving headfirst into the grandbaby pool?"

"Ah, but the moment is fleeting! And you know how fast time flies when you're having fun," she replied with a knowing smile, the kind that said she wouldn't let it go that easily. I knew this dance too well—my mother, a master choreographer of family dynamics, always eager to lead the way toward her own happily-ever-after for me.

Lucas intervened, placing a reassuring hand on my shoulder. "Julia's got plenty of time for all of that. Right, Jules?"

"Right!" I echoed, desperate to cling to the brief shield of support he provided. "The theater is my focus now, and there's so much more to explore."

"More like so much more to juggle," my mother countered, her tone teasing yet sharp. "You're not as young as you used to be, and theater can be so... unpredictable."

Before I could retort, the crowd began to disperse, laughter echoing against the theater walls as patrons shared their thoughts on the performance. I could see our cast members starting to gather for a toast, the air thick with the mingling scents of sweat, perfume, and popcorn—a unique fragrance that only the theater could conjure.

"Let's join them!" I urged, sensing the urgency to dive back into the joy that filled the room. I couldn't let the specter of future expectations cloud the moment. Not tonight.

As we approached the makeshift gathering of our troupe, the energy was infectious. Glasses clinked, and shouts of "To the show!" rang out, each cheer building upon the last. I felt a sense of belonging, a deep-rooted connection to this eclectic group of artists who had become like family.

I lifted my glass high, a grin plastered across my face. "To the show and to all of you, my wonderful, talented family! May we always find the courage to take the stage, no matter what comes next."

"To the show!" they echoed, and I felt a swell of warmth, knowing we had created something beautiful together. As the celebration continued, I caught sight of Lucas leaning against the wall, an amused smile playing on his lips.

"Look at you, the queen of the stage and the crowd," he said, a teasing lilt in his voice. "Don't let it go to your head."

"Too late," I shot back, mockingly preening as I enjoyed the banter between us. The laughter felt easy and effortless, like slipping into a favorite pair of shoes.

But as the night wore on, I couldn't shake that niggling sense of uncertainty. Each triumphant laugh hid an undercurrent of doubt. Would this moment be a stepping stone to greater things, or a fleeting interlude before the curtain fell once more? I took a deep breath, pushing the weight of those thoughts aside for the moment, determined to immerse myself in the laughter and joy around me.

And just as I began to lose myself in the jubilant atmosphere, the front doors swung open. A gust of cold air swept through the theater, and my heart leapt at the unexpected sight of someone standing in the doorway. My stomach dropped. What was he doing here?

The familiar silhouette against the doorway sent a shockwave through the jubilant atmosphere, my heart racing as I processed the sight before me. Noah stood framed by the entrance, his presence stirring memories I had long since tried to tuck away. The flickering lights cast shadows across his sharp features, accentuating the tension in his jaw as he scanned the room, his gaze settling on me.

"Look who decided to grace us with his presence," I muttered under my breath, half-amused, half-annoyed, trying to mask the sudden swell of emotions that accompanied his arrival. The laughter around me faded into a dull roar, my mind racing with questions. Why now? Why here?

Lucas caught my eye, his expression shifting from playful to cautious as he sensed the change in energy. "Do you want me to handle this?" he asked, his voice low, the protective edge clear in his tone.

I shook my head, a mix of determination and dread swelling within me. "No, I'll talk to him." As I stepped away from the crowd, the air grew heavy with unspoken words and unresolved feelings. My heart thudded against my ribs, a wild bird desperate to break free, as I approached the man who had once been a source of joy and heartache in equal measure.

Noah's presence was magnetic, drawing attention even in a room full of celebrating artists. His dark hair tousled just enough to appear effortless, his confident stance painted him as someone who had never truly faded from the stage of my life. "Julia," he said, his voice rich and smooth, like a fine whiskey. "You look... incredible."

"Thanks. And you look... like you walked in from a different decade." I tried to keep my tone light, but the sarcasm danced dangerously close to resentment. I crossed my arms, my defenses rising instinctively.

He chuckled, that familiar glint in his eyes almost disarming. "I figured I'd bring a little retro flair to your opening night. I heard it was going to be a big deal."

"Word travels fast in this town," I replied, my heart rate still racing. "What exactly are you doing here, Noah? I didn't think you'd come back, especially after..."

"Especially after I hurt you," he finished for me, his gaze steady, holding mine as if he was trying to bridge the distance we had both created. "But I've changed, Julia. I wanted to see the theater again—your theater—and I wanted to see you."

I swallowed hard, grappling with the emotions threatening to bubble to the surface. Memories of our laughter, late-night discussions, and whispered dreams collided with the pain of his departure. "You could have called," I said, more bitter than I intended. "You could have said something. Instead, you just left."

"I know," he admitted, his voice softer, laced with regret. "And I can't change the past. But I've realized how much I miss this place, and how much I miss you."

I glanced back at the celebration, where Lucas was deep in conversation with our lead actress, his laughter ringing clear. The contrast between the two men in my life was stark. Lucas had shown me what it meant to build something from the ground up, to create joy from the ashes of disappointment. Noah had once been my muse, my wild card, but now he felt like an echo of a dream I had almost forgotten.

"What do you want from me, Noah?" I asked, my voice firm, the pulse of the celebration still thrumming in my ears. "You can't just waltz back in here and expect everything to be the same. I've moved on."

"Have you?" he challenged, stepping closer, the heat of his presence igniting old sparks I had thought extinguished. "You've moved on to a new production, but have you really moved on from us?"

The crowd's laughter faded into the background, the world narrowing to just the two of us. I could feel the warmth radiating from him, a reminder of everything I had lost. "I'm happy now," I insisted, though a tremor in my voice belied my confidence. "I'm doing what I love."

"And I'm proud of you," he said, his expression softening. "But you can't deny that what we had was special. It was... intense."

"Intense doesn't always equate to good," I shot back, a mix of frustration and longing spilling from my lips. "It can burn you alive if you're not careful."

"True, but you can't deny the heat." He took another step closer, the tension between us palpable. "You still feel it, don't you?"

I was trapped in his gaze, the way his eyes sparkled with that familiar mischief, a reminder of the countless moments we shared. And just as I opened my mouth to respond, a loud cheer erupted from the crowd, startling me back to reality. The party continued, but my world had shrunk to this moment, this crossroads.

"Julia!" Lucas's voice sliced through the haze, pulling me from my reverie. He approached, his brow furrowed, the lightheartedness replaced by concern as he looked back and forth between me and Noah. "Everything okay?"

"Just catching up," Noah said smoothly, his charming facade firmly in place, as if he had rehearsed this scene. I could see the subtle way he shifted his weight, his posture a blend of confidence and something else—defiance, perhaps.

"Catching up?" Lucas repeated, skepticism lining his words as he slid his arm protectively around my shoulders. "Right. I didn't realize we were having a reunion."

"Lucas, it's fine," I interjected, trying to defuse the tension coiling around us like a serpent. "Noah was just leaving."

"Am I?" Noah asked, arching an eyebrow, a playful challenge in his tone. "I'd like to think I'm just getting started."

"Maybe this isn't the time or place," I suggested, my heart pounding as the tension thickened. "We're in the middle of a celebration. Can't we all just enjoy the moment?"

Noah's gaze flickered with something unreadable, and I could sense a storm brewing beneath the surface. "I came here for you, Julia. You know that."

"Then maybe you should consider how this looks," Lucas snapped, his protective instincts flaring. "You can't just walk back into her life and expect everything to fall into place."

"Is that what you think?" Noah replied, his voice low and smooth, yet edged with frustration. "You think I'm here to ruin things?"

"No," I said, cutting through their escalating tension. "I just want this night to be about celebrating what we've built, not what was lost."

The atmosphere thickened with unspoken words, and I could feel the weight of the moment pressing down on me. I glanced at Lucas, who remained steadfast, a pillar of strength, and then back at Noah, whose expression shifted, the playful facade cracking just enough for me to see the vulnerability beneath.

Before I could speak again, the fire alarm blared to life, a shrill, chaotic wail that shattered the fragile equilibrium we had established. Panic surged through the crowd, people scrambling toward the exits, laughter turning to shouts of confusion.

"Is it a drill?" I shouted over the din, adrenaline surging as I turned toward the exit.

"No idea!" Lucas replied, eyes wide, scanning the room. "We need to get everyone out!"

As we began to move, Noah's hand shot out, grabbing my arm with a grip that was both firm and desperate. "Julia, wait! We can't leave things like this."

But I was already swept into the maelstrom of panicked voices, my thoughts swirling as I tried to focus on the chaos around me. "We'll talk later!" I yelled back, but his eyes bore into me, and for a moment, everything else faded.

Then the crowd surged, and I lost sight of him, swept away by the throng, the blaring alarm echoing through my mind. As I reached the doorway, the scent of smoke tickled my nostrils, a sudden wave of dread crashing over me. Something was wrong. This wasn't just an alarm—it felt ominous, like the beginning of something I couldn't escape.

Outside, the night sky glimmered with stars, the crisp air a sharp contrast to the frenzy inside. But the moment was fleeting, the sound of the alarm still ringing in my ears, a harsh reminder that everything could change in an instant. I turned back, scanning the throng of bodies, searching for familiar faces. Where was Lucas? Where was Noah?

And then, from the corner of my eye, I caught a glimpse of a figure emerging from the smoke-filled doorway behind me. My breath caught in my throat as I strained to see, adrenaline coursing through my veins. I felt my heart racing, an uneasy mixture of hope and fear rising within me. Would this moment reveal the answers I desperately sought, or would it plunge me deeper into uncertainty?